EVERY PRECIOUS THING

It was supposed to be a fun weekend, a celebration of a marriage and growing family. Alan Lindley couldn't have been happier...until his wife Sara disappeared.

Asked by a mutual friend to help look for her, Logan Harper is sure he'd discover a wife who simply wants out of the marriage.

What he finds instead is a woman who didn't exist, a diabolical plan, and people who would do anything to keep it a secret, including taking the life of the person most important to him.

What would you do for those precious to you?

ALSO BY BRETT BATTLES

THE PROJECT EDEN THRILLERS
Novels
Sick
Exit Nine (late 2011)

STANDALONES
Novels
The Pull of Gravity
No Return (January 2012, US)

Short Stories
Perfect Gentleman

FOR YOUNGER READERS
THE TROUBLE FAMILY CHRONICLES
Novels
Here Comes Mr. Trouble
You're in Big, Mr. Trouble (late 2012)

EVERY PRECIOUS THING

BRETT BATTLES

A LOGAN HARPER THRILLER

For my brother and sister,
Darren and Dawn,
who've had to put up with me
their whole lives

1

"IT'S NOT HERE," Sara Lindley said as she dug through her purse.

Her husband Alan looked over her shoulder into the bag. "It's gotta be there somewhere."

"It's not," she told him, her tone of desperation growing. "It's gone."

"But you had it earlier."

"I *know* I had it earlier. But I'm telling you it's gone now."

"Could you have left it somewhere? One of the shops?"

She was already shaking her head before he finished. "I never took it out."

"Are you sure? Maybe you did but didn't realize it."

She looked at him, exasperated. "Now why would I have done that?"

"I don't know. Maybe someone asked you for ID?" he suggested, trying to keep his voice calm. "I'm just trying to think of possibilities."

Sara closed her eyes and took a breath. "I know. I'm sorry. Here." She held out the purse to him. "You check."

Not taking it, he said, "Honey, I believe you."

"A second set of eyes is always a good thing."

He almost smiled at that. It was something he'd said to her in the past. He let her give him the purse, then carefully searched through it. She'd been right. Her passport was definitely not there.

"Oh, God," she said as he handed the bag back to her. "What are we going to do?"

Alan looked at the traffic that was backed up on the road beside them, each car waiting its turn to reenter the United States from Tijuana, Mexico. Unlike those in the vehicles, he and his wife had left their car in a stateside parking lot and walked in.

"Let's retrace our steps, and see if someone found it," he suggested. "Maybe you just dropped it somewhere."

Though the frown on her face made it clear she didn't think their chances of success were very good, she said, "Okay."

Up until that point, it had been a wonderful day, finishing off an equally wonderful weekend. They were celebrating, after all. While they'd been married for nearly a year, the final piece that solidified their life together had just been completed the previous week. He was now officially the father of Sara's two-year-old daughter, Emily. They were truly a family now, and nothing would ever take that from them. He couldn't have been happier.

Leaving Emily with Rachel and Kurt—his sister and brother-in-law who lived in Simi Valley—he and Sara had traveled south from their home in Riverside for a pre-anniversary romantic getaway. They'd spent Saturday in San Diego, splitting time between the beach and the zoo, then on Sunday, at Sara's suggestion, had gone even farther south to Tijuana. The plan was to drive back home that evening.

But now, Riverside might as well have been on the other side of the world, because without Sara's passport, she wasn't getting back across the border.

It took over an hour to check all the places they'd visited earlier, but no one had seen Sara's dark blue booklet.

"I'm sorry," she said, trying to hold back tears. "I don't know what happened."

Alan put his arms around her. "It's okay. Don't worry about it. We'll just explain that it was stolen. I'm sure it happens all the time."

"But they're not going to let me back through," she argued.

"They'll have to."

"No, they won't, Alan."

She was starting to get worked up again, but he knew she was right. A decade ago, a person could pass back and forth across the Mexican border with just a driver's license, but that all changed when the towers came down. These days, no passport, no entry into the States.

"There's got to be an American consulate in town," he said. "Someone there will know what to do."

"Alan, I'm so sorry."

He locked eyes with her and smiled again. "Sweetheart, it's okay. Really."

"I'm such an idiot."

"No, you're not."

"I am."

He chuckled. "Well, you're my idiot." He looked around. "I'll grab a cab. I'm sure the driver will know where the consulate is."

As he started to raise his arm, she said, "Oh, no."

"What?"

"I don't have any other ID on me. Since we were together, I didn't think I'd need my wallet. My driver's license...it's in the car. I'll need that to prove who I am, won't I?"

It took all his will to suppress a groan.

"I'm sorry," she said. "Since I had my passport, I thought that would be enough."

"It's okay, don't worry about it."

"Don't worry about it? We *need* it."

"I know." He paused for a moment. "Here's what we'll do. I'll go back and get it, while you find out where the consulate is. We'll meet..." He looked around. There was a restaurant across the street with a bar that spilled out onto a patio. He pointed at it. "Over there. You can grab a drink while you wait."

"Do I look like I need a drink?"

"I think we both do," he said, giving her an encouraging

smile. "Now which bag should I look in?"

"The red one," she said, after a moment's hesitation. "In the pocket on the side."

He gave her a hug and a kiss. "I'll be as quick as I can."

As he started to move away, she pulled him back.

"I love you," she said, kissing him again.

"I love you, too," he told her. "Now stop worrying. It'll all be fine."

"I know it will."

——— ———

AS ALAN CROSSED back into the States, he explained to the officer what had happened, hoping that maybe the guy would tell him just to bring her through. What he got instead was a confirmation that a trip to the consulate was in their future.

By the time he reached their car, nearly thirty minutes had passed since he left Sara by the restaurant. Anxious to get back, he immediately unlocked the trunk and popped it open.

For a second he thought he was at the wrong car, but his key had worked, and there, against the side, was his suitcase. But where were Sara's bags?

He leaned in and looked beyond his luggage, but it was a ridiculous gesture. No way her bags could have been behind it without him noticing.

Thinking maybe he'd put them in the backseat and forgotten, he rushed around and looked inside the cab, but of course they weren't there. He *hadn't* forgotten. He'd put them in the trunk when he'd put his own bag there.

He returned to the rear of the car and looked into the trunk once more. Why would someone only take Sara's bags and leave his?

He was just about to pull out his cell phone so he could tell Sara what was up when he noticed the corner of an envelope sticking out from under his suitcase. He pulled it out, then nearly dropped it again when he saw his name written on the front in his wife's handwriting.

With more apprehension than he'd ever felt in his life, he opened it and read the letter inside.

> Alan,
> Don't come looking for me. You won't find me. I wish I could have told you in person, but I might never have left. Whether you can accept it or not, this is for the best. Please don't let this affect your relationship with Emily. She's blameless, and now, more than ever, she needs a father. She needs you. I love you. Believe that or don't, but I do.
>
> I hope that one day you will be able to forgive me.
> Sara

He read it twice, the words so hard to understand that it almost seemed as if they were written in a foreign language. When he finally finished he stared at the paper, his mind in a haze.

A voice started deep down in his gut—a whisper at first, but soon a scream that flooded his skull, jerking him back to the here and now.

"No!" it yelled. "No!"

He looked toward the border crossing.

The word then spilled from his lips. "No!"

Leaving the trunk of his car wide open, he started to run.

2

LOGAN HARPER WAS having lunch with his dad in the break room of Dunn Right Auto Repair and Service when Joy stuck her head in and said, "Harp, you've got a call. Line three."

"Tell them I'll call back when I'm done," Logan's dad said.

"They said it's important."

Harp frowned as he set his sandwich down and stood up. "Who is it?"

"Someone named…um…Mueller, I think."

"Mueller?" Harp looked at Logan. "Your uncle Len."

With a smile, Harp walked over to the phone mounted on the wall, and punched the button for line three.

"Len? What's going on?"

The smile on Harp's face froze, then faltered. "Oh, no," he said as he closed his eyes for a moment.

Logan rose quickly from his chair and went over to him. "You all right, Dad?"

Harp shook his head and waved him off. He said into the phone, "When?…I'm so sorry…I understand. Don't worry about it…Of course. What time?…We'll be there."

When he hung up, he just stood there, staring at nothing.

"Dad?" Logan said.

A second passed, then another, and another. Finally, Harp looked over. "What?"

"What's going on?"

His father hesitated. "It's…Len. He passed away this morning."

Len Mueller wasn't a blood relative, but that didn't matter. He was as much an uncle to Logan and a brother to Harp as any man could have ever been. The Mueller family and the Harper family had lived on neighboring farms back in Kansas where Harp had grown up. Len had been best friends with Harp's older brother Tommy. They had both served in World War II, and while Len had come back—minus two fingers on his left hand—Tommy hadn't returned at all. Len had done what he could to fill in for Tommy—helping Harp, advising him, teasing him, and eventually serving as best man at Harp's wedding.

Now he was gone, and with him Harp's connection not just to one man but two.

Two and a half days later, Logan and Harp drove up the coast to Marin County, north of San Francisco. They stayed in a motel in Sausalito that overlooked the bay, then headed to Mill Valley the next morning for Len's memorial service.

Church first, then a line of cars made their way out to the cemetery where at least three dozen people gathered around the gravesite. Sons, and daughters, and grandsons, and granddaughters, and a few old friends like Harp and Logan. Len had been a kind man, easy with his laugh and his smile. They had all hoped Len would live forever.

Because of his military service, an American flag was draped over the casket, and a four-person honor guard stood at the ready.

"You holding up okay?" Logan whispered to his father.

Harp's response was no more than a quick nod. Logan could feel every breath his dad took—the shallow, shuttering intakes, the deep gasps, and the pauses in between.

As soon as the reverend finished speaking, the honor guard

surrounded the casket, raised the flag, and with practiced preci-
sion, folded it into a neat, tight triangle. The servicewoman who
ended up with the flag walked over to where Len's five children
sat and reverently handed it to Michael, who, at sixty-two, was
Len's oldest.

The reverend said a final prayer as the casket was lowered
into the grave. One by one, the mourners walked by the opening
in the ground, dropping in a handful of dirt as they passed.

As Harp's turn came, Logan rose with him, putting a hand on
his dad's back to steady him.

"I'm okay," Harp said, then walked to the grave unaided.

When he dropped in his dirt, he paused a second and said
something Logan couldn't hear before he continued on. Logan
tossed in his handful of soil and followed his father, catching up
to him just before he reached Logan's electric blue El Camino.

"I don't know if I can go over there," Harp said once they
were inside the car.

Logan knew his father was referring to the reception that was
about to start at Len's house. "We can go back to the motel if
you'd rather," he suggested.

Harp sat silently for a moment, then said, "It would be rude
not to stop by at least."

"Don't worry about it, Dad. They'll understand."

Harp looked at him, his face a mix of uncountable emotions.
"You think so?"

"Yeah, I do."

His father thought about it, then nodded.

WHEN THEY PULLED into the motel parking lot, Harp
said, "Maybe we should have gone."

"We still can, if you want."

"I just don't know."

Logan hated seeing his dad like this. Harp was always the
positive one, the one who kept things going and encouraged oth-

ers to keep their heads up. And to Logan especially, he was also invincible, a stone that shouldn't crack. That's how most children saw their parents. Even when Logan's mother had died, Harp had kept up a strong façade though Logan knew his dad had been deeply affected by her passing. Of course Harp had been younger then, more in control. Now he'd reached an age where he was outliving his friends, including the brother who was not his brother.

"Why don't we go for a walk?" Logan suggested. "We can grab a coffee, look at the houseboats. They'll be at Uncle Len's for hours. If you want, we can go over after we get back."

Harp almost smiled. "Yeah. I'd like that."

Most of Sausalito's famous houseboats were located along piers at the north end of town. It was a long walk, but it turned out to be just what Harp needed. After a while he started talking, telling Logan stories about Len, about Kansas, and even a couple about his brother Tommy—a subject he'd always been less open about. By the time they grabbed a coffee on their way back, Harp seemed if not himself then at least improved.

"I don't know about you, but I'm up for an early dinner," Logan said. "Maybe catch a movie on TV after?"

Harp said nothing for a moment. "I'd like to stop by the cemetery on our way home in the morning."

"Sure, Dad. Whatever you want."

"Okay," Harp said, looking relieved. "That sounds good."

As they crossed into the motel parking lot, Logan said, "There's that Indian restaurant here that's supposed to be pretty decent, and I thought I saw a sushi place when we drove in."

Harp lit up. "Sushi sounds good." He'd developed a fondness for California rolls in recent years. "Let's—"

His pace slowed to a stop as his gaze locked onto something in the distance. Logan turned to see what it was.

Standing near his El Camino was Callie Johnson, Uncle Len's youngest child and only daughter, still wearing the same black dress she'd had on earlier. She was somewhere in her mid-fifties now, and when she'd been a young undergrad at Cal Poly in San Luis Obispo, she'd make a few extra bucks by occasionally driving up to Cambria and babysitting Logan.

Harp shook off his surprise and walked quickly toward her.

"Callie. I'm…I'm sorry I didn't stay around. I just…"

"It's okay, Uncle Neal," she said, using Harp's first name. "I couldn't hang around there, either."

"Well, uh…we're about to grab some dinner. Would you like to join us?"

"I don't want to interfere."

"You won't be interfering," Logan said, coming up behind his father. "I'm sure Dad would like a little more company than just me."

"Well, now that he mentions it…" Harp said.

She smiled and nodded. "All right. Thank you."

———————

LOGAN ORDERED SPICY tuna, while Harp went for his usual. Callie, not as experienced at sushi, decided on the sampler plate.

As they waited for their food, Harp said, "I can't tell you how sorry I am about your dad."

"Thanks," she said. "I know he meant a lot to you, too."

"He was a special man. I don't know what my life would have been like without him."

Callie bit the inside of her lip, obviously attempting to keep her emotions in check. Finally she said, "He left something for you."

Harp looked surprised. "For me? What?"

"I don't know." She opened her purse and withdrew a padded envelope about an inch thick. "It was in a box of things Dad told Michael and me about. He said once he was gone, we should open it and we'd know what to do. There were packages for several people inside." She looked at the envelope and then handed it to Harp. "This one has your name on it."

Written across the front in thick black ink was FOR HARP. Below this was his address in Cambria. Harp stared at his name for a moment, then looked at Callie and said, "Thank you."

As he started to set the package on the seat beside him, she asked, "Aren't you going to open it?"

Logan was sure Harp wanted to wait until he was alone, but Callie was Len's daughter, and the package was, in essence, one of his last messages. She'd want to know what was inside, too.

Harp also seemed to sense this. "Sure," he said, and set the package on the table.

A single strip of packing tape held the package closed. Harp carefully ripped it off, then reached inside the envelope and pulled out the contents.

A book. An *old* book.

Harp looked at it, his face growing in wonder. "Oh, my god," he said.

"What is it?" Logan asked.

Harp turned the book so Logan and Callie could see it. It was a hardcover, and though torn a little at one end, the dust jacket was still intact. Arched across the top portion was the title *Lost Horizon*, below this was a brown illustration of some buildings on a mountain, and at the very bottom was the name James Hilton.

Logan had read *Lost Horizon* in high school. It hadn't been an English class requirement. It was something Harp had suggested he read. And while the story was long dated even then, Logan had enjoyed it enough to read it again in college.

In almost fearful anticipation, Harp opened the cover, sucked in a breath, then touched the inside near the top.

Softly, Logan said, "Dad?"

Harp looked at him, his eyes brimming with tears, and showed Logan what he'd found.

Written on the inside cover in pen was TOM HARPER.

Harp's big brother. Logan's uncle whom he had never met.

"I haven't seen this since before he left for…before he left home," Harp said. Logan knew his father had only been ten when his brother joined the navy during the war. "He used to have me read parts out loud to him when he was working around the farm. Said it was good practice for me."

Logan had never known that. He thought *Lost Horizon* was a book his father had wanted him to read just as a whim. How wrong he'd been.

"He took this with him," Harp went on. "I thought it got lost over there."

Callie said, "My dad once told me the day Tom's plane didn't return was one of the worst of his life. He must have found the book in Tom's things and saved it. He probably meant to give it to you long ago."

"I didn't realize they actually served together," Logan said.

Harp nodded absently, his attention still on the book. "They were both ordnancemen on PBYs, just on different planes."

Callie picked up the discarded packaging and looked inside. "There's something else," she said. She withdrew a white, business-sized envelope and handed it to Harp.

This was nowhere near as old as the book. On the front was scrawled MANILA.

"What's that mean?" Logan asked.

Instead of answering, Harp looked inside the envelope, then closed it again without showing it to anyone else.

"It's nothing," Harp told him. He put the book and the envelope back into the package, and set it on his lap, out of sight.

There were so many questions Logan wanted to ask—about Uncle Tommy, about the book, about the envelope—but Harp was a million miles away.

After their food finally arrived, and they'd started eating, Callie glanced at Logan. "Dad mentioned your, uh, trip a few months ago."

"My trip?" Logan asked.

"Where you helped that girl? Brought her back?"

Logan looked at his father. "I didn't know we were sharing that with other people."

"You can't seriously think I wouldn't have told Len," Harp said.

Logan frowned, and turned back to Callie. "I got lucky, that's all. There's not much of a story to tell."

She hesitated a moment. "I'm not asking you to tell me the story. I'm asking you for help."

3

"HELP? WHAT KIND of help?" Logan asked, hoping he was wrong about where Callie was going.

"It…it actually wasn't my idea. It was Dad's."

"Len?" Harp said, looking at her with interest.

She nodded. "When he went into the hospital last weekend, the doctors told us it was very unlikely he'd be coming out. My brothers and I took turns sitting with him so that he was never alone. He slept a lot, but there were a few times when he'd wake and want to talk." She smiled at the memory. "He and I, we've always talked a lot, and when I became a lawyer, it seemed as if we talked more than ever. Every time I ran into a problem case, he was the first one I turned to. I can't remember a time when he didn't suggest something I hadn't thought about." She paused. "One night at the hospital, he wanted to talk about how work was going, and about any issues I might be having.

"I told him I did have one case that had reached a point where I didn't know what to do next. Unfortunately, it wasn't something that could be fixed with a creative motion in court or a well-written letter on firm stationery. He said he wanted to hear about it anyway, so I told him. When I finished, I thought he'd fallen asleep, but apparently he was thinking. After a bit, he opened his eyes and said, 'You need to talk to Harp.'"

As she said his name, Harp rubbed a self-conscious hand across his mouth.

Callie shifted her gaze to Logan. "That's when he told me about what you did for that girl, that you'd gone clear to Asia to find her."

"It wasn't as big a deal as he probably made out," Logan said.

Harp frowned. "Don't listen to him. It was a big deal. If Logan hadn't been there…" He shook his head.

Callie's eyes were still on Logan. "I've come to a dead end. I'm hoping there might be something you could do."

"I'm sure there is. We'd be happy to look into it, won't we, Logan?" Harp said.

Logan adjusted himself in his chair. What he'd done for Harp's friend Tooney, bringing the man's granddaughter back, had happened because if he hadn't done something, no one would have. He wasn't so sure that was a good habit to get into. Then again, Callie was basically family. You didn't turn your back on family.

"What exactly are you hoping I'll do?" he asked.

"Find my client's wife," she said.

Her answer did nothing to dissipate his discomfort. "If you think I'm some kind of missing persons expert, you're mistaken."

"Technically, she's not missing."

"Technically?"

Callie took a moment to collect her thoughts, then said, "My client's name is Alan Lindley. A month and a half ago, he and his wife Sara went to San Diego for a long weekend. On their last day, they decided to visit Tijuana. He says they had a wonderful time, but as they were headed back for the border, Sara realized she'd lost her passport and didn't have any other ID. Alan crossed the border alone to get her driver's license out of her luggage so they could get her a temporary passport, but when he got to the car, her things weren't there. Only a note telling him she was gone."

"Oh, that's horrible," Harp said.

"I'm sorry for your client, Callie, but people leave marriages all the time," Logan said.

Harp shot him a look. "Logan, where's your compassion?"

"I have compassion, Dad. But if this woman left, she must have had her reasons."

"I'm not finished," Callie said. "They went to San Diego because they were celebrating."

"Wedding anniversary?" Harp asked.

Callie shook her head. "At the time, their first anniversary was still a month away. Sara came into the marriage with a daughter. Emily is two now. What Sara and Alan were celebrating was that his adoption of Emily had been finalized the week before."

"She didn't take the girl with her, did she?" Logan said.

"No, she didn't."

Logan shrugged. "I'm still not sure what I can—"

"Naturally, Alan was distraught," Callie said, cutting him off. "He couldn't understand why she'd left. By his account and others I've interviewed, they had a great marriage. He came to me because he wanted to find her, not to bring her back if she didn't want to come back, but to find out why she left. I was thinking it was going to be mostly a divorce case. We have other lawyers in the firm who handle those, but since Alan was one of my personal business clients, I agreed to help track Sara down. I did the obvious thing—hired a detective to look into it."

"So what did the detective find out?" Harp asked.

"Nothing."

Logan nodded, expecting as much. "She probably stayed in Mexico. That would make it hard for her to be found."

"No, you misunderstand me. He didn't find *anything*. Sara Lindley doesn't exist."

A thick silence descended on the table.

After several seconds, Logan said, "Maybe your detective didn't know what he was doing."

"I don't waste my money," Callie said, her tone serious. "I've used Joe Fulkerson dozens of times. He definitely knows what he's doing. Alan's wife has no history."

Harp leaned forward. "That doesn't make sense."

"Maybe it was a scam," Logan said. "Did she take any of his money, or something valuable?"

"No," Callie said. "The only things missing were a few of her possessions and pictures."

Logan's brow furrowed. "Pictures?"

"That's the last thing. When Alan got home, every picture in their house that Sara was in was gone. Even the digital shots on their computer had been permanently erased from the hard drive."

"*What?*"

"That's not all. Out of all Alan's friends and family, only his sister had a picture with Sara in it, and she was just in the background. Apparently, Sara was good at avoiding camera lenses."

"But that's…that's crazy," Harp said.

Callie simply shrugged.

"Have you gone to the authorities?" Harp asked.

"That's…not an option," she said.

Harp looked confused. "Why not?"

But Logan knew the answer. "Emily."

Callie nodded. "Exactly."

Harp was still lost. "Emily?"

"Sara's been using a false identity," Logan explained. "Which means the marriage, I'm pretty sure, is invalid."

"It is," Callie said.

"And if the marriage is invalid, then the adoption…"

Harp stared at Logan for a moment before it hit him. "Oh… oh, no."

"If I were to get the authorities involved," Callie said, "they'd have no choice but to take Emily away. I have a good friend in the FBI, but I don't even dare ask her for advice. She'd ask me questions I couldn't answer." She looked at Logan again. "If this were a simple matter of a wife ditching her marriage, my dad would have never brought you up. But after what we've learned, both

Alan and I are concerned that Sara is in trouble. If she is, Alan wants to help her, but he can't if he can't find her. That's what I'm hoping you can do. Find her, see if she's in trouble, then let me know."

Logan looked down at his food. He still had four pieces of spicy tuna left, but he was no longer hungry. "I'm not sure what more I can do that you haven't already done."

"Maybe there is nothing," she admitted. "But you'll come at it with fresh eyes, and given what I heard happened in Thailand, from an angle that is less…rigid than mine."

He glanced at his father, and could see that Harp was fully behind the idea. Helping Callie—and, through her, the memory of Len—was all the motivation his father needed. And if his father felt that way, could Logan really say no?

"I guess…I could at least talk to Alan. We can see where it goes from there."

Callie reached out and put her hand over Logan's. "Thank you."

4

CALLIE CALLED ALAN and set up a meeting for the next afternoon. The problem was, Alan lived in Riverside, about an hour's drive east of Los Angeles, and at least seven hours from San Francisco. Logan and Harp decided that since Cambria was halfway between the two, the best thing would be to drive home for the night, check in at the shop in the morning, then finish the trip to Alan's.

"I can be there if you need me," Callie offered.

Logan shook his head. "We should be okay."

"You're sure?"

"Unless you think it would be better."

"Alan's a good guy, just a little wound up about things."

"I'd be surprised if he weren't."

"If you need me, just call my cell," she said. "I'll be at Dad's house. We're going to go through some of his things, but it won't be a problem if you'd like to talk."

Harp put his arm around her back. "We'll call only if necessary."

She paused, then smiled. "I can't thank you both enough. Alan's always been a good client, but honestly, he's not the reason I want to do this. It's Emily. Someday, when she's older, she'll want to know what happened. I'd like Alan to be able to tell her."

"I'll do what I can," Logan said.

Driving south, Logan listened absently to a ball game on the radio, the announcers' voices helping him focus on something other than how the hell he was going to help Alan Lindley. At some point, he heard paper rustling, and looked over to see Harp reading the copy of *Lost Horizon*.

"You want me to turn the radio down?" he asked.

There was a delay of several seconds before his father glanced up. "What?"

Logan pointed at the volume control. "Is this too loud for you?"

Harp shifted his gaze to the dash as if he'd just noticed the radio was on. "No, it's fine," he said, returning to his book.

Logan lowered the volume anyway, but if his father noticed, Harp made no comment.

"That's not going to make you sick, is it?" Logan asked a few minutes later.

Another delay before another "What?"

"Reading in the car. It's not going to make you sick?"

"No." Harp's tone made it clear he thought that was a stupid idea.

Another few minutes passed. "Dad. What was the envelope Len left?"

Harp kept his eyes on the book. "Just something your uncle and I talked about once."

Logan could tell it was a lot more than nothing, but he had no idea what it could be. The envelope had said MANILA. As far as Logan knew, Harp had never been to the Philippines, and if it was the name of someone his father knew, it wasn't anyone Logan had ever met.

But he didn't push. His father had had a heavy couple of days. Len's passing was tough enough, but the book seemed to have affected him even more.

When Harp was ready, *if* he ever was, he'd tell Logan what was so important about the envelope.

———————

LOGAN WAS THE first one to arrive at Dunn Right Auto and Repair the next morning. That wasn't unusual. Unless he was taking the day off, he was always the first one in. He turned on the lights, opened the bay doors, and started the coffee maker. He then went into the office and checked the work orders on the vehicles he'd had to leave for the others to take care of while he was up north with Harp.

With one exception, all his projects had been completed and picked up by their owners. Reentering the garage, he saw that Joaquin, the garage's head mechanic, had arrived.

"Thought you weren't coming back until this afternoon," Joaquin said.

"Change of plans. I see no one got to Mrs. Galloway's Miata."

"Are you kidding? I tried to get Artie on it, but neither him nor Manny would touch it."

"What about you?"

"I'm not touching it, either."

The fact that the Miata needed a new transmission wasn't the problem. It was Mrs. Galloway. To say she was a pain in the ass would have been an understatement. Whenever she brought her car in, it was a scramble to see who could make themselves scarce first.

"One of you is going to have to deal with it now," Logan said.

"What are you talking about?"

"As soon as Dad gets in, he and I have to go out of town again."

"Not It!" someone yelled out behind them.

Joaquin and Logan turned toward the bay door. Manny had just walked in, his bag lunch in one hand, sunglasses in the other.

"Where you going now?" Joaquin asked Logan.

"Hey, not It," Manny said again. "You guys heard me, right?"

Joaquin gave him a quick glance, then looked back at Logan, waiting.

"It's a…family thing," Logan told him.

"How long?"

"Don't know. Could be a few days."

Joaquin groaned. "Fine." In a louder voice, he said, "Manny, you get the Miata."

"Hey, that's not fair," Manny said. "I called not It."

"Yeah, and last I checked in the mechanics guidebook, there's no not-It rule."

Manny glared at Logan. "Thanks a lot."

"Don't look at me," Logan protested.

"You're the one leaving, aren't you?"

Though Logan was tempted to help get the Miata project started while he waited for Harp to show up, doing so would mean he'd have to go home again to get cleaned up. Instead, as soon as Joy, their office manager, got in, he helped her go through some paperwork and put together a supply order that she could call in later.

When he'd dropped his father off the night before, they'd agreed to meet at eight a.m., but it wasn't until almost eight thirty when Joy said, "Your dad just pulled up."

Harp had lost his driver's license a few years earlier, and relied these days either on the high school kids he hired to chauffeur him around, or rides from his friends.

Today's victim was Barney Needham, a retired doctor and Harp's fellow member of a small group of elderly men who called themselves WAMO, which stood for Wise Ass Old Men, and yes, they knew the letters were in the wrong order.

As Logan stepped outside, his father was transferring a couple of suitcases into the back of the El Camino.

"Dad, we're not going to be gone that long," Logan said.

"This isn't all mine," Harp said, as if it should be obvious. "One's Barney's."

"Barney's?"

"He didn't have anything to do, so I invited him along," Harp explained.

Logan came within half a second of saying he didn't think that was a good idea, but then checked himself. Perhaps it wasn't such a bad thing. While Logan appreciated his father's interest in Alan's problems, Harp had the habit of unintentionally getting in the way sometimes. If Barney came along, maybe they could keep each other entertained.

Logan shrugged. "One of you will have to sit in the middle."

"Not It!" Barney yelled out.

5

THEY BREEZED THROUGH L.A. but got caught behind a traffic accident in Corona that slowed them to a crawl for about twenty minutes. Finally they pulled into the driveway of Alan Lindley's house in Riverside, not far from the University of California campus. The neighborhood was old and quiet, the houses probably built in the 1960s or '70s.

Heat assaulted them as they climbed out of the El Camino. Riverside was on the edge of the desert, and summers could get pretty toasty.

The door swung open before they reached it. Standing just inside was a man in his late thirties. Hugging his leg and peeking around from behind him was a little girl.

"Logan Harper?" the man asked.

"Yeah," Logan said, holding out his hand. "You must be Alan."

A quick nod accompanied the handshake.

"This is my dad, Harp," Logan said. "And our friend Barney."

"Harp. Barney," Alan said, shaking each man's hand. He reached down and hoisted the girl up. "This is Emily."

"Hi, Emily," Logan said.

The girl tucked a knuckle into her mouth, then turned and planted her face firmly in her father's shoulder.

"Come on in," Alan told them.

He led them through a small entryway into a large, open-plan living area. The furniture was a cross between the new and the old, an eclectic mix that worked well together. On the wall hung a TV playing a cartoon, the one with the sponge character Logan had seen on T-shirts.

Alan set Emily on the couch. "Daddy's going to talk to his friends for a few minutes, okay?"

She looked at Logan and the others warily.

"You want some goldfish?" Alan asked.

Emily's eyes brightened and she nodded. "Goldfissss, yes!"

Alan looked at Logan and the others. "Give me a second."

He went over to the kitchen area, and returned a few minutes later with a small plastic bowl of orange goldfish crackers.

"Here you go, sweetie." He handed the bowl to Emily, and she immediately settled back on the couch and popped a cracker into her mouth, her attention now fully on the TV.

Alan watched his daughter for a moment, then said, "Why don't we go over here?"

He led the group to the dining room table, a long oak affair that looked like it could have once been a door to an old church.

Once they were all seated, Alan said, "Callie tells me you can help find Sara."

Logan raised a palm. "I think it's a little too early to know that yet. If I can, I will."

"I'll take whatever you can do."

Alan's desperation wasn't limited to his face. It encased him like a parka.

Across the room, Emily laughed at the TV. Her father's gaze flicked to her, his eyes softening for a moment before worry filled them once more.

"Why don't we start at the beginning?" Logan said. "How did you and Sara meet?"

"My job keeps me pretty busy," Alan said. According to Callie, Alan ran a small accounting firm. "To keep it from driving me crazy, I got in the habit a few years ago of attending some of the free talks they give at the university. I've always enjoyed history, so anytime they had a lecture like that, I was probably there. It was a great way to not think about numbers. Sara and I met at a discussion about the terracotta warriors. You know, in China?"

Logan nodded.

"She was with a couple people I knew. We all got to talking, went out for coffee, and, well, she and I started hanging out."

"Did she start talking to you first? Or you her?"

The muscles in Alan's face tensed. "I know what you're thinking, but she didn't come after me. I went after her. Hard. She tried to break up several times while we were dating, but finally she gave in."

Logan knew there were manipulators who could make a person like Alan think they'd done all the work. Was Sara one of these? He had no idea, but knew it was best not to share that thought at the moment.

"I love her," Alan said. "I love her more than I've loved anyone in my life. Well, except maybe for her daughter...*our* daughter."

"Tell us about the day she disappeared."

Alan gazed down at the table, then told them about the afternoon in Tijuana. When he was through, Logan took a moment before he asked the next question.

"Who do you think took the bags out of your car?"

"I've thought about that a lot," Alan said, frowning. "But I have no idea."

"Could it have been one of her friends?"

"Sara didn't have a lot of friends. Just a couple of the women here in the neighborhood, and a few people at the office. My accounting agency is small, but we do a good business. Sara worked there part-time, office management stuff."

"What about the people she was with when you met her that

first time?"

"She'd actually only met them at another lecture, and were just sitting together. After we started dating, she didn't really see them much anymore."

"But did you check them out?"

"Of course I did," Alan said angrily. He paused. "Sorry."

"It's okay."

"It's just…I've talked to everyone I've ever seen her with. No one knows what happened to her."

"Could be one of them is lying."

"I guess so, but I never got that sense."

"Was there anyone you couldn't find? A friend or acquaintance you haven't been able to talk to?"

Alan shook his head. "I've talked to everyone I can remember. I realize someone must have helped her. I just have no idea who that could be."

"Can you show me the note?" Logan asked.

Standing, Alan said, "It's in my bedroom. I'll be right back."

"Why don't I come with you?" Logan suggested. He wanted to take a look at the rest of the house, and try to get a sense of what Sara's place had been within it.

Alan nodded. "Sure, okay."

Logan followed him into a hallway, and up some stairs to the second floor. The upstairs hallway was lined with framed photographs, or rather, it would have been if not for the dozen or so empty nails spaced sporadically among the pictures that were left. Remembering what Callie had told him, Logan guessed the blank spots were places where photos Sara had been in once hung. Six weeks on, and Alan had not replaced them with anything. Was he hoping she'd come back and everything would return to the way it was, including the wall? Or did he want the physical reminder that his wife was gone? Most likely, the emotional wound was still so raw he didn't have the energy to do anything about it.

The master suite took up the whole south end of the floor. In addition to the normal things a bedroom had, there was also a sitting area and a sliding glass door that led out onto a balcony.

Logan waited near one of the chairs while Alan stepped into a walk-in closet. A moment later, he reemerged holding a wooden jewelry box.

"This was my mother's," he said. "I gave it to Sara right after we got married."

He opened it, revealing an empty, black velvet-lined tray. He lifted this out and put it on the chair. Underneath, sitting on more velvet, was a folded envelope.

Alan removed it and handed it to Logan.

Carefully, Logan pulled out the letter and read it. Nothing in it seemed to shed any new light on the situation.

"This was the only thing left in the car?"

Alan was looking wistfully at the letter. "Yes. Everything else was gone."

"Callie told me about the missing pictures."

Alan's face dropped. "You saw the hallway."

"Yeah."

"She cleaned out the photo albums, too. Even the computers."

"I assume they weren't gone before you left on your trip."

"No. At least not the ones on the wall. The photos in the albums could have already been gone, and maybe the ones on the computer, too. I didn't regularly check those."

Someone had come into the house while Alan and Sara were gone. The same person who'd taken Sara's luggage? Or were there more than one other person involved?

"So everything she was in?"

"All but one with Sara in the background. It isn't great, but…"

"Callie mentioned that."

"It wasn't mine. It was my sister's. I had her email it to me after Sara left."

"Could you forward it to me?"

"Of course."

"Besides the photos, what else did she take?"

Alan absently glanced at the closet. "Not much. She left most of her things here."

"Really?" Logan asked, surprised. "What about the stuff from the place where she lived before moving in with you?"

"She was in a furnished apartment. None of it was hers." They were both quiet for a moment, then Alan said, "Yeah, I know. I guess that should have been a red flag, huh? But she said she was new to the area, and didn't have any stuff yet."

A red flag, yes, but... "Don't beat yourself up about it. I don't think anyone would have thought twice about it. I wouldn't have. Where did she say she'd moved from?"

"Back east. Philadelphia."

"Did you meet any of her family? Old friends?"

Alan shook his head. "Said she was an only child, and that her mother had died a few months earlier. That was the reason she'd moved out here, you know, to start fresh."

"What about her father?"

"She said he left when she was young, never really knew him. So it was just her and Emily."

"Well, then, what about Emily's father?"

"Sara told me he was a guy she'd gone out with a few times, but it didn't work out. She never even told him about Emily."

All nice and neat and packaged so that it sounded believable while being extremely difficult to disprove.

Logan handed back the note. "Thanks for letting me see this."

Alan returned it to the bottom of the jewelry box, and put the box back into the closet. When he came out, he hesitated in the doorway. "There was something else she left."

"What?"

Looking like he really didn't wand to discuss it, Alan said, "It's...in Emily's room."

Without another word, he headed into the hallway.

Emily's room was near the top of the staircase. There was a dresser and a toy chest and a kid-sized bed, but the star was the walls. They had been turned into a giant mural of rolling hills and rivers and castles. There were knights on horses, a prince and princess in a carriage, and kids playing in a field. This wasn't some amateur job done by a person with limited skill. This was a beautiful, detailed work of art.

"Sara painted it," Alan said, as if reading the question on Logan's mind. "Took her three months to finish."

"It's amazing."

"It is, isn't it?" For a few seconds it seemed that Alan had forgotten about everything else, and was simply enjoying what his wife had created.

To Logan it was more than just a mural on a child's wall. It was an attempt by a mother who knew she wouldn't be around for long to leave something lasting for her little girl.

About two feet down from the ceiling, a narrow shelf ringed the room. On it were dozens of small stuffed animals. Dragons and bunnies and bears and turtles and several other creatures looked down into the room, guarding it from some imaginary evil. Alan used the frame of Emily's bed to step up and reach between two of the animals. When he came back down, he was holding a small, square box.

"This was at the foot of the bed when I got home," he said.

He opened it. The first thing Logan saw was a photograph of Alan holding a younger Emily in his lap. They both appeared to be laughing. Alan pulled the picture out, revealing a ring underneath. Turning the photo over, he held it so Logan could read the message scrawled on the back.

Pls. give the ring to Emily when she's old enough. Tell her it was always worn with love.

Logan didn't want to ask, but he knew he had to. "Her wedding ring?"

Alan nodded. "This is the picture she used to keep in her wallet. It was right in front so anytime she opened it, she'd see us. Why would she leave this here?"

Logan didn't immediately reply. Some definite ideas were running through his mind, but he wasn't sure how much he should say because there was no way to know if he was even close to being right. He realized, though, he had to say something.

"If you ask me, I'd say she didn't leave you."

Alan stared at him. "She's been gone for a month and a half. It sure looks that way to me."

"What I mean is she didn't leave *you*. Yes, she's gone, but you're not the reason. There's something else going on. Something that made her think she had no choice but to go. I don't think it has anything to do with you."

Alan seemed unsure.

"Look at it this way. When people go on the run, the thing they fear even more than getting caught is for anything to happen to those important to them." Logan moved his gaze to the mural. "Look at the wall. That's the work of a parent who truly loves her child, and wanted to give her something special. The woman who painted this, if she was leaving her husband because she wasn't happy…" He pointed at the wall again. "This woman would have taken her daughter with her. She left Emily with you because she knew Emily would be safe here."

"I…want to believe that," Alan admitted. Logan could tell he'd been hoping that was the case.

Logan touched the photo still in Alan's hand. "Believe it."

———————

TEN MINUTES LATER, Logan, Harp, and Barney climbed back into the El Camino. Logan started the engine, but didn't put the car in gear.

"Well?" Harp said.

Logan eyed the house, saying nothing.

"Are you going to help him?" his dad asked.

Logan remained motionless for several more seconds, then he put the car in reverse.

"Yeah. I'm going to help him."

6

THE SKY HAD grown dark as the thunderstorm moved in. Nearly every afternoon they'd come, big billowy towers of clouds around lunchtime that turned into a dark menacing mantle covering the sky a few hours later. Sometimes the rain would last only a few minutes, sometimes for an hour or more, but always, there was the lightning.

And the thunder.

Sara knew she should have been used to it by now, but she wasn't. Every time the thunder clapped she'd jump, then pull the blanket tight around her as she huddled on the couch, as far from the windows as she could get. That was the only place she felt even remotely safe.

She'd tried the bathroom once. It had only the one frosted window, and not being able to see turned out to be worse. So she stayed in the main room, and cowered as the bright flashes and thunderous roars of each storm ran its course.

As much as it terrified her, it was, in an odd way, her favorite part of the day. For however long a storm would last, she could forget about everything else, and think only of the light and the sound and the rain and the darkness. Because when the clouds cleared away, the real world returned, and when that happened, everything came rushing back.

Even when she tried to draw, something that had always been her escape before, she couldn't forget and would end up pushing her sketchbook away.

Her overriding worry was that she had waited too long to disappear. It didn't matter that nearly seven weeks had passed without anything happening. They'd already been closing in, forcing the change of plans and hastening her departure.

"A quick trip to celebrate," she'd suggested. She smiled, though inside she'd never felt more horrible. "Just the two of us, in San Diego." She had already arranged for Rachel to watch Emily, and though she knew her husband had work he'd been planning on doing that weekend, she'd convinced him to go.

But even rushing things, had it been too late? If yes, she didn't know what she'd do. The pain would be…unbearable.

Outside everything suddenly glowed white. She didn't see where the lightning struck, but it was *close*. She barely blinked when the house rattled with an explosion of thunder.

She didn't even know she was yelling until the noise in the sky began to die. Without a doubt, that was the closest she'd come to being hit since she'd arrived.

Putting her hands over her head, she curled into a ball.

All she could think about was the nightmare outside.

Terrifying and nerve-fraying.

And freeing.

If only for a little while.

7

"I CAN'T TELL you how much I appreciate this," Callie said over the phone. "Anything you need, just let me know and I'll take care of it."

"I'd like to talk to that PI you hired," Logan told her. He was sitting in the El Camino in the parking lot of the University Place Inn. Harp and Barney were in the office arranging rooms for the night.

"Absolutely. Let me give him a call and see when I can get you in."

"Thanks."

Three minutes later, Logan's two traveling mates walked back outside. Instead of getting in, Barney headed down the walkway along the three-story motel, while Harp walked around to the driver's window of the El Camino, motioning for Logan to roll it down.

"We're on the first floor near the back. One twenty-three and one twenty-four," Harp said. He handed one of the keys through the window, then headed off after his WAMO buddy.

As soon as Logan was parked in front of the rooms, they all got their bags out of the back and split up. Logan's room was a balmy eight-two degrees, so he fiddled with the thermostat until the air conditioner clicked on. The temperature was just starting to get bearable when his phone rang.

"Fulkerson said he'd see you whenever you could get to his office," Callie told him.

"Hold on." Logan searched for paper and a pen, finding them in the nightstand drawer. "All right. What's his address?"

She gave it to him. "Call me if you need anything else. Whatever it is, I'll make it happen."

When Logan stopped by Harp and Barney's room on the way out, his dad, of course, wanted to come along, but Logan told him it would be easier if he saw Joe Fulkerson on his own.

As he was starting up his car, Harp rushed out of his room.

Logan leaned through his open window. "Dad, I promise I'll tell you everything when I get back."

"What?" Harp said, confused.

"I need to do this alone."

"You already made that clear. I just…I just forgot something."

Now it was Logan's turn to be confused.

Harp pointed toward the passenger side of the truck. Sitting on the bench seat was the padded envelope Callie had given Harp back in Sausalito. Logan could see the copy of *Lost Horizon* sitting just inside it. He picked up the package and passed it to his dad.

"Thank you," Harp said, clutching it with one arm against his torso.

Logan could see a million thoughts and emotions racing through his father's eyes. He wished he knew the right thing to say, something that would get his father to open up and talk, but he was afraid anything he might try would cause Harp to clam up completely.

So Logan simply smiled and said, "No problem."

JOE FULKERSON'S OFFICE was in an old, brown, brick building several miles from the university. The sign on the door said FNR Investigations, and it appeared to take up half of the fourth floor.

Logan waited in the lobby for less than two minutes before an older Latina led him into the inner workings of FNR. The few single offices he saw were along the outside walls, taking up prime window territory. Most of the employees, though, seemed to work in a large bullpen area of high walled cubicles.

Fulkerson was not in a cubicle. He had a corner office that looked toward the smog-hidden mountains. His desk was an old metal monstrosity that seemed out of place with the rest of the furnishings. Joe was sitting behind the desk, squinting at a computer monitor. He was a thin, middle-aged man who'd buzzed what little hair he had left on his head as close to his skin as he could without shaving it off. It was what Joaquin back at Dunn Right liked to call the full Captain Picard.

"Mr. Fulkerson?" the woman said. "This is Mr. Harper."

Fulkerson immediately rose from his chair, a large smile appearing on his face. With unnecessary enthusiasm, he came around the desk and extended his hand.

"Mr. Harper. Thanks for coming down."

They shook.

"You can call me Logan."

"And I'm Joe." Fulkerson glanced at the woman. "Thank you, Mary."

She smiled and left.

Fulkerson motioned toward the guest chair in front of his desk. "Please, have a seat." Once they were both settled, he said, "Would you like anything to drink? Coffee? Tea? Water?"

"I'm fine, thank you."

They looked at each other for a moment, then Fulkerson leaned forward. "So Mrs. Johnson says you have some questions?"

"Yes, about the Lindley case," Logan said.

"Right." Fulkerson looked at his computer screen, moved the mouse, and clicked a few keys on the keyboard. "What can I help you with?"

"First off, I would love to take a look at the report."

Fulkerson's smile turned stale. "I believe Mrs. Johnson has copies of that at her office."

"She probably does," Logan agreed. ""But I'm not at her office, I'm here. And she said you'd be happy to help me."

The private detective was having a hard time holding on to what was left of his smile.

"Is it a problem?" Logan asked.

"Of course not." He picked up his phone and punched in a number. "Mary? Can you print out a copy of the Lindley file and bring it in here, please?" After he hung up, he stood. "I'll walk you out to the lobby. My secretary will bring you the report as soon as she's done."

Remaining in his seat, Logan said, "Actually, I have a few questions I'd like to ask."

"Like what?"

Logan eyed him for several seconds. "Sit down, Mr. Fulkerson. I'm not here to assess your performance or take work from you or anything like that. I've been asked to provide Alan Lindley with some help, and that's all I'm trying to do."

With reluctance, Fulkerson lowered himself back into his chair. "If Mrs. Johnson requires more help on the Lindley case, my agency is fully capable of providing that."

Logan almost laughed. "I'm betting your *agency* does a lot of business with Mrs. Johnson's firm. Is that right?"

"The relationship between our companies is none of your business," Fulkerson said, but the narrowing of the man's eyes told Logan he'd been right.

"I don't give a damn about the relationship. I have nothing to do with it. And just so we're clear, I haven't been hired for *anything*. I've been asked to help. That's it."

"Right. You do this job gratis, and then use that to leverage yourself into more work. I've seen people do that a million times. Go ahead and try, but don't expect me to assist."

"Fair enough." Logan retrieved his phone.

"What are you doing?"

"Just give me a second." He found the number he was look-ing for and placed the call. As soon as it was answered, he said, "Callie? It's Logan."

Fulkerson tensed a little at the use of Callie's first name.

"How did the meeting go?" she asked.

"I'm actually sitting here with Joe right now."

"Joe? He must really hate you."

"That seems to be my take. Mind if I put you on speaker?"

"Not at all."

Logan activated the speaker function as he set the phone on the desk. "Are you still there?"

"I'm here," she said, her voice coming out clearly.

"Hello, Mrs. Johnson," Fulkerson said. "I think there might be some kind of misunderstand—"

"Let me fill her in first," Logan jumped in. "You can correct anything I get wrong. Callie, I'm calling because we have a little problem you might be able to help with. Joe here seems to think I'm angling to take future work you might otherwise send his way. Is that right, Joe?"

"Well, I'm not sure I'd put it that way," Fulkerson stammered.

"It's how you just put it to me. Anyway, I tried telling him I have no interest in taking work from him, but he doesn't seem to believe me. And, because of that, he's, well, reluctant to provide additional help."

Callie said, "Is that right, Mr. Fulkerson?"

"Mrs. Johnson, your firm and FNR have had a very close working relationship for several years. I would hate to see any-thing damage it."

"Good," Callie said. "Then you'll give Mr. Harper whatever help he needs. Mr. Harper is not now, nor will he ever be inter-ested in taking over any of the work you do for us. Mr. Harper is strictly a specialist I've brought in on this. You will treat him with the same respect you would treat me. If you do not, then the relationship you are so worried about will indeed be in trouble. Is that understood?"

"Of course," Fulkerson said, looking uncomfortable. "Like I said, it was simply a misunderstanding. Of course I'll give Mr. Harper whatever help he requests."

"That's *any* help, Mr. Fulkerson. If you incur any cost, just forward them directly to me."

"I completely understand." The mention of potential revenue brightened his demeanor considerably.

"Are we finished here?" she asked.

Logan looked at Fulkerson, who nodded.

"Yep," Logan said. "That about covers it."

"Just call if you need anything else."

"Will do, Callie. Thanks." He disconnected the call, and looked at the detective. "So we're good?"

"Yes." Fulkerson still wore some of his earlier resentment, but he'd obviously gotten the message.

"Excellent. How did you determine Sara Lindley wasn't who she said she was?"

"All that's in the report."

"I'm sure it is," Logan said, waiting.

Fulkerson sucked in a breath, and blew it out through his teeth. "Various ways. First we checked the background she'd given her husband, but could find no trace of her prior to when she'd moved to Riverside. Then we checked with the management company that runs the apartment building she was living in when she and Mr. Lindley met. From them we were able to get a copy of her rental application, which, we'd been told, had been thoroughly checked and approved. None of the previous addresses or jobs she listed actually exist, but since they were back east—"

"Philadelphia?"

Fulkerson gave Logan an obligatory smile. "Right. Because of that, the management company relied strictly on phone calls. Turns out all the phone numbers she listed were for disposable phones you can pick up at any convenience store."

"Let me guess," Logan said. "None of them are active anymore."

"Not a single one."

"Did you check the addresses?"

"Mr. Harper, we do know how to do our job. Of course we checked them. In fact we went so far as to hire an investigator in Philadelphia to visit each location. The addresses themselves existed, but the businesses they were supposed to represent never did."

That was consistent with what was already clear—whoever Sara Lindley really was, she didn't want anyone to find out. "What else?"

"Driver's license, fake. Social Security number, valid, but was actually issued to a woman killed in a car accident overseas three years ago. The Social Security Administration doesn't even know that yet."

The door to the office opened and Mary reentered. She set a gray, nine-by-twelve-inch envelope on Fulkerson's desk, and retreated without saying a word.

"Your copy of the report," Fulkerson said, nodding to the envelope.

Logan grabbed it and pulled out the sheaf of about two dozen pages, stapled together in the upper corner. The top sheet was an assignment report, detailing the information Callie had given FNR. Logan flipped to the next page.

"Are you going to read that now?" Fulkerson asked. "Mrs. Johnson's firm isn't my *only* client. I do have other things that need my attention."

Logan was tempted to meticulously go over every page, but the only thing that would accomplish was pissing off Fulkerson again. As satisfying as that might be, it would only make things more difficult. He did a quick thumb-through of the pages, stopping only on the summary of potential leads near the back.

"Did you follow up on any of these?" he asked.

"Any of what?"

Logan turned the report around and pointed at the list of five items. Three were derived from information they'd gathered from Alan, no more than offhand comments or feelings—Sara's desire to go to San Francisco, her interest in art, and something she'd said once about the Midwest that made Alan think she'd spent considerable time there at some point. The other two were based on mobile phone records, calls Sara had made to Alan that were pinpointed to cell towers nowhere near Riverside. One was in the Laguna Beach area, while the other was at the far side of the state, in Braden near the border with Arizona. A follow-up conversation with Alan revealed he had no knowledge of these trips.

Fulkerson leaned forward so he could read the summary better. "Yes, of course we did. We had people looking out for her in San Francisco, but at the time the investigation was called off, we'd had no sign of her. As for her interest in art, I'm sure you can imagine how ambiguous that is. Short of putting someone in all the museums and art galleries on the West Coast, there was little we could do on that front. And a similar thing can be said about the potential Midwest connection."

Logan had figured as much about all three. He was more interested in the phone calls. "And these?"

Fulkerson nodded. "We sent investigators to both places. Out of the two, Laguna seemed the most promising. There's a thriving art community there, so it also checks that box."

"And?"

"And we found nothing at either place."

"How long were your investigators there?"

"Long enough."

"How long?"

"A day at Laguna. A couple of hours at Braden."

"Why only a couple hours?"

"It's a small town, and chances were she was just passing through on the interstate, perhaps stopped to get some gas."

"On her way to where?"

"That, we have no way of knowing. If she hadn't made that

call, we wouldn't have even known she'd gone out that way."

"Doesn't seem to me like enough time spent in either place."

Logan could sense Fulkerson trying not to glare at him. "You'll have to take that up with Mrs. Johnson."

"Why is that?"

"We recalled our people because she decided to put the investigation on hold."

Emily again, Logan realized. Either Callie or Alan had begun to worry that the more Fulkerson and his team looked into things, the more likely word would get to the wrong people that the adoption wasn't legitimate.

He glanced through the rest of the report, but didn't see anything that needed clarification at the moment, so he smiled and stood up. "Thank you for your time. I'll call you if I need anything else."

The look on Fulkerson's face was not what Logan would call excited.

8

LOGAN FOUND A Starbucks, grabbed a cup of coffee, took the only empty table left, and then carefully went through Fulkerson's detailed report. By the time he was done, his barely touched coffee was lukewarm.

While the notes on the investigation filled out a few things he was hazy on, it had provided no new information. What it did do was make Logan think more about the out-of-character phone calls Sara had placed from Laguna Beach and Braden. They were the only halfway decent leads. But were either of them important?

The only way to know for sure was to check both places, and given the distance between them, it would go a lot faster if he had help. While Harp and Barney might be able to assist Logan wherever he went, he was not about to send them off on their own.

He considered his options, then pulled out his phone.

"Yes?" a gruff voice answered after a single ring.

"Dev? It's Logan Harper."

"Logan," Dev Martin said, brightening. "How ya doin'?"

"I'm okay. You?"

"I got nothing to complain about."

Like Logan and Harp, Dev Martin also lived in Cambria. He

was in his sixties, but looked at least ten years younger. A former Marine and Vietnam vet, he'd kept himself in great shape. There were few people, no matter their age, who'd want to mess with him. Dev and his network of former servicemen had proved extremely useful when Logan was looking for Tooney's granddaughter, Elyse.

"Good to hear." Logan paused. "Let me cut right to it. I'm wondering if you might be able to help me out with something."

Dev let out a low laugh. "Didn't think this was just a social call."

Logan explained the situation and what he needed.

"Braden or Laguna Beach, huh?" Dev said. "Let me make a call, and I'll get right back to you."

"Thanks, Dev."

"No worries."

Less than five minutes later, Dev called back. "Chris Pepper," he said. "Goes by Pep. He was Navy, but don't hold that against him. Lives in Victorville, so could be in Braden in a couple of hours."

"Thanks, Dev. That sounds perfect. "

"Told him expenses would be covered."

"No problem," Logan said. "Give me his cell number and I'll text him the picture we have of Sara. It isn't great, but it's all we got."

"He'll do what he can with it," Dev said, and then rattled off the number.

"How soon can he get out there?" Logan asked.

"I assumed you wanted them out there right away, so I already gave him the go ahead. If he's not on the road already, he will be soon."

———————

IT WAS ALMOST six p.m. when Logan left the coffee shop. He thought Alan would still be at the office, but since he was close to the accountant's house, he decided to try him there. When no one answered his knock right away, he guessed that he would have to come back later.

Then he heard a voice, distant and muffled. "Coming!"

A few seconds later, the deadbolt slid free and the door opened.

"Logan," Alan said, surprised. "Come in. Come in." He moved out of the way so Logan could enter, then shut the door behind him. "Sorry. Emily took a late nap, and I guess I fell asleep in the chair."

"I didn't mean to wake you," Logan said.

"Are you kidding? I shouldn't be sleeping at all. I've got too much work to do."

"Yeah, I was beginning to think you were still at the office."

Alan hesitated before saying, "Emily goes to this nursery school in the mornings. She's been attending since...well, before, so I thought it best that she kept going. While she's there I go into the office. Then, unless there's no way around it, I work the afternoons here."

Alan could have easily afforded a nanny, but Logan could see that wasn't even an option for him. He was trying to make Emily's life as unchanged as possible, and while Sara was no longer there for her after nursery school, he was.

"I won't take up much of your time," Logan said.

"Whatever you need." Alan smiled. "Callie told me you'd agreed to help."

"I'll do what I can, but don't get your hopes up. The agency Callie used to try to find Sara seems pretty first rate. I don't have their resources so I may not find out anything at all."

"I realize that," Alan said. "I'm just happy someone's trying."

There was an awkward moment, then Logan said, "I'm here because I was hoping I could borrow the letter Sara left for you."

Alan looked surprised. "Why do you want that?"

"I just want to make a copy of it. I'll bring it back to you in the morning."

"Okay," Alan said, drawing the word out. "I still don't understand why, though."

"It's the only good sample of her handwriting that you have. I may not need it at all, but in case I do…"

Alan nodded. "Of course. Wait here and I'll get it."

He returned a little while later with the letter. Logan held out his hand to take it, but Alan hesitated.

"Please," he said, finally giving Logan the note. "Don't let anything happen to it. It's…the last thing, you know?"

"I understand," Logan said. "Thank you." He took a step toward the door.

"What are you going to do now?" Alan asked.

"Check a few things Callie's PI was working on."

"And if that doesn't work?"

"I'll figure that out then."

Logan walked through the entry and opened the door.

"If you need me for anything, anything at all, just call," Alan said.

"I will."

"I don't mean just questions. If Sara's in trouble, I want to help."

"Let's find out what's going on first. I promise—if there's something you can do to help, I'll let you know."

The answer didn't seem to completely satisfy Alan, but he nodded as if he knew it was the best he would get.

Logan wished there was something more encouraging he could say, but he wasn't going to lie. So instead, he nodded a good-bye then stepped outside with the note.

9

CHRIS "PEP" PEPPER dove into the search for the run-away mom with focused determination. Dev had warned him that things might not be as they appeared, so he should avoid any preconceived notions.

While Pep understood what Dev was trying to say, there was no way his own past couldn't help but influence his feelings. His childhood was fine enough, his mother distant but physically there. It was his brother Marko's kids that he couldn't keep out of his mind.

Pep's sister-in-law, Ann, had not run off unexpectedly. She'd been killed while crossing a street to get change for a parking meter. Just like that, Marko's kids lost their mother. Pep had seen how her absence affected them. Marko had tried to do the best he could, but his kids would always be living with that absence.

Pep knew Ann would have given anything to stay with her children, but that wasn't a choice she'd been given. Sara Lindley, on the other hand, *did* have that choice. Whatever trouble she might be in, how the hell could the best answer have been abandoning her child? No matter how much he tried to rationalize it as he drove across the Mojave Desert, he couldn't come up with a good answer.

He arrived in Braden at around eight thirty p.m., and spent the first two hours going around to restaurants and motels showing the picture Logan Harper had sent him. It was obvious the image of the woman had been cropped from a larger photo and enlarged to focus on her. She was a bit fuzzy and not fully facing the camera, but it was enough to get a pretty good idea of what she looked like. Unfortunately, no one had recognized her so far.

As the night grew late, he switched his focus to the several bars scattered around town.

"What're you drinking?" the bartender asked. It was the third bar Pep visited.

"Just want to show you something, if you don't mind," Pep said.

He already had his phone in his hand, so he brought up the picture and turned it so the bartender—an old, leather-skinned guy who looked like he'd been birthed from the desert itself—could see it.

"Ever see her before?"

The man looked at the screen, shrugged, and said, "I have no idea. People come in and out of here all the time."

Pep would have missed it if he hadn't been looking at the man's face when he glanced at the picture. For a brief second, the man's eyes widened. He *had* seen the woman before.

"You sure?" Pep asked.

The man stepped back from the bar. "Yeah. I'm sure."

Pep frowned and shook his head. "You're lying."

"Hey, buddy. I don't like being called a liar."

"Then tell me the truth when you answer the question. Have you seen her before?"

The bartender shrugged noncommittally.

So that's how the guy wanted to play it. Pep pulled a twenty-dollar bill out of his pocket and set it on the bar. "Tell me," he said, his fingers securing the bill in place.

The guy looked at Pep, then at the twenty, and smiled. "I

don't know. She looks like someone who came in here a couple times."

"Looks like, or is?"

Another shrug, but one that seemed to indicate the latter more than the former.

Pep picked up the twenty and folded it as if he were going to put it back in his pocket.

"Hey, what are you doing?" the bartender asked.

"I don't pay for guessing games."

"A twenty's not that much."

Now it was Pep's turn to shrug. He stepped toward the door.

"Wait a minute," the bartender said.

Pep paused.

"Yeah. I've seen her."

Walking back to the bar, Pep asked, "When?"

"A year or two ago. Came in a couple times."

That was not the answer Pep had been expecting. "A year or two? Why would you remember someone who came in here a couple times that long ago?"

"She, um, came in with someone I know."

"Someone here in Braden?"

"Maybe."

Pep took a step back like he was going to leave again.

"Okay, yes. Your friend there came in with a woman named Diana Stockley."

"And who is she?"

"Works at The Hideaway. It's another bar. She should be there if she's working tonight." He held out this hand. "So can I get my twenty now?"

———————

THERE WAS A woman behind the bar at The Hideaway when Pep walked in. From the other bartender's description, she had to be Diana Stockley.

The Hideaway was packed, so the woman was kept busy, running around and making drinks. Pep took a seat at the bar. Over a twenty-minute period, he started up a conversation with her without ever letting on he knew her name or of her potential connection to Sara. Finally he showed her the picture, but unlike with the old man, there wasn't even a hint that she'd ever seen Sara. So had the other guy been pulling a fast one just to get the money out of him? Or was this woman the one who was lying?

"Sorry. Who is she?" Diana asked.

"You don't know her?"

She shook her head. "No. She a friend of yours or something?"

"Hey, Diana. How 'bout another beer?" someone called from the far end of the bar.

"Excuse me," she told Pep, and walked off.

Pep hung at the bar for another quarter hour but was unable to grab any more time with the woman, so he began showing the picture around to the customers. Those that paid him attention showed no sign of having ever seen Sara. Finally, he decided he wasn't going to get much further that night. He'd go find a room, come back early the next evening before the place got busy, and maybe he could have some quality time with the bartender to find out for sure if she knew anything or not.

The parking lot of The Hideaway was small, and had been packed when he arrived, so he'd had to park along the side of the road a block away. When he got to his car, he unlocked the driver's door and pulled it open.

"You're looking for Sara?"

Pep turned. The voice had come from down the gap between two abandoned buildings, but it was too dark to see anyone.

"Who's there?" he called out, instantly alert. He'd only been showing Sara's picture, not giving out her name.

"I...I know where she is."

"Tell me who you are," Pep said.

"I can't. They'll kill me if they find out I'm here."

"Who'll kill you?"

"Never mind. I…I shouldn't have…shouldn't have come."

Footsteps moved toward the back of the building, quickly fading to nothing.

Pep ran after them. "No. Wait. Please, just tell me where she is. I need to—"

The board hit him square in the face, twisting him to the ground. Immediately, someone jumped onto his back, holding him down and hitting him in the ribs and head and kidneys. Stunned by the initial blow, he could do little to fight back.

"Stop looking for her," a voice whispered in his ear as the world started to close in on him.

Then another blow, and another.

If the voice said anything more, Pep didn't hear it.

10

LOGAN'S EYES SNAPPED open.

His phone was vibrating loudly against the nightstand, smacking against the hard surface. At home, a small tablecloth covered his stand, dulling the noise. That was definitely not the case here. He might as well have turned the ringer on.

He snapped it up and tapped the ACCEPT button.

"Hello?"

"Sorry to wake you." It was Dev.

Logan swung his feet off the bed, and glanced at the clock next to where the phone had been. It was 3:42 a.m. "What's going on?"

"It's Pep."

Pep? It took Logan a second, then he remembered—Pep, the man who Dev had arranged to check out Braden. "Did he find her?"

"He's in the hospital."

"Hospital? What happened?"

"I just got off the phone with a nurse a few minutes ago. Said Pep had asked her to call me. Apparently someone beat him up outside a bar. She tells me he wasn't drunk. Pep, I mean. The other guy—they don't know who he was."

"Did you get a chance to talk to him?"

"No. But apparently he said he'd been showing a picture around."

Sara's picture.

"I'm heading out there, but it's going to take me a good six hours at least," Dev said.

The hotel where Logan, Harp, and Barney were now staying was in Laguna Beach. At this time of night, they could probably reach Braden in about half the time.

"We'll meet you there," Logan said.

———————

BY THE TIME Logan was able to get Harp and Barney up and out the door, it was after four, so they didn't reach Braden until a quarter after seven. Even at that early hour, it was easy to tell the day was going to be a scorcher. Already the temperature was north of ninety-five degrees.

As they drove into town, they caught a glimpse of the Colorado River to the east, its wide, blue stripe at odds with the brown landscape that surrounded it. The city limits sign listed the town's population at 4,763. There was nothing gaudy or fancy about the place, just a working-class town full of people struggling to carve out an existence from one of the harshest environments on the planet. It wasn't a place Logan would ever choose to live—not a judgment, just an observation.

Following the instructions from the GPS on his phone, they exited I-40 and made their way to the Braden City Medical Center. Like the town itself, it was small—three one-story structures connected by covered walkways. The buildings were made of tan concrete blocks, textured on the outside to give them a rough-hewn look, and were surrounded by low-impact desert landscaping.

The hospital's lobby was about the size of Dunn Right's garage back home. Behind a counter along the far wall were two nurses and an older woman who appeared to be the receptionist.

"Can I help you?" the woman asked as they walked up.

"Thank you, yes," Logan said. "A friend of ours was brought in last night. Chris Pepper?"

Without even looking at her computer screen, she said, "Was he the one who was in that fight?"

"That's what we understand."

"We don't approve of drunks in our town."

"I was told he wasn't drunk."

She gave him a pitiful you-can't-believe-everything-you-hear look. "He *was* near a bar."

Logan forced a smile. "Is it possible to see him?"

She was shaking her head before he even finished. "You'll have to come back. Visiting hours don't begin until eight."

He'd been afraid of that. "Is there at least a way to find out how he's doing? We've driven for several hours to get here."

Looking doubtful, she said, "Have a seat, and I'll check."

"Thank you."

They found chairs not far away.

"I don't like her attitude," Harp said.

"Sometimes people get set in their ways," Logan said. "Only see the things they want to see."

Both Harp and Barney stared at him.

"Are you talking about *old* people?" Barney asked.

"We're not the only ones who can get set in our ways," Harp added.

Logan scoffed. "Did I say anything about old people?"

"It was implied," his father argued.

A grunted laugh escaped Logan's mouth. "Whatever you want to believe, Dad."

Before anyone could say anything else, the door to the left of the reception counter opened, and a woman wearing a white doctor's coat exited. She was short, with blonde hair and tired-looking eyes that Logan guessed meant she was closer to the end of her shift than the beginning. When she glanced at the receptionist, the older woman nodded toward Logan and the others.

"I understand you're friends of Mr. Pepper's, is that correct?" she asked as soon as she drew near.

All three stood.

"Yes," Logan said.

She held out her hand. "I'm Dr. Ramey."

"Logan Harper." They shook. "This is my dad, Harp, and our friend, Barney Needham."

"Barney's a doctor, so don't hold back," Harp told her.

"Harp!" Barney said.

"Dad!" Logan chimed in at the same time.

"What?" Harp asked.

Logan took a breath, then said to the doctor, "How is he?"

"Better than when he came in. He's got two broken ribs, a fractured cheek, numerous cuts and bruises. He definitely didn't come out the winner."

"What about the other guy?" Logan asked.

"As far as I know, the police are still looking for him."

"Was he drunk?" Harp asked, his eyes flicking toward the receptionist.

She hesitated. "Typically, that would be confidential, but I don't think it would be a problem to tell you he had no trace of alcohol or drugs in his blood."

"So he *wasn't* drunk," Harp said.

"No. He wasn't."

Harp looked at the receptionist again, his eyes hard and narrow. "You should tell your staff that so they'll stop making false accusations."

The doctor looked back at the woman, sighed, and turned to Harp. "I'll have someone talk to her." Her tone made it sound like this wouldn't be the first time.

"I know visiting hours aren't for a while yet," Logan said, "but is there any chance we can see him now? We came straight here the moment we arrived in town."

Dr. Ramey considered it, then nodded. "Sure. For a few minutes."

"Thank you," Logan said.

"This way."

As she led them to the door, the receptionist looked over with both surprise and disapproval. Harp stared back at her, then said in a whisper loud enough for everyone to hear, "He wasn't drunk."

They passed examining rooms, a nurses' station, and a lunchroom before turning down the hallway that served as the ICU. Dr. Ramey explained that while Pep's life wasn't in danger, it was still important to keep an eye on him in case there was any internal damage they hadn't been able to diagnose. She asked them to wait a moment then went off to talk to one of the nurses.

When she returned, she said, "All right, he's awake. Remember, not long."

"We'll remember," Logan promised.

"On the other side of that curtain," she said, pointing at one of the patient stalls lining the right side of the corridor.

Pep's bed had been raised so that he wasn't completely flat on his back. One of his eyes was swollen shut, and the other looked like it wanted to be. There was a bandage across his chin and another on his forehead above his left eyebrow. But even then, the look on his face was stoic, as if nothing had happened.

"Pep? I'm Logan Harper, Dev's friend. How you feeling?"

"Mr. Harper. Kind of you to come by." There was a dreamy, drug-induced quality to the man's voice.

"I'm Harp."

"And I'm Barney."

The corners of Pep's mouth turned up a fraction of an inch. "Hey."

"Can you tell us what happened?" Harp asked.

"What happened when?"

Logan gave him a smile. "We hear you were in a fight."

"Fight? Oh, yeah. You mean last night. Not sure you could call it that. A fight takes two people. As far as I can remember, I

66

was only a spectator. Or the punching bag. I guess that would be more accurate, huh?"

"Did you see him?"

"If I did, I don't remember."

"Did he take anything?" Logan asked. "Was it a robbery?"

"Don't know. Haven't checked. The nurse says I still have a wallet, but my phone…" He seemed to lose focus.

"What about your phone?"

"It, uh, got broken in the fight."

"Did he say anything to you?"

Pep concentrated for a moment. "Just that he knew where Sara was."

"That's it?"

Pep was quiet for a moment. "I…I'm not sure."

Whatever drugs Pep had been given were clearly starting to affect him. "Can you tell us why you were there?"

"Getting my car."

"Why was your car there?"

"Oh…uh…was showing the girl's picture…around…at bars."

"Any luck?" Harp asked.

Pep looked like he was going to say something, then his eyes fluttered, and he slipped out of consciousness.

11

AFTER WEEKS OF silence, there were nights Sara would forget to bring the phone into the bedroom with her when she went to sleep. That's why she didn't hear it the first time it rang several hours before she woke.

When it rang the sixth time, she was still in bed but awake, feeling the weight of another day ahead of her. The sound had been faint, almost imperceptible, but after so long in the cabin, hearing all the noises the walls and the surrounding woods made, the ring was like a fire alarm.

She jumped out of bed, raced into the other room, and grabbed the phone off the couch, afraid she'd arrived too late.

"Hello?" she huffed. "Hello? Hello?"

"Where the hell have you been?"

"What do you mean? Here. Where else would I be?"

"I've been calling you for hours."

"I...I didn't hear the phone ring."

"Sara, you *have* to hear it."

"I'm sorry. I'll turn the volume up."

There was a pause, then her caller said, "Things are happening."

Sara tensed.

"You need to be ready in case you need to move in a hurry. You remember the escape route?"

Sara closed her eyes, her shoulders sagging at the inevitability of it all. She had hoped they'd succeeded, that she had made a clean disappearance. But…

"I remember," she said.

"Good."

Her caller hung up.

Sara stared at the wall. Just moments before she had been suffocating at the thought of living through another boring day of nothing. Now she would give anything for another one like that.

God only knew if she would ever have another quiet day.

12

THEY FOUND ROOMS at a place called the Desert Inn Motel, and spent most of the day either hanging out there or at the hospital, waiting for Pep to regain consciousness.

Dev arrived just before noon, but even his presence wasn't enough for Pep to fight through whatever drugs the doctors had given him.

When visiting hours ended at eight, they drove back to the motel, ready to call it a night. Everyone but Logan.

"We'll probably put on a movie, if you want to join us," Harp said as they approached the room he and Barney were sharing next to Logan's. Dev's was downstairs, at the other end of the building.

Logan gave his dad a smile. It wasn't hard to see from the heaviness of Harp's eyelids and his lethargic pace that he wouldn't make it to the end of whatever movie he and Barney were planning on watching.

"Thanks, Dad. Think I'll pass."

Harp nodded. "See you in the morning, then."

They hugged.

"'Night, Logan," Barney said, looking nearly as tired as Harp.

"'Night, Barney."

The two older men went into their room, and Logan went into his.

That afternoon, he'd left the others at the hospital while he made a visit to the police station. The first thing he found out was that while the police were still dubious about Pep's level of involvement in the fight, no charges had been filed because there were no witnesses, and they had no idea who Pep's sparring partner had been.

The second thing was that Pep had been found on Thatcher Road, near some abandoned buildings, and about a block from a bar called The Hideaway. According to the cop he'd talked to, Pep had been leaning against the empty building, half conscious at best, when someone driving by had spotted him and stopped. The officer hadn't given Logan the address, but he'd described the buildings as adjacent to some railroad tracks.

In his dad's room next door, the TV went silent. Just to make sure there was no chance Harp or Barney would hear him, he waited for another hour before slipping out quietly.

Since Dev's old Jeep Cherokee was large enough for all four of them, they'd earlier left the El Camino at the motel and used Dev's SUV to shuttle to and from the hospital. Planning ahead, Logan had purposely parked his car far away from his dad's room, so that as he started it up now, there was no way Harp would hear it.

Less than ten minutes later, Logan pulled to a stop on the other side of the street from the abandoned building Pep had been leaning against when he was found. The structure looked like it was one medium-sized earthquake away from tumbling to the ground, and the same could be said for the ones on either side of it, too. The only place that seemed to be in decent shape was The Hideaway. In fact, Logan was willing to bet it was the only building still in use on the street, its parking lot filled nearly to capacity, with another half dozen cars strung out along the road.

He climbed out of the car, and walked over to the empty

building. The cop had said the fight—or ambush, depending on one's point of view—had taken place around the side, between the building and the one next to it.

Using the LED flashlight on his key ring, Logan hunted around until he found the spot where Pep had been attacked. It was only about a quarter way down the wide gap between the two properties, but far enough in so that passing motorists wouldn't have noticed anything.

There were dark smudges in the dirt where blood had soaked in then dried in the heat of the day. He did a quick three-sixty, but other than a few beer cans and fast-food wrappers, the ground was bare. If this had been a crime scene in L.A.—or even Cambria, for that matter—everything would have still been taped off. Apparently the Braden police had seen no reason to do so. That decision was backed up by the fact that, except for a few footprints probably made by investigators and by Pep and his assailant, no one else had been around.

Logan crouched down and slowly moved his flashlight across the dirt. The area where the fight occurred wasn't as disturbed as one might expect. The impression of a prone body, some marks that could have been knees or elbows, a few footsteps, and that was it. How anyone might think this was anything but a one-sided mauling, Logan had no idea. Pep had gone down at the start, and not pulled himself back up until it was over.

Logan moved the light in a wider arc, revealing more spots of dried blood marking the trail Pep created as he'd struggled to get to the front of the building. Standing, Logan slowly walked farther back. There he found two sets of footprints—one leading from the rear of the building to the disturbed dirt, and one headed in the opposite direction. It was clear they were both made by the same person. The tread was heavy and wide, not a tennis shoe, more like a hiking or working boot, and by the length Logan figured the person who wore them had to be at least six feet tall. He followed the prints all the way behind the building, finally losing them on a slab of cracked concrete. He circled it, looking to see if they started up again on another side, but found nothing.

Since Pep wasn't missing anything, this certainly hadn't been a robbery. A random beating? Could be. Some local thug sees an out-of-towner on his own and thinks easy target. It wouldn't even be close to the first time that ever happened.

The problem Logan had was separating the attack from the fact Pep had been asking around about Sara.

With nothing more he could learn at the fight scene, he returned to the El Camino, and drove a block down to The Hideaway, parking in a recently vacated slot behind the bar. The building utilized what appeared to be the most popular building material in town—concrete blocks. But unlike the ones making up the walls of the Braden City Medical Center, there was no artistic texture to The Hideaway's blocks, just flat gray stones holding up a flat roof.

As Logan got out of his car, a pickup truck and an old Plymouth sedan pulled into the lot, taking the last two spots. A middle-aged couple climbed out of the truck and waited until a woman traveling by herself got out of the sedan. Logan slowed his pace, waiting until they entered the bar, then went in a few seconds behind them.

The Hideaway wasn't as much of a dive as the exterior had led him to believe. The bar itself was set up along the wall to the right. The rest of the space was taken up by a dozen or more tables, most of which were occupied.

Somewhere a jukebox was playing an old seventies rock hit, "More Than a Feeling" by Boston. Judging by the look of the clientele, Logan guessed most of them had come of age when the song was released. Not an old crowd, but not a young one, either.

Logan snagged one of the few stools left at the bar, then caught the attention of the bartender. She gave him a nod and mouthed, "Be right there."

She was younger than most of her customers, probably no more than thirty. Her face was tanned and creased around the eyes, no doubt from squinting at the desert sun. She finished filling a pint of beer, set it in front of one of the other customers, and walked over to Logan.

"Evening," she said.

"How you doing?" he asked.

"Fine, thanks. What can I get you?"

"What do you have on tap?"

"Bud, Bud Light, Heineken, Sierra Nevada."

"I'll take a Sierra Nevada."

"You got it."

She walked back to the taps and pulled his drink. "Five bucks," she said as she set it in front of him.

He put six on the bar.

She smiled. "Thanks."

He gave her a nod as she walked off.

Taking a drink, he scanned the room, wondering if anyone there knew anything about Sara or what had happened to Pep. Maybe they all did, or maybe no one.

When he'd worked his way through most of his beer, the bartender returned.

"Another?" she asked.

"Sure," he replied.

A moment later, she walked back with the full glass, and Logan put six more bucks on the bar.

"Can I ask you a question?" he said.

She gave him a look like she knew exactly what he had in mind. "Not interested."

"Sorry?"

She leaned forward, and whispered so only he could hear. "You're not my type."

"Okay," he whispered back, "but that's not what I was going to ask."

Her eyes narrowed, wary but curious. "So what, then?"

"My name's Logan." He held out his hand.

She shook it, but said nothing.

Okay, he thought. "Did you hear about that fight last night?"

Now her curiosity turned into full-on suspicion. "Why? The bar had nothing to do with that."

"I didn't say it did."

She remained quiet.

"I'm not trying to cause trouble. It's just that the guy who ended up in the hospital is a friend of mine," Logan said.

He sensed a sudden shift in her demeanor, a distancing.

"Sorry to hear that," she said.

"I don't suppose you know who attacked him?"

"Attacked? I heard it was a fight."

"Not really. I don't think my friend even got a blow in."

"Sorry, don't know who *attacked* him. I don't even know who your friend is."

"I think you might have met him."

She shrugged. "I meet lots of people."

A woman walked up to the bar. "Hey, Diana. Can I get another rum and Coke?"

"It would have been last night," Logan went on. "Not long before he was beaten."

"Excuse me," the bartender—Diana—said to Logan.

She went off and made the woman her drink, but she didn't immediately come back over. Logan waited, leaving his second beer untouched. Finally she returned.

"So what?" she asked.

"I'm sorry?"

"So what if I might have met him? If he came in for a drink, yeah, I would have. Why's that important?"

"He was looking for a woman."

She snorted. "Like that never happens here."

Logan pulled out his phone and accessed the picture of Sara. "A specific woman." He turned the phone so that Diana could see it. "She's missing."

The bartender looked at it for a moment, then nodded. "Yeah, I remember your friend now. He didn't want a drink. He just showed me that picture."

"And?"

"I told him I'd never seen her before," she said. "I'm sorry about your friend, but I wasn't paying him that much attention."

She started to move off.

"Wait," Logan said. "Did he show the picture around? Maybe piss someone off? Anything like that?"

"Like I said, I wasn't paying attention to him," she said, shrugging. "Enjoy your beer, and have a nice night."

13

THE FLIGHT ARRIVED in Los Angeles at 11:44 p.m. Though it was on time, Dr. Erica Paskota glanced at her watch, annoyed. By the time she retrieved her rental car—with the special package that had hopefully been slipped into the trunk—waited for her two men who weren't scheduled to arrive for another thirty minutes, then drove the three-plus hours to Braden, she wouldn't arrive until after four a.m. at best.

Her man on the scene had been watching the woman for four weeks, but there had been no sign she'd had any contact with the target. Erica had begun to assume it was a dead end, but had left her watcher in place because caution was the best course.

Then there'd been the beating the previous night. The watcher had not seen the actual fight, but he *had* seen the man in the bar not long before he was attacked. That, in itself, wouldn't have been enough to draw the doctor's interest, but the picture the injured man had been showing around was.

Someone else was looking for the same person she was. Why? Who was he? And the woman bartender they'd been watching—did she actually know something?

Whatever the answers, this needed to end *now*. It had been going on way too long. Though she had other matters that required her attention, she could no longer trust this issue to anyone else. She had decided to fly out herself and lead the search. It was the only way she could be sure of a satisfactory ending.

She glanced at her watch again, even more agitated than before. She was sure the ending she craved lay to the East, but she wasn't getting there any faster as her plane endlessly taxied through LAX.

14

FOUR MORE BARS and Logan found himself no better off than he'd been when he left The Hideaway. It was almost midnight when he walked into the fifth, a place called the Sunshine Room. It was in a low-slung building connected to the Sand Castle Motel just off the main drag.

The Sunshine Room did not live up to its name. The interior was almost as dark as the desert night outside. Whereas The Hideaway had elevated itself above dive-bar status, the Sunshine Room seemed to embrace its seediness.

It was only large enough for four tables and the bar. A handwritten sign on the wall read: RESTROOM OUTSIDE AROUND BACK. The toilet's location didn't seem to help eliminate the stale odor of piss and beer that hovered in the room.

Logan walked over to the laminated bar, where a tired old man stationed on the other side looked annoyed by the fact he had a new customer.

Instead of asking Logan what he wanted, he merely looked at him, waiting.

Logan used his now familiar opening line. "What do you have on tap?"

"Beer." The man's voice was scratchy.

"Okay. Sounds good." It was Logan's seventh beer that night, but beside the first one, he'd only taken a sip or two of the others so he didn't really care what the man brought.

The bartender filled a glass with something that almost looked like water, and set it on the bar. "Four fifty."

Logan pulled out a ten.

When the bartender returned with his change, Logan pulled out his phone and turned it so the man could see the screen. "Did a guy come around last night and show you this picture?"

The bartender glanced at Sara's photo, then looked at Logan through narrow eyes. "You a cop?"

"No."

"You kind of look like one."

"Army," Logan said. "Once."

"That could be it, I guess." The man jutted his chin at the phone. "So what's the deal?"

"My friend got beat up last night near The Hideaway. I think it was because of this."

The man shook his head, said, "I don't know nothing," and started to turn away.

It was clear, though, that he did know something. "What did you tell him?"

Swiveling back, the man said, "Didn't tell him nothing. Nothing to tell."

"So he *was* here."

The bartender frowned. "I guess. So what?"

"My friend wasn't doing anything wrong. There was no reason for him to get beat up like that."

"Then that makes it all the worse, don't it?"

This time, the old man did walk off, not stopping until he reached the far end of the bar, where he started wiping down the counter. After a moment, Logan got up and walked over.

"What did you tell him?"

"Already told you. Nothing."

Logan stared at him, his face immobile.

The corner of the man's mouth twitched. "Maybe you should leave."

Logan remained silent.

The man opened the cash register and pulled out a five-dollar bill. "Here's your money back. I don't want it. Now get out."

Logan heard a chair behind him scrape across the floor. He didn't know if it was someone coming to the bartender's aid or heading for the exit, but there was no need to find out.

"Sure," he said. He took a step back, leaving the money on the bar. "Thanks for your help."

LOGAN'S ALARM WENT off at five minutes to two a.m. Though the El Camino's seat wasn't exactly the best place to sleep, it was better than the metal truck bed in back.

He was in a parking lot behind an insurance office across the street from the Sunshine Room. He got out and walked over to the corner of the building and peeked around it at the bar. The lights were still on, and a few cars remained in the lot, but they wouldn't be there for long. Two a.m. was closing time in California.

He watched patiently as people trickled out and drove away. Finally there was only an ancient VW Bug left, so he guessed it must belong to the bartender. He climbed back into the El Camino, and pulled out onto the side street, his lights off.

Leaning over, he popped open the glove compartment, intending to look for a piece of paper he could write the VW's license number on. Just inside was a white business-sized envelope. Sara's note. He didn't remember putting it in there and guessed he must have left it on the seat, and Harp or Barney stuck it in the box so it wouldn't be lost. This was not something he could write on, so he lifted it to see if there was anything underneath.

That's when he realized it wasn't Sara's note. It was the envelope Len had left his father.

He knew he should just ignore it, but he'd seen how the contents had affected Harp. Maybe if he knew what was inside, he could figure out a way to help. He hesitated, then pulled open the flap.

He'd been expecting a letter or a picture or something like that. What he found was another, though smaller, envelope. The paper had browned and felt stiff. He couldn't help noticing the postmark in the corner: May 14, 1944.

The addressee was Tommy Harper, and the sender was Neal Harper. A letter from Logan's dad to his uncle.

He took a breath and flipped it over.

A letter that had never been opened. The reason was obvious. It had been sent right around the time Uncle Tom went missing.

No wonder it had hit his father so hard.

Carefully, Logan put it back the way he'd found it.

What he knew of his uncle's time in the navy was little. Tom had served as an ordnanceman on a PBY, which was a plane that landed on water, picking up downed pilots and inserting commando units in places where no other aircraft could get. He also knew Tom's plane had simply disappeared while returning to its base in Perth, Australia, from a mission in southern Indonesia. That was pretty much it.

Logan had always been wary of bringing up his uncle to Harp because anytime the subject had arisen, his father's normal, easygoing manner would dim, almost in reverence.

Refocusing on why he was sitting in his car in the middle of the night, he found an old map in the back of the glove box, wrote the VW's license number on it, and waited.

Twenty minutes passed before the old guy finally came out. He shuffled over to the VW like someone who'd lived hard and was now just marking the days. It took him two tries to get the Bug started, but when he did, he wasted no time hitting the road. Logan gave him a five-second lead before following.

The town wasn't big, so even though they drove clear to the other side, it was only seven minutes before the bartender pulled into the driveway of a small, boxy house. As he did, Logan coasted his El Camino to the curb a block away and killed the engine.

The neighborhood had a weariness born from decades existing in the hot, arid desert. Almost half the houses on the block had FOR SALE signs in their front yards, and many looked like their tenants had already moved out.

This wasn't a neighborhood of trees or hedges, but of poorly growing grass and dirt, so Logan had a clear view of the bartender entering his house. Once the front door closed, he quietly exited his car.

The first thing he did was to check for any indication that someone else also lived there, but there was very little outside. As far as vehicles went, the VW was it. After a quick scan to make sure no one was watching, Logan jogged up to the fence at the side of the house, and took a look over it. More dirt, a couple of forgotten lawn chairs, and a pile of scrap metal in the back corner.

He lifted the latch and opened the gate. It groaned a little, but not enough for anyone but him to hear. The first thing he noticed once he'd rounded the back of the house was a concrete patio butting up against the building's foundation. Sitting in the middle was a rusting Weber grill, a lonely monument to a past real or imagined. There was only one door along the back of the bartender's home. It was at the top of a three-step staircase on the left, near where he'd come in, a window filling its upper half.

Logan checked the knob. Locked.

If he'd had the right tools with him, he could have picked it easily enough, but he didn't. He glanced back at the yard, his eyes settling on the discarded lawn chairs. They were the metal kind, with the plastic straps that served as seat and backing. Only the plastic had rotted away, leaving just the frame and a few tattered fragments. He walked over and picked one up, checking its heft.

Perfect, he thought.

He carried the chair to the edge of the patio, took careful aim, and threw it at the grill as hard as he could. While the base of the

Weber remained standing, he scored a direct hit on the top. It flipped off, tumbled through the air a couple times, and clattered loudly onto the concrete.

Logan immediately raced back to the house, hiding around the corner. Barely five seconds passed before he heard hurried footsteps thundering through the house and then stopping just on the other side of the door. He could imagine the bartender looking through the window, trying to see what had caused the noise.

A moment later, the door opened.

"What the hell?" the man muttered.

As soon as the man descended the steps, Logan peeked around the side. As he'd hoped, the bartender was heading for the patio, his back to the door. Without hesitating, Logan slipped over to the stairs, then into the house. Moving quickly now, he passed through a kitchen, a small dining room, and entered a slightly larger living room.

Outside, he heard the man pick up the chair and call out, "Who's out here?"

Logan crossed into a tiny hallway and headed straight into the only bedroom.

From the look of the bed covers, the man had already been lying down when the chair hit the grill. A quick scan of the room revealed the only practical hiding place was the three-foot space between the bed and the far wall. As he dropped into it and tucked himself tight against the bed, Logan heard the distant thud of the kitchen door closing.

Less than a minute later, the bartender walked back into the bedroom, muttering under his breath. There was a metallic groan as the bed compressed under the man's weight. Holding his position, Logan listened until the man's breathing became deep and regular. Finally, he extracted himself and stood up.

He found the man's wallet on the dresser. According to the driver's license, the guy's name was Brian Pearson, and he'd just celebrated his fifty-ninth birthday the year before. That was surprising. He looked a hell of a lot older to Logan.

Putting the wallet back down, Logan approached the bed and gave Pearson a shake.

"Wake up."

The bartender's breath caught, but he remained asleep.

Logan shook him again. "Hey, Brian. Wake. Up."

This time, Pearson opened his eyes with a start. He began to push himself up, but Logan shoved him back to the mattress.

"What's going on? Who—"

"What did you tell him?" Logan asked.

"Huh? What are you talking about? Who the hell are you?"

"Brian, answer the question. What did you tell him?"

The man's eyes widened. "You're...you're that guy from earlier."

"Answer the question."

"Jesus. This is my house. Get the hell out!"

Again Pearson tried to rise. This time when Logan pushed him back, he left his hand firmly on the man's chest, holding him in place.

"I told you there was nothing to tell," Pearson said.

"You told me a lie, Brian."

"I didn't," he said, but his eyes were clearly saying the opposite. "Wait. How do you know my—"

"Are you the one who had him beat up? Is that why you don't want to say anything?" Logan asked. "I'd be happy to return the favor if that's the case."

"No, no! Please. I didn't touch him. I didn't even know about the fight."

"I don't think I believe that," Logan said, shifting more weight onto Pearson's chest.

"It's the truth! I just sent him over there, that's all."

Logan eased back a little. "You sent him? Why?"

"Because of the picture. Why else? I'd seen the woman before, a few years ago."

"Do you know her name?"

He shook his head. "No. I never talked to her. Just saw her with someone."

Logan narrowed his eyes. "Who?"

When Pearson didn't answer right away, Logan pressed down again.

"Okay, okay," the man said, nearly coughing. "Her name's Diana. Diana Stockley."

Diana? "Is she the bartender at The Hideaway?"

"Yeah," Pearson said, surprised. "You know her?"

Ignoring the question, Logan said, "You're telling me you saw the woman in the picture and Diana together?"

Pearson nodded. "Came in a couple times on Diana's nights off. Like I said, a year or two ago. After that, I never saw the woman again."

Logan was silent for a moment. "Where does she live?"

"The woman? I have no idea."

Logan shoved him in the chest again. "Diana."

"Oh, uh…near the high school. I…I can give you her address."

LOGAN LEFT A shaken Brian Pearson with the promise of a return visit if the man said so much as a word to anyone about their conversation. Then he drove to Diana's house.

While the homes in her neighborhood were a bit newer and better taken care of, the number of FOR SALE signs was about the same. Braden was apparently in the midst of downsizing.

The Hideaway's bartender actually lived in one half of a duplex with a nice shade tree out front and some decent grass in the yard. The house was located on the corner, and had three cars parked in the shared, double-wide driveway, so there was no telling if Diana lived alone or with someone.

Her unit was the one on the left, farthest from the intersection. Logan walked up the stone path to the covered porch, and peeked through the window beside the door. The lights were off and all was quiet, so he assumed she must be asleep. He took out his flashlight, focused it to a tight beam, and aimed it through the glass.

On the other side was a typical living room, albeit one that could use some straightening up. Clothes and a couple of boxes lay haphazard on the couch and the nearby stuffed chair. A few more boxes were scattered across the floor.

He doused the light and turned his attention to the door, once again wishing he had proper lock-picking tools. As he'd done at Pearson's house, he tried the knob. Tools, he realized, weren't going to be unnecessary. The door was unlocked.

He pushed it open wide enough so he could stick his head in. The mess wasn't contained to what he'd seen through the window. There was stuff everywhere. Even in the kitchen at the other end of the living room, he could see that all the doors to the cabinets were hanging open. It felt like the place had been systematically ransacked.

With growing dread, Logan stepped inside, made his way over to the hallway, then paused.

Dead silence.

Son of a bitch.

Hoping Diana was just a light sleeper, he tiptoed down the hall, running his light through the bathroom as he passed. It, too, had been strategically picked over. There were two more doors at the end of the hall. The first led to a small bedroom that contained only a bed and a nightstand, and nothing else.

The last door opened into the master bedroom. Diana's room. It turned out to be the messiest in the whole place.

It was also unoccupied.

Diana was gone, and Logan had a very strong feeling she wasn't coming back.

15

DIANA HAD BEEN caught by surprise. She'd convinced herself that if nothing had happened by now, they had acted in time, and everything was going to be all right. But that unrealistic dream had shattered the moment a man walked into The Hideaway with a picture of Sara.

Diana had been smart enough to avoid the guy for the most part, but that didn't mean she wasn't on the verge of panic the whole time he was there. That's why she had foolishly allowed herself to sneak away for a moment and call Richard.

Dumb. Dumb. Dumb.

At the very least, she should have waited until she got home to make the call.

Damn him! His heart was in the right place, but even more than she did, he let his emotions control his actions at the worst possible times. Of course, when a situation had anything to do with Sara, they both had emotions that ran about as high as they could get.

Richard didn't tell her what he'd done until the next morning. He didn't know if he'd killed the man or just knocked him out. The only thing he did know was that he'd destroyed the phone the picture was on. She didn't have the heart at the time to point out there had to be other copies out there.

Once he confessed, she immediately called the hospital, saying she heard there'd been a fight near the bar, and was wondering if anyone had been hurt. What she learned was that a man *had* been brought in, but his condition didn't appear to be life threatening. What little relief Diana took from that was outweighed by the fact that the man had come into The Hideaway and asked about Sara at all.

She and Richard should have skipped town then, but she wanted to keep an eye on things. "Just a few days," she'd said.

Then, the very next night—*that* night—another man came into the bar, and on his phone was the same picture of Sara. This time she did wait until she got home to call Richard.

"We're leaving," she told him.

"What happened?"

"Another one showed up."

"Where is he?" She could hear what he was thinking in his tone.

"No," she said quickly. "We're getting out of town. Now. We leave him alone. Understand?"

She raced through her duplex, going through all her possessions, and grabbed only what she needed. Before leaving, she scrawled a note to her landlord, then added a postscript for her boss as an afterthought. She stuffed the message in an envelope and put it on the kitchen counter. She would have liked to talk to Mary Ralston, The Hideaway's owner, but there just wasn't time. Maybe someday she'd call her and explain.

It wasn't until she was twenty miles out of town that she remembered the picture taped to the underside of her nightstand drawer. There were times when she'd look at it every night before she went to sleep, and other times when she'd go weeks without remembering it was there. It was a comfort, a reminder of the important things.

Though it would be hard for anyone to find, eventually someone would. And if it was the wrong person? She could not let that happen.

She called Richard, and told him to wait for her in Kingman, Arizona.

"You're going to confront him, aren't you?" he said.

"Absolutely not."

"Then what are you doing?"

Ahead she spotted a turnaround in the center medium, and slowed to take it. "Please, just wait for me. I'll get there as soon as I can."

Braden was even deader than it had been when she'd left not long after two a.m. As she turned onto her street, she noticed a blue Chevy El Camino parked at the curb in front of her house. It had definitely not been there earlier.

Fully alert, she drove past her driveway, parked at the curb half a dozen houses down, and made her way back on foot. She approached the side of the house, and peeked through the kitchen window. From there, she had a partial view through the living room and into the hallway that led to the bedroom.

For a few seconds she saw nothing unusual, then a burst of light briefly cut through the darkness at the far end of the hall. When it came again, its source, a flashlight, moved all the way into the hall, and started heading back toward the living room. She ducked down and leaned against the wall, unsure what to do. Part of her wanted to sprint back to her car and race away, but the picture...she *had* to get the picture.

As silently as possible, she retreated to the street and ducked behind an old Dodge van parked on the other side.

Nearly twenty minutes later, the front door of her duplex opened. Since her porch light was off, she couldn't get a good look at the man who stepped out, but as he walked toward the car at the curb, he passed into the light of the corner streetlamp.

It was the guy who'd come into the bar earlier that night. Not a surprise.

She stayed rooted to the spot until long after he'd driven

away. Finally, she forced herself to move. Once inside her former home, she spent only as much time as needed to get the picture and get out. A minute later, she headed for the freeway, but just before she reached the on-ramp, she pulled to the side of the road.

There was an opportunity here, she realized. The man would be under the impression she'd left town. Even if he hadn't read the note, which she believed he must have, the signs of her departure were there. She could use this to her advantage and stay in town, spying on him—where he went, whom he talked to. She could turn the tables on them, know what *they* were doing, and control the situation instead of being controlled by it.

Her mind made up, she called Richard again, and had him meet her just on the Arizona side of the border. Since locals would know her car, but no one had seen the rental he was using, she wanted to switch vehicles with him. That turned out to be easy. The harder part was convincing him to leave his gun with her.

"If you need a gun, then you need me," he said.

"It's just in case."

"Then you need me, *just in case*."

It took nearly all the energy she had left to convince him to go back to Kingman and wait until she contacted him again.

As she drove back into Braden, she donned a hoodie and then searched through town for the El Camino. It wasn't difficult. The car was easy to spot. As she'd figured, it was parked at one of the town's motels. She found a spot at the other end of the lot, and dropped her seat back as far as it would go.

It had been a long day, and the one that had already begun was sure to be another. A few hours' sleep—that would be a good idea.

But just a couple, she thought as her eyelids grew heavy. *Just a couple*.

16

LOGAN ROLLED OVER and forced himself to check the time: a few minutes before eight thirty a.m. Total amount of sleep: three and a half hours.

The night before, after he'd confirmed Diana was gone, he had gone through her place room by room. Any guilt he would have felt for the intrusion was negated by the desire to find Sara. Given what Brian Pearson had told him about Diana, and the fact she had run after Logan and Pep showed her Sara's picture, there was no question in his mind that the two women were connected.

How and why were something else entirely. Unfortunately, Diana's place revealed few clues on either front. The only real thing of interest was a letter he found on the kitchen counter.

Dear Mr. Hackbarth,

I apologize for not giving notice, but as you must realize, I've had to move out in a hurry. I realize I've left the place in a mess, so I don't expect you to return my security deposit. Feel free to sell anything I've left and keep what you make.

Again, I apologize, but it couldn't be helped.
Diana

P.S. If you could, please let Mary Ralston know I won't be coming back to The Hideaway.

There was no doubt in Logan's mind—Diana Stockley was gone.

If only he'd known about her connection to Sara when he'd originally talked to her. He'd been so damn close.

After a quick shower, he threw on some clothes and called Callie. Though talking to Diana was currently no longer an option, she could still be useful. The line rang once, then voicemail kicked in.

"It's Logan," he said. "I've got a name I'm hoping you can check out. Diana Stockley. She was apparently seen in Sara's company a couple years ago in Braden. That's where I am now. Last night, after I started asking around about Sara, Diana skipped town. If you could find out anything on her, where she's from, any previous addresses, that would be a big help. Thanks, Callie."

After he hung up, he went in search of the others, finding them downstairs in Dev's room.

"Anyone up for some breakfast?" he asked after Barney let him in.

"Breakfast?" Harp said. "We ate over an hour ago. We *did* knock on your door first, but I guess you were out on your run."

"You've got to be careful exercising in this heat," Barney told him.

Logan was in the habit of taking an early morning run every day. If that's what they thought he was doing, that was fine. He wasn't quite ready to tell them about his late-night excursion yet. Besides, details like that tended to worry his father.

"We've been waiting for you so we can go to the hospital," Harp said. "I called over. Pep's got his own room now. So if you're hungry, you can get something at the cafeteria."

He picked up the copy of *Lost Horizon* and headed outside.

"I had their egg salad sandwich yesterday," Barney said as he stood up. "Wasn't bad."

As they walked out to the Cherokee, Dev strolled up next to Logan and said in a low voice, "I'm guessing you *missed* your morning run. Unless that was your dad who went joyriding in your car last night and didn't come back until a few hours ago."

Few things ever got by Dev.

Logan took a second then said, "We'll talk later."

"I'll be around."

PEP WAS STILL asleep when they arrived. Logan had been hoping to finally talk to him about what happened, but it looked like that would have to wait a little longer.

He sat there with the others for a half hour, then caught Dev's eye and said, "Can you give me a ride back to the motel so I can get my car?"

Dev immediately stood up. "Sure."

"What do you need your car for?" Harp asked. "We just got here."

"I'm trying to find Sara, remember?"

"Yeah, but we don't have any leads."

"And I won't find any just hanging around here."

"Well, Pep will be able to help."

"And when he wakes up, I'll come back to talk to him."

Harp nodded, conceding the point. "You know what's best. Call us if you find something."

"I will."

BORROWING A PHONE book from the hospital receptionist—a different woman than the one the day before—Logan found a listing for a Mary Ralston and three for men with the last name of Hackbarth. He wrote down the addresses and phone numbers for each, then he and Dev headed out.

As they pulled out of the parking lot, Dev said, "If I have to sit in that hospital all day, I might have to throw someone through a window, so how about I tag along with you?"

"I was going to suggest the same thing," Logan told him. It wouldn't hurt to have someone along just in case he needed a little assistance, and Dev was more than capable on that front.

He gave Dev directions to Diana Stockley's house and told him about his late-night visit. Several minutes later, they walked up the pathway to Diana's front door.

The reason Logan wanted to start with the duplex was to see if anyone had discovered she was gone yet. It would help him decide what his next move should be.

Looking through the window, everything appeared the same as when he'd left. Chances were no one was yet aware of her departure. Still, just to be sure, he wanted to check that the note was still on the kitchen counter. He took a quick glance through the neighborhood, then pulled out a napkin he'd stuffed in his pocket when he picked up a bagel from the cafeteria earlier. He first wiped the knob to remove his earlier prints, then used the napkin to open the door.

While the note was still there, the envelope was closer to the center of the counter than where he remembered leaving it. Of course, it had been late, so it was possible he'd knocked it there without even realizing it as he walked away.

A quick check of the rest of the house revealed nothing new. As he and Dev started to leave, an idea came to him.

He motioned for Dev to wait, then went back and grabbed the envelope. Dev raised an eyebrow, but said nothing as they returned to the car.

Using the list Logan had created at the hospital, they visited the first of the Hackbarth addresses. As they parked, Logan immediately knew they could dismiss this one. The house was empty—no curtains, no furniture, no car.

In the driveway of the neighboring house, a woman was removing grocery bags from the trunk of her sedan.

"Stay here," Logan told Dev. He climbed out of the Cherokee and walked part of the way down the sidewalk toward the woman.

"Excuse me," he called out. When she looked over, he pointed at the empty house. "Was that the Hackbarth residence?"

"Still own it as far as I know."

"It looks empty."

"That's because it is. Why do you want to know?"

"I'm looking for Mr. Hackbarth."

"Well, if that's the Mr. Hackbarth you want, you're four months too late."

"Moved?"

"Died."

"Oh. Sorry. I didn't know."

She shrugged. "Didn't talk to him much. He was pretty old. Mostly stayed inside."

As she returned to what she was doing, Logan took another step in her direction. "Sorry, one more question."

She stopped and looked at him.

"There's a duplex not too far away from here owned by a Mr. Hackbarth," Logan said. "I thought it might be your neighbor."

"That would have to be one of the sons. My bet would be Mark. He's the real estate guy. Got an office over on Center Street, I think."

"Perfect. Thank you."

"You thinking of buying it?"

"I'm…looking around at the moment."

She pulled out the last grocery bag and shut the trunk. "Well, if you *are* buying, you'd be the only one. Whatever price they're asking, offer half."

THE HOME ADDRESS for Mark Hackbarth had been the next one on Logan's list, but instead of heading there, he instructed Dev to drive over to Center Street.

"There it is," Logan said.

It was the third real estate office they'd passed. Like the others, the names of the agents were painted on the window. Right at the top of the new office's list was Mark Hackbarth.

Once they were parked at the curb, Logan grabbed the envelope from Diana's place and the two men got out. Logan had almost reached the office door when he realized Dev wasn't with him. He looked back and saw that the former Marine was still standing near the car, staring down the street.

"What is it?" Logan asked.

Dev didn't move for a moment, then he turned and walked toward the building. "Probably nothing," he said. He motioned at the door. "Shall we?"

The temperature inside was a good thirty degrees cooler than out—almost too cold, in Logan's opinion. The real estate office consisted of five desks in two rows of two with the odd desk centered up front. Three were occupied.

The woman sitting at the one nearest the door smiled as they walked in. "Welcome to Desert Horizons Realty. How can I help you gentlemen?"

Logan smiled back. "We're looking for Mark Hackbarth. Is he in?"

Before the woman could say anything, a man sitting at a desk in the back jumped up. "I'm Mark."

He walked toward them, all smiles and energy, and thrust out his hand. As Logan shook it, he could sense desperation hiding behind Hackbarth's welcoming demeanor. Given all the FOR SALE signs in town, it seemed likely that trying to sell real estate here was like sucking blood from a dried-out corpse. The man had to be on the edge of financial collapse.

"How are you doing? Mark Hackbarth. And you are?"

"Logan Harper. This is my associate, Dev Martin."

"Associate? Well, okay," Hackbarth said, as if it were immensely interesting. "Why don't you come on back and have a seat."

When they reached his desk, Hackbarth dragged two guest chairs over and motioned for Logan and Dev to take them.

"So, Mr. Harper, Mr. Martin, what can I do for you?" Hackbarth said as he dropped down in his own chair.

Logan set Diana's envelope on the desk, Hackbarth's name facing up. "To start, you can see what's inside this."

Hackbarth's happy expression turned perplexed, then concerned. He leaned back. "Is it a subpoena or something like that?"

"No. Nothing like that. At least I don't think so."

"What is it?"

"That's what we're hoping you can tell us. We found it leaning against the door of a house we went to check."

"What house?"

"Part of a duplex," Logan said. "On Sage Lane."

"At the corner?"

Logan nodded.

"I own that."

"Then I guess that explains why the envelope has your name on it."

Hackbarth looked at him for a second, then down at the envelope. Finally, he pulled open the flap and removed the letter. As he read, he grew visibly upset. When he reached the bottom, he put it down.

"One moment," he said. He rose and walked rapidly back to the woman at the front of the room. Though he was obviously trying to keep his voice down, it was easy enough for Logan and Dev to hear him. "Call Frank. Have him go over to the duplex and check unit two. I think my tenant just skipped."

"Which one's that?" the woman said.

"Just call Frank."

When he returned, he was having little luck masking his anger. "You found this against the door?"

"Yes," Logan said.

Hackbarth shook his head and muttered, "Great." He then

looked at Logan again, his eyes narrowing. "So why exactly were you at my duplex?"

"We were looking for Ms. Stockley."

"Why was that?"

Logan paused and looked briefly at Dev as if he were gauging whether he should say anything more. When he did speak, he drew it out, like there was more to what he was saying than the words coming out of his mouth. "She borrowed some money from our corporation, and has missed the last couple payments."

Right on a cue they hadn't discussed, Dev leaned forward, his face impassive.

"I guess you could say we're on a collection call," Logan continued. "My father isn't going to be very happy when I tell him she's gone."

"Your father isn't the only one," Hackbarth said.

Logan was silent for a moment. "While I'm sympathetic with your situation, it's of no importance to me. *Finding* the woman is. Any cooperation I get in doing so will, naturally, be appreciated."

"Whoa," Hackbarth said. "I don't have any idea where she went."

Logan kept his gaze steady and his voice calm, but direct. "Of course you don't. If you did and didn't tell us, that would just be stupid. And you're not stupid. I can see that."

The fingertips of Hackbarth's left hand began to tap nervously on the desk. "I'd love to help you, but I've got my own problem to deal with right now."

"That's where we're in luck. At the moment, our problems are similar," Logan said. "And the few minutes you spend helping me would be helping yourself."

"I don't see what I could possibly do for you that would help."

Logan allowed himself a quick, controlled smile. "I assume Ms. Stockley filled out a rental application, and perhaps other documents containing personal information."

Hackbarth looked really nervous now. "Well, of course, but I'm not sure if I should—"

"Mark?" the woman up front yelled.

They all looked over. She was standing at her desk, a phone held to her ear.

"Frank was in the neighborhood, so he's there now," she went on. "Definitely looks like your renter cleared out. Says the place is a mess."

Hackbarth took a deep, seething breath, and turned back to Logan. "Let me get her file for you."

17

ERICA SAT BEHIND the wheel of her car and fumed. They had missed the woman by what couldn't have been more than a few hours. *Unbelievable!*

Though Erica had made good time at the rental agency at LAX, and Clausen and Markle—her two men—had arrived on schedule, it was still after four thirty in the morning when the three of them finally arrived in Braden.

She had decided during the drive that they could no longer risk simply observing the woman. Either the bitch knew something or she didn't, and now that someone else was snooping around, Erica couldn't prolong this irritation. She needed it sewn up, and she needed it done now.

That's why she was here, to make sure no one screwed up this time.

Half an hour before they arrived in town, she had called Cecil Frisk, the man who had been watching Diana, and told him to meet her at the woman's house. Though Frisk had obviously been half asleep when they talked, he was wide awake and parked a block away from the woman's place when Erica and her team arrived.

It should have gone nice and smooth. At nearly five a.m., even a bartender would be asleep.

But when they went in, instead of finding Diana in her bed, she wasn't even in the house.

How the hell did that happen?

Erica was the one who found the note. When she read it, she'd come very close to ripping it up on the spot. Extreme self-control was the only thing that helped her return it to its envelope.

It had taken her over two years to find Diana again. *Two years!* Once she had, she'd sent Frisk out to monitor her, with the hope that Diana would lead them to the other one. But then tonight, while Frisk *slept*, Diana had skipped town.

Incompetency!

Frisk was lucky she didn't have him killed on the spot. Once more her cool nature prevailed, and all four of them retreated to her car where they would wait and see what happened.

Now, for the thousandth time since the sun had risen, she looked down the street at Diana's duplex.

"You all right?"

Erica glanced at Frisk in the passenger seat. "I'm fine."

"You look a little...pissed off."

She locked eyes with him. "Really? And that surprises you?"

"No...I...I—"

"Company," Clausen announced, pointing between the front seats and out the window. He and Markle were sitting in the back.

A Jeep Cherokee had just pulled to a stop in front of the duplex. Momentarily forgetting her anger, Erica watched as two men exited the car and walked up the pathway to Diana's place. One of the guys was probably not much more than thirty, while the other was older and harder to pin down.

She wondered if one of them was the landlord mentioned in Diana's note.

"You want us to get in closer?" Clausen asked.

"Do it," she said, nodding.

Clausen and Markle got out of the car and disappeared into

the neighborhood.

"Maybe I should go, too," Frisk suggested.

"*You* stay here."

At the house, the two new arrivals stepped over to the door, then the younger one took a quick look around the street, obviously making sure no one was watching. Erica froze as the man's gaze moved in her direction.

"Hold still," she ordered Frisk.

Given the distance, the guy wouldn't be able to discern them from the rest of the car if they remained motionless. Apparently satisfied, the man pulled something out of his back pocket—a piece of cloth or paper— and used it to cover his hand as he grabbed the doorknob.

That certainly wasn't landlord behavior.

She watched the men step inside the house. Their visit wasn't a long one. When they came back out, the younger one was carrying something that looked very much like the envelope Diana had left behind.

Erica called Clausen.

"Yes?" he answered, his voice low.

"Where are you?"

"In the backyard."

"You don't have to whisper. They're getting into their car."

"I thought it sounded too quiet in there." Clausen's voice returned to normal.

"I think they took the note. Check, then meet us back at the motel."

"Will do."

Erica waited until the other car left, then pulled onto the street to follow them.

18

INSTEAD OF MAKING Logan and Dev go through the documents there, Hackbarth let them photocopy everything so they could walk out with their own set. Once they finished, they headed for Mary Ralston's place.

It turned out she lived in a trailer park in the northwest corner of town. Surprisingly, it was the most well-maintained neighborhood Logan had seen in Braden, the trailers showing little sign of the wear and tear the nearby permanent homes displayed.

Mary Ralston's place was a white double-wide right in the middle of the park. Since there was no car in the driveway, Logan thought she might not be home, but as Dev turned off the engine, the trailer door opened, and a woman around Dev's age stuck her head out.

"So are we going all Sopranos again?" Dev asked. "Or trying something different?"

"I guess that depends on whether or not our friend Mark Hackbarth has called and told her about us."

It turned out that Hackbarth had called, but hadn't said anything about Logan and Dev, just that Diana had left town.

"I figured it was going to happen someday," Mary said. She

was sitting in a cloth-covered recliner, while Logan and Dev sat on the couch. "Diana's always been kind of the restless sort."

"How long had she been in Braden?" Logan asked.

"About two years now. She and I, we've had our differences on occasion, but she's a hell of a bartender."

"Did she work for you the whole time she was here?"

"Yep. I ran an ad in the local paper. She called me up, I tried her out, and that was that."

"So she *was* here before she got the job," Logan said, thinking the woman had misunderstood him.

Mary shook her head. "No. She called me from somewhere in Arizona, I think. Can't remember exactly. Think she said she found the ad on the paper's website."

"She have any friends here you know of?"

"A few different people. Lately she'd been hanging around with Tessie Carter, I think."

Logan typed the name into a note on his phone, then accessed the picture of Sara. "Have you ever seen this woman before?"

Mary looked at the picture for a second, then glanced around until she spotted a pair of glasses on the coffee table. "Can you hand me those?" she asked Dev.

Dev passed them to her. "Here you go."

"Thank you. My close-up vision is shot. Growing old sucks sometimes."

"Tell me about it," Dev agreed.

She gave him a smile, and looked back at the picture.

"You might have seen her with Diana about two years ago or so," Logan suggested.

"She *is* familiar." She continued to examine the photo. "Wait, wait. There was this…friend who visited her from out of town. What was her name?" She stared at the floor for a moment. "Sandy? Sally. I don't know. Something like that."

"Sara?" Logan suggested.

"Maybe." She pointed at the picture. "That could be her, but I'm not a hundred percent."

"And you haven't seen her since then?"

"No. Don't think so."

"You see anyone else with them at the time?"

She thought for a moment. "If I did, I don't remember."

"Is there anything else about Diana that might help us find her? Something she might have said? Family she might go to?"

"No family that I know of. Certainly none in Braden. She said her mom died a few years ago, but otherwise…" She shrugged. "She's a pretty private person. Never really talked much about herself."

Logan hesitated, then said, "If you don't mind me saying, you don't seem as mad as I expected, given she just quit on you."

"Annoyed that I'll probably have to cover a few shifts myself, yeah, but I can't be mad at her. Diana's a good person, but I always felt like there was something missing, you know, like she was looking for something that she would probably never find."

———

AS THEY WALKED to the car, Dev tossed Logan the keys. "You drive."

Logan gave him an odd look, but said, "Okay," thinking that maybe Dev was just tired of being behind the wheel.

But as they exited the mobile home park, Dev swiveled in his seat and stared out the rear window.

"What is it?" Logan asked.

Turning back around, Dev seemed to contemplate something. Finally he said, "I think someone might be following us."

Logan's gaze flicked to the rearview mirror. "Who?"

"There's a gray sedan about a block back."

Logan searched the street behind them. "Okay, I see it. You sure?" The car was too far back for him to see the people inside.

"No, I'm not. Have you seen how many gray sedans there are in this town?"

"Then what makes you think we're being followed?"

"It *looks* like the same one I saw when we visited the real estate place, and before that, not long after we left the woman's house. But I don't know."

Logan frowned. He considered making a few quick turns to see if the car was really tailing them, but decided doing that might scare the person off. If they pretended like they hadn't noticed, and just kept tabs on the other car, there was a better chance they might learn something useful. He told Dev what he wanted to do, and the former Marine nodded as if he'd been thinking the same thing.

Mary Ralston had told them Tessie Carter was working at the Wallace Wash Mini Market out near the interstate. As Logan pulled into the store's small lot and parked, Dev positioned himself so he could see out the back without seeming too obvious.

"There they go."

"They?"

"There're two people inside."

"Did either of them look this way?" Logan asked.

"No. Kept facing straight."

"Recognize them?"

Dev shook his head. "Never seen them before. A man and a woman, both white. Her hair's cut short." Dev touched his neck about halfway between his head and shoulder. "About to here. Think it's brown. But she was driving, so harder to see. The guy's hair was close-cropped, lighter, almost blond."

"How old?"

"She could be anywhere from thirty to fifty. Sorry, best I can do. The guy's younger, late twenties at most."

"Where are they now?"

"They kept going straight through the next intersection, like they were going to get on the freeway." Dev craned his neck. "Can't see them anymore."

Maybe it *was* nothing. Braden was small, with only so many roads a person could use, and the route they'd just taken *had* been the logical route to the highway. They'd just have to see if the car showed up again.

The Wallace Wash Mini Market was a kind of low-rent 7-Eleven—older shelves, worse lighting, and fewer choices. Behind the counter was a woman with vibrant auburn hair and too much black eye makeup. Her clothes of choice were a Lady Gaga T-shirt and a short black skirt.

Logan caught Dev's eye, then subtly motioned to the opening in the counter that allowed whoever was behind it to get out. With a single nod, Dev walked toward it as Logan grabbed a bag of beef jerky and approached the cash register.

The woman took the bag, scanned it, said, "Anything else?"

"Can I ask you something?"

She stared at him, bored.

"Are you Tessie Carter?"

A spark in her eye. "I don't know you."

"That's right. You don't."

She pulled back from the counter. "Then how do you know me?"

Logan raised his hands in front of his chest, palms out. "I just want to ask you a few questions."

"About what?"

"Diana Stockley."

"Did that bitch send you?" she spat. "You can tell her that if she wants to talk to me, she should have the balls to do it herself."

She moved toward the opening in the counter, but Dev was there, blocking her path.

"What the hell?" she said. "Get out of my way!"

"Diana didn't send us," Logan told her. "We're trying to find her."

"Does it look like she's here? Her place is on Sage Lane. Try there."

"We did."

"Well, then wait until she goes to work. The Hideaway. She starts at six."

"According to her note, she left town and isn't coming back."

Logan's phone buzzed in his pocket, but he ignored it.

The anger on Tessie's face morphed into disbelief. "What are you talking about? What note?"

"The one she left her landlord. Said he could sell whatever was left in the house."

"No," she said. "No, you're wrong. She's not gone. She probably just went on a trip." She paused, her face hardening. "I don't even know you. You're probably lying."

"I wish I was, but I'm not. You can ask Mary Ralston. She's the one who told us you were a friend of Diana's."

"Mary…? No, no, you've got to be wrong. Diana wouldn't leave, not without…"

Suddenly she whipped around and grabbed the cell phone that was sitting on the back counter. She found a number and called it.

"Mrs. Ralston?" she said a moment later. "Sorry to bother you. This is Tessie. Tessie Carter. Look, um, there's some random guy here trying to tell me that Diana's le—" As she paused to listen, her expression grew worried, then pained. "Are you kidding me?…No. No…All right. Okay…Okay."

She hung up, and absently set the phone back down. Her eyes began to lose focus, and she leaned against the back counter, seemingly forgetting they were even there.

Logan and Dev shared a confused look. This was a much stronger emotional reaction than Logan had been expecting. It was almost as if—

Oh, damn.

He motioned for Dev to move out of the way so he could get behind the counter. He then stepped in next to her. "I'm sorry. I didn't realize there was something going on between you."

"Well, there's not," Tessie blurted out. "Not anymore."

"What happened?"

"That's none of your business!"

Logan paused. "We just want to talk to her. We think she knows a friend of ours we're trying to find, a friend who's in trouble. Diana might be able to point us in the right direction.

That's all. Anything you could tell us that will help us find her would be great."

"I told you, I have no idea where she is. I haven't talked to her in almost two months."

Two months? "Is that when…?"

"When we broke up?" She tried to sound accusatory, but the sadness that had taken over her face wasn't selling it.

"Yes," Logan said.

She dipped her head and nodded. "She…she started going out of town on her days off. That was usually *our* time, you know. When I asked where she'd gone, she'd give me some half-assed answer that I knew wasn't true, so one day I followed her."

"Where did she go?"

"All the way to Riverside, of all places."

The nape of Logan's neck started to tingle. He didn't trust his own voice, so he said nothing.

"She met with this other woman there. I watched them have coffee, but when they left, I lost them in the traffic. I drove around for a while, but couldn't find them again, so I came home. That night I asked her if she was seeing someone else. When she said no, I told her what I saw." Tessie looked at Logan. "She totally freaked out. Told me she never wanted to see me again. She hasn't talked to me since."

Not wanting to do so, but seeing little choice, Logan pulled out his phone and showed her the picture of Sara. "Is this the woman she met?"

Tessie stared at the image, her eyes welling with tears. "Fuck," she said to no one, then nodded. "They ran off together, didn't they? God, I'm such an idiot."

Logan kept his voice soft. "I don't think Diana was cheating on you with this woman. This is our missing friend," Logan said, keeping his voice calm. He didn't know if he was right, but he felt that he was. If Diana had been involved with Sara, then why hadn't Sara been here with her?

"I saw them together."

BRETT BATTLES

"You saw them getting coffee. That's all," he said. "Now think, Tessie. Do you know where Diana might have gone? Maybe she went back to where grew up?"

"She never talked about her past. I got the feeling it wasn't all that great."

"Were there any special places she mentioned? Places she liked to visit?"

She was silent for a moment. "Buenos Aires. Said she wanted to live there someday. She…she talked about us going together."

Buenos Aires was a long way away, and if Sara was already there, he might as well pack up now and go home.

"Anyplace else?"

She thought about it, then shook her head. "Nothing that I can remember."

IF LOGAN WASN'T convinced before, he knew if he found Diana, Sara wouldn't be far away.

"Our friends are back," Dev said.

They were in the Cherokee again, with Logan once more in the driver's seat. He looked in the rearview mirror. The same gray sedan was a block back, and Logan recognized the silhouettes of the driver and her passenger.

He stuffed his hand into his pocket and pulled out the keys to the El Camino. "Here," he said, handing them to Dev. "I'll try to lose them for a few seconds near the motel. You jump out, but make sure they don't see you."

Dev smiled. "Then I follow them."

"Exactly."

"They're going to wonder why there's suddenly only one of us."

"No, they won't," Logan said. "Lean your chair back as far as it will go, but take your time so they can see what's going on. Then lie back, and get them used to seeing only me."

19

"READY?" LOGAN ASKED as they neared the motel.

Dev grabbed the door handle. "Ready."

Logan checked the rearview mirror again. The other car was still a full block behind them.

"Don't worry about trying to catch up right away," Logan told him. "Call me once you get going and I'll tell you where we are."

Just beyond Desert Inn was a small intersecting street that was mostly blocked from view by one wing of the motel. Keeping their pace steady, Logan flipped on his turn signal so as not to alarm the other driver with any sudden movements.

"Here we go." He slowed through the turn. As soon as the building was between them and the sedan, he slammed on the brakes and shouted, "Now!"

Dev shoved the door open and hopped out in record time. The second he was clear, Logan took off again, accelerating until he matched the speed he'd been traveling at earlier. In the mirror, he could see Dev race across the sidewalk and crouch behind a car parked at the curb. He'd barely ducked down when the sedan appeared around the corner.

"Stay with me. Stay with me," Logan muttered under his

breath.

As the sedan came abreast of Dev's position, Logan watched to see if the others looked over, but both remained focused on him the whole time.

Two minutes later, Dev called.

"I'm south of the motel," Logan said, using the speakerphone. "You remember seeing that Sonic Burger on Center Street?"

"I remember it."

"I'll drive by that in three or four minutes."

"Which way?"

"Away from the freeway."

"I'll be waiting."

Five minutes later, Dev called again. "I'm on you."

Logan had been keeping an eye on his rearview mirror, but had seen no sign of the El Camino. When he looked this time, he caught a glimpse of blue in the distance.

It was time for part two of the plan.

"There's a diner coming up in a couple blocks. I'll use that." If it was like before, their unwanted shadow would drive by, but this time Dev would be tailing *them* to see where they went.

Rosemary's Eats sat in the middle of a lot, surrounded on all four sides by parking. Logan pulled in and grabbed an empty spot along the side, then turned and acted like he was talking to someone reclined in the chair. He kept a casual eye on the road as the sedan slowly passed. As soon as it was out of sight, he grabbed the photocopies of Diana's rental file and went into the restaurant.

He sat at a booth in the back corner near the restrooms, out of view of the front windows.

"Something to drink?" his waitress asked as soon as he was settled.

"Water's fine." She set a menu in front of him, but before she could leave, he said, "Do you have a BLT?"

"Sure."

"I'll take that." He handed back the menu.

"Fries?"

"Yeah. That's fine."

As soon as she was gone, he pulled out his phone and reconnected with Dev.

"What's happening?"

"They doubled back after a couple of blocks, then parked on a side street just across from you."

"What about you?"

"I'm in a strip mall a block away."

"You can see them?"

"Absolutely."

"That means they can see you, too."

"Doubtful."

Given Dev's track record, Logan was willing to buy that. "Call me if something changes."

"You got it."

Logan set the photocopies in front of him. The first was the rental agreement, listing Diana Stockley as the tenant, and Hackbarth Holdings as the landlord. It was boilerplate stuff, skewed heavily in favor of the landlord. There were the terms, the rent, the security deposit, and, at the end, signatures—Diana's, tight and clear, and Mark Hackbarth's, large and important.

"Here you go," the waitress said, setting his sandwich and fries in front of him. "Can I get you anything else?"

"No, this will be great. Thanks."

Logan started in on his BLT as he moved on to the next document—the application. This one was more interesting. Under employment history, Diana had listed The Hideaway as her current employer, and someplace called Harkin Services as her most recent job prior to that, but had given no address or phone number for the latter. Next was a listing of previous addresses. There were slots on the form for four, but Diana listed only two. One was another address in Braden that corresponded to her first year in town. The other was a place in a town called El Portal, California. The name sounded familiar to Logan, but he couldn't recall where it was. The dates she'd lived there, though, were the same dates she'd put down for Harkin Services.

But all that information paled when compared to the nine-digit number in a box near the top—her Social Security number.

Logan grabbed his phone, intending to email Callie the number, but before he could, he was greeted with a message saying he'd missed a call. *Right*, he remembered. His phone had rung when they'd been talking to Tessie. Turned out the caller was Harp.

Before calling him back, Logan accessed his email, composed the message for Callie, but stopped himself before hitting SEND. He quickly looked through the rest of the photocopies to make sure there wasn't anything else that could be useful, and was glad he did. The last page was a copy of Diana's driver's license. Not only was there the license number, but also her middle name and date of birth. If that didn't help Callie dig something up, nothing would. He added all this to the message, and sent it on its way.

That done, he called his dad.

"Logan. Oh, good." Harp sounded agitated.

"What's wrong?"

"I don't know. I…" He paused.

"Dad, are you okay?"

Still nothing.

"Dad?"

"Logan. I…I can't find the letter."

"What?"

"The letter Len left me. I can't find it. It was in the book, but I checked a little while ago and it's not there. I need you to come back, and take me to the motel. It's got to be in the room, don't you think?"

"Whoa, Dad. Relax."

"How can I relax? I can't lose it."

"You didn't lose it. It's in my car."

Silence. "Your car?"

"I saw it in the glove compartment."

"I didn't put it there," Harp said. Logan could hear the phone move around, and his father's voice became more distant. "Logan says it's in the glove compartment of his truck."

Even farther in the distance, Barney responded, though Logan couldn't make out what he said.

Harp again. "You're kidding me, right? When?" A pause. "I swear to God, Barney, if I was forty years younger, I'd kill you right now...no, I would. Don't talk to me right now." Harp's voice got louder again. "Barney put it there. He...forgot. If you get a chance, drive by a drugstore and pick up some ginkgo!"

Trying to ease his father's tension, Logan said, "The important thing is it's not lost."

"I want you to bring it to me. Can you do that?"

"Not right now, but later."

"Why not?"

"I'm a little busy at the moment."

He could hear his father take a deep breath. "As soon as you can, okay?"

"Sure, Dad." Logan's phone beeped; Dev on the other line. "I've got another call. I'll talk to you later."

"Thanks, Logan. Barney, I cannot believe that you—" The line went dead.

Logan switched calls.

"He's on the move," Dev said. "The woman was on the phone, and as soon as she hung up, they took off."

"Which way?"

"South."

"In a hurry?"

"No. Normal speed."

"You're still following them?"

"Roger that."

"Sounds like this is a good time for me to sneak away while they're not looking."

"Definitely."

HARP JUMPED UP when Logan entered Pep's hospital room. "Thought you said you couldn't come right away."

"I didn't bring the envelope with me," Logan said.

"Why not?"

"It's still in the El Camino."

"And?"

"I was in the Jeep. Dev's got my truck."

Harp looked past Logan at the door. "Is he on his way?"

"Dad, relax. It's safe, all right? We'll get it later."

Harp frowned. "I wish you had brought it with you."

Logan touched his dad's shoulder. "It won't be long. I promise."

"So where *is* Dev?" Barney asked.

"Doing something for me," Logan said.

"You found something out?"

"Working on a few things." Logan paused. "How's Pep?"

"I'm fine. Thanks for asking," Pep said from the bed.

Logan walked over. The bruises on Pep's face had darkened, making him look worse, but the swelling had gone down around his eyes.

"Another couple weeks and you'll be as good as new," Logan told him.

"I'm fine now. I just want to get out of here and help you guys."

"We're okay at the moment. Just take your time and get better."

"What will really make me better is a conversation with the guy who put me in here."

Logan nodded sympathetically. "You didn't tell me that you went to The Hideaway because the bartender at the Sunshine Room sent you there."

"Doesn't surprise me," Pep said. "I barely remember that you were here at all."

"The guy told me he sent you to see the bartender."

"Yeah. Her name's…um…uh…"

"Diana," Logan said.

"Right. Diana. I tried to talk to her when I got there, showed her Sara's picture, but she acted like she'd never seen her then walked off. I started to think maybe the other guy was just giving me a line to get a few extra bucks out of me."

"You paid him?"

"I slipped him a twenty."

"How long did you stay at The Hideaway?" Logan asked.

"I don't know, another thirty minutes or so. She was my best lead by far, but she was always busy so I couldn't get any time with her. I showed the pictures to some of the customers but wasn't having any luck, so I decided to get some sleep and come back earlier the next night when the place wouldn't be so busy."

"And after you left?"

"When I reached my car, someone called out from between some buildings, gave me the impression he had information about Sara." Pep's lips pressed together in a tight line. "It was stupid. I wasn't thinking danger. I was thinking I'd found something that was going to help." He frowned. "If I were a little younger, he wouldn't have gotten me like that."

"He may have tried something else," Harp suggested. "Like a knife or a gun."

"You saying my age saved me, old man?" Pep asked.

"It's possible."

Pep cracked a smile. "Maybe. Anyway, as soon as I was far enough away from the street, he whacked me in the head."

Logan hesitated, then said, "Diana's gone."

"What?" Pep and Harp said almost in sync. Barney, though silent, looked just as surprised.

"I did the same thing you did, just in reverse," Logan explained. "The Hideaway, *then* the Sunshine Room. So when I talked to Diana, I had no idea about any connection to Sara. Unfortunately, when I finally found out and tracked her to her house, she'd left town."

"When did you do all this?" Harp asked.

"Last night."

"Last night? Well, maybe she just wasn't home."

"No. She was gone."

"You're sure?"

"Trust me, Dad. I'm sure."

"Of course I trust you."

Logan's phone vibrated in his pocket. Dev again.

He stepped away from the bed to answer it. "What's going on?"

"You're not going to believe this," Dev said.

"What?"

"They went to our friend Mark Hackbarth's office."

"Really?"

"Stayed inside for about ten minutes. After that they went back by the diner, but didn't stay. My guess is that when they didn't see the Cherokee, they had no reason to hang around."

"Did you lose them?"

A grunted laugh. "No, I didn't lose them. They're at a motel near the highway. A place called The Happy Traveler. You want the room number?"

"You can tell me when I get there."

20

DIANA SAT UP with a start. Sweat covered her brow and soaked her shirt. The pleasant desert night had been replaced by Braden's typical one-hundred-degree-plus day, turning Richard's rental car into a sauna.

But it wasn't the heat that bothered her at the moment. It was the position of the sun itself. It was higher in the sky than she'd expected. She grabbed her phone and looked at the time.

A quarter after ten?

She'd slept for over six hours.

With a sense of dread, she looked out to where the El Camino had been parked, and saw that it was…still there.

"Thank you, Lord," she said, relieved.

Maybe the guy—what had he called himself? Logan?—maybe Logan had slept in, too. Even if he hadn't, she knew he wouldn't be too far from that car. It was a beauty, more so in the daylight where its paint job sparkled under the desert sun.

Kitty-corner to the motel was a gas station she'd used a few times. It had a restroom around back that you could enter without going through the store. She drove over, pulled her hoodie tight around her face, and made a beeline for the women's room.

After relieving herself and cleaning up as best she could, she returned to the motel, parking this time a few slots away from the El Camino.

When an hour and a half passed with no sign of Logan, she decided he must have gone somewhere without his car. She wasn't worried, though. He'd be back. But after another forty-five minutes, it turned out she was wrong. At first she barely looked at the tough older guy who'd entered the parking lot, but then he got into Logan's truck and drove off.

She couldn't imagine that there were *two* electric blue El Caminos in town, so she had no choice but to pull out after it.

Following vehicles always looked easy on TV. Cops and PIs and even amateurs seldom ever lost the car they were tracking. In real life it turned out to be another matter—for Diana, anyway. She was a bartender, after all, not a stock car driver. She made it through two traffic lights before the El Camino disappeared.

She drove through the town, but couldn't find the car.

"Dammit! Dammit! Dammit!" she said as she pounded the steering wheel, adrenaline and dread racing each other through her body.

When she finally calmed down, she did the only thing she could do—return to the motel and hope that the El Camino showed up again.

21

LOGAN RECRUITED BARNEY to drive him to Dev's location. Harp, not wanting to be left out, came along for the ride. Whatever spat they'd had over Len's envelope seemed to have been forgotten. On the way, they picked up a burger and a drink for Dev, then parked a few blocks from the El Camino.

"Don't forget to call us if you need any help," Harp said as his son got out. "And...the envelope?"

"Next time you see me, I'll give it to you. I promise," Logan told him. He looked at Barney. "Park behind our motel. If you guys need to go out again, walk or wait until we get back. Don't take the Jeep." He had told them on the way over about being followed, so they all understood the car was marked.

"Be careful," Barney said.

Logan watched them drive off and then walked through the quiet neighborhood until he reached the street where Dev was parked. Beyond the El Camino he could see the motel the others were apparently using. Other than a family trying to cool off in the pool, the place looked almost deserted. Satisfied no one was casting any attention in his direction, Logan approached his truck and got in the passenger side.

"Here," he said, handing over the bag and setting the drink caddy on the seat between them. "Anything new?"

Dev shook his head. "They've been inside since I called."

"Which room?"

"Second floor, third from the left. Number twenty-seven."

Counting the doors, Logan found the room, but there was no way he could read the number mounted outside.

"You have binoculars or something?" he asked.

"Took a little walk," Dev said, chewing his burger. "The car's parked right below it." He handed a piece of paper to Logan. "That's the license number, but it won't get us much. It's a rental."

"Have you seen anyone else with them? Another woman, maybe?"

"Nope. Just the couple we already saw."

Logan was working under the theory that these people were either friends of or working for Diana. He'd been hoping Dev had spotted her and solidified the connection.

His phone vibrated on the seat where he'd set it. The display read BLOCKED.

"Hello?" he answered.

"Logan?" It was Callie.

"Hey. I was beginning to worry something happened to you."

"Sorry, flew back down this morning, then got pulled into some meetings at the office. I did get your message, though."

"What about the email I sent a little while ago?"

"Email?" she said. "Haven't seen it yet. What was in it?"

"I found Diana's Social Security and driver's license numbers."

"Great," she said, excited. "That'll help a lot."

"Logan," Dev said, pointing through the windshield.

"Hold on, Callie."

Across the street, two people had just exited room twenty-seven.

"That's them?" Logan asked Dev.

"Yeah."

They watched the woman and the man walk along the breeze-way and disappear inside an enclosed staircase. A few moments later they reappeared downstairs and walked over to the sedan.

"What do you want to do?" Dev asked.

Logan brought the phone back up to his ear. "Callie, I apologize, but I have to call you back."

"No problem," she said. "I'm here."

"Thanks." He hung up.

Across the street, the sedan's taillights flared on.

Logan grabbed some napkins out of the hamburger bag and reached for the door. "Follow them. If they start heading back this way, call me."

"What are you going to do?"

Logan pushed open the door. "A little recon."

A BLOCK DOWN from the motel, next to the interstate, was a combination gas station/mini-market. Logan made that his first stop. He went rapidly up and down the aisles looking initially for paperclips, but settling in the end for a plastic box of various-sized safety pins. He then circled around the back of the motel to avoid the office, and took the stairs at the far end up to the second floor.

When he reached number twenty-seven, he turned his head and held his ear near the door, listening in case someone had stayed behind. All was quiet.

Just to be doubly sure, he rapped on the jamb.

"Housekeeping," he said.

Silence—no squeaks from beds or feet walking across the room.

He retrieved the package of safety pins, selected two of the largest, then bent them all the way open, creating spears—or tools, in this case—to pick the lock. They were far from the best, but the lock was a cheap one, and within thirty seconds it willingly gave way.

Inside the room, the air had the undisturbed stillness that confirmed he was the only one present. Though dim, there was enough sunlight seeping in from around the curtain for him to see. Along one wall were two queen-size beds separated by a nightstand, and against the opposite, a dresser with a TV on top. At the back of the room was a closet, and next to it a nook that went further back to a countertop with a sink. Though he couldn't see it from where he stood, he knew there would be a door near it to the toilet and shower.

He checked the dresser first. On top were a few brochures laid out neatly next to the TV. Tourist stuff, probably left there by the Chamber of Commerce, hoping to entice guests to spend more than just the night. Quietly, he slid open the drawers one by one, but all were empty.

The nightstand was next, but it, too, revealed nothing that hadn't been there before the current occupants had checked in. Moving into the sink area, he found that the soap had been unwrapped, but there were no toothbrushes or shaving kits or anything like that.

The door to the toilet and shower room was open. A used towel on the floor, but that was it.

The closet was the only place left, so he pulled it open. Inside was a single suitcase. He'd expected to find two bags at the very least, one for the woman and one for the man, but this was it.

Using another napkin, he laid the suitcase on its side, unzipped it, and lifted up the top. It was the woman's bag—blouses, skirts, pants, underwear, bras. The clothes were precisely folded and stacked as if they were on display at Macy's. Without removing anything, he slipped his hand under the garments and slid it around, checking for anything hidden underneath.

While there was nothing along the bottom, he did find a black makeup bag tucked against the far side. Looking inside it, he could see lipstick, eyeliner, and several other items that were similar to those his ex-wife used to have. As he closed the makeup bag, his thumb brushed against something stitched on the side.

Though he could feel it, in the semi-darkness of the room, he couldn't see anything.

He carried the bag into the toilet area and flipped on the light. Initials, sewn on with black thread. No wonder he couldn't see them. They blended in perfectly with the bag itself.

E. P.

Two possibilities, he thought. Either they were the woman's initials, or the initials of the bag's particular brand. He couldn't think of a brand that fit, but he wasn't well-versed in women's wear or cosmetics, so it was very possible he was just unfamiliar with it.

He put the makeup bag back exactly where he'd found it, closed the suitcase, and returned it to the closet. With everything as it was, he scanned the room, making sure he hadn't missed anything.

He checked in with Dev. "Where are they?"

"A restaurant two miles from the motel. Been inside five minutes. Figure they'll be here at least an hour."

Good. "You didn't happen to see if either of—"

A knock on the door froze Logan where he stood. As soon as it stopped, a male voice called out, "Dr. Paskota. Thought you said you were going out."

"Logan?" Dev said.

"Someone's at the door," Logan whispered as loudly as he dared.

"I'm on my way."

As Logan hung up, there was another knock.

"Dr. Paskota, are you in there?"

A second man said, "You sure you heard her?"

"Thought I heard *someone*," the first replied.

"I didn't hear anything."

"Dr. Paskota? Mr. Frisk?" the first voice said. Another knock. "I swear I wasn't hearing things."

"This place is a dump. It was probably just a TV in another room turned up too high."

Silence.

"I think we should check," the first man said.

22

LOGAN MOVED QUIETLY into the bathroom and closed the door. Above the shower was a frosted glass window about four feet long and two feet wide. Not great, but he had little choice.

From the main room, he could still hear the others working on the front door. They were obviously not as skilled at picking a lock as he was, but even so, they were likely to be through in no more than a minute, two tops.

He stepped into the shower, unlatched the window, and slid the pane as far to the left as he could. A screen, brown after years cooking in the sun, covered the opening. The only thing holding it together was a memory of what it had once been, so it put up little defense against the single punch that ripped through it.

Logan tore at the hole, widening it, then anchored himself against the wall and swung his legs up, kicking his feet through the opening. Just as his ankles passed outside, he heard the front door open.

He shimmied backward until only his shoulders and head were left inside. He could hear the men talking, but couldn't understand what they were saying, nor did he much care at the moment.

His only goal was getting out. Fast.

His plan was to slide out the window, then hang on to the frame with one hand while closing the open pane with the other to remove any signs of his presence. The idea had sounded good in his head, but it failed in practice. His fingers barely paused on the lip of the frame before he was headed straight for the ground.

His army training kicking in, he rolled as he hit the dirt, popped to his feet, and began running along the rear of the motel.

"Hey! You! Stop!" It was the first man's voice, clear and unhindered. Logan had no doubt the guy was sticking his head out the bathroom window, but he wasn't about to look back and check. "Hey! I said stop!"

If the man was really expecting his words to work, he was sadly disappointed. Logan picked up his pace and sprinted the rest of the way to the corner.

Right would take him toward the front of the motel and Center Street, but it was also the direction from where the others would be coming. So Logan went left into a low-rent neighborhood of rundown homes. There were fewer FOR SALE signs than he'd seen elsewhere in town, but the amount of vacancies seemed to be the same.

At the first intersection he came to, he went right. Ahead, on the other side of the street, several men were gathered around a truck with its hood up. Whatever conversation they'd been having stopped when they saw Logan, and they stared at him as he ran by.

"Where you going so fast?" one of them called out, eliciting laughter from his friends.

As he neared the next intersection, Logan heard feet pounding the pavement somewhere behind him. This time he did look. A man—thin, late twenties, good shape, decked out in nice pants and a white, long-sleeved button shirt—had his eyes glued on Logan, so there was little doubt he was one of the men from the motel.

Logan turned right again, figuring he could risk heading for Center Street now. He wiped the back of his hand across his forehead, clearing away a layer of sweat. Though it was after five p.m., it was still hotter than hell, and running wasn't helping.

His phone began vibrating. Without slowing, he worked it out, and checked the screen. DEV.

"I just pulled up to the motel. Are you still in the room?"

"I'm…a couple blocks…east," Logan said between breaths. "Running. Got company behind…me."

"On my way. Don't hang up."

Logan looked back. The other guy hadn't turned the corner yet, so, with any luck, Logan would reach the main road before his pursuer came into view. Seconds later, that plan fizzled.

"Son of a bitch," he muttered under his breath.

Another man had just come around the corner from the Center Street end. He was also dressed in nice pants and long-sleeved shirt. Even discounting the similar clothes, the growing sneer on the guy's face was enough to convince Logan the two men were together.

Skidding to a halt, he said into the phone, "I don't have a lot of time here," then slid it into his pocket without disconnecting.

He couldn't go forward, and couldn't go back, leaving only the homes lining either side of the street. He took a quick look left and right. While the house on the right appeared occupied, the one on the left seemed to be another of the abandoned variety.

Logan went left, racing across the dead grass in the front yard, and hopping over the rotting wooden fence that surrounded the back.

"What the hell?"

It turned out the house on the left wasn't empty after all. A fat guy with a salt-and-pepper goatee and balding head was sitting next to a barbecue, drinking beer and cooking a steak.

"Get out of my yard!" the man said. "This is private property!"

He made a movement like he was going to get out of his chair, but he never quite pushed himself all the way up.

"Sorry," Logan said, not breaking stride.

"Where do you think you're going? I said get the hell out of here!"

Logan leaped just before he reached the back fence, grabbed the top with his hands, and vaulted himself into the neighboring yard.

Though no one was outside this time, there was a dog. It was small, a Yorkie or Maltese or something like that. Whatever it was, it didn't look happy that someone had intruded into its kingdom. Rapid-fire yaps spewed from its mouth as it ran toward Logan, halting just far enough away so that it could make a mad dash if Logan turned aggressive.

"Dude! This isn't a freeway!" It was the man from the other yard again, not yelling at Logan this time, but at someone else who'd dared enter his domain.

Logan reached the front fence next to the house, found the gate, and popped it open. As he passed through, the yappy dog almost got out, but he forced it back and closed the gate tight. A few seconds later, he was on the new road, running once more toward Center Street.

He retrieved his phone. "Are you still there?" he asked.

"Yeah. Where are you?"

"Coming up on Center Street. I'm about three blocks from the motel."

"I'll be right there."

Logan didn't slow until he turned onto the sidewalk that lined the main drag. On the corner was a shoe store, and next to it an ice cream shop. He went a half-dozen feet past the shop, stopped, doubled back, and went inside. A handful of customers were waiting in line. Logan positioned himself against the wall, and acted like he was reading the menu above the counter.

He raised his phone and whispered, "Ice cream place near the corner. I'm inside."

"I see it," Dev said. "Stay there."

Less than ten seconds later, the El Camino pulled to the curb and parked. Logan disconnected the call, but just as he was about to step outside, Dev held up a hand and stopped him.

Two seconds later, one of the men chasing him raced by without pausing to look inside.

Dev follow the man with his eyes, then looked back at Logan and nodded. Logan bolted out the door and climbed quickly into the El Camino. As soon as he was inside, he ducked below the dash so the others wouldn't spot him. Dev pulled leisurely out into Center Street's sparse traffic.

"Anything?" Logan asked.

Dev took a moment before he answered. "No."

"Drive around. Let's make sure we didn't pick up a tail."

After several minutes, and multiple changes in direction, Dev said, "We're clean."

"Let's go back to the motel," Logan said. "I've got a call to make."

––––––––

"EVERYTHING OKAY?" CALLIE asked.

"We seem to have stirred something up," Logan said. He was alone in his room, pacing between the bed and the window. Dev had returned to the other motel to keep an eye on things there.

"What?"

"That's a great question."

He brought her up to speed. When he finally finished, she said nothing for a moment.

"Your friend, Mr. Pepper. He's going to be all right?"

"No permanent damage."

She paused again. "I...I didn't expect anyone to get hurt."

Neither had Logan. "Well, I think we've at least confirmed the fact that this is more than just a wife with second thoughts."

"She *is* in trouble, isn't she?"

Instead of answering, Logan asked, "Were you able to learn anything from the stuff I sent?"

"I did a rough background check on Diana Stockley."

"And?"

"To start with, that wasn't the name she was born with. She changed it a little over two years ago. Before, it was Diana Baudler."

There was that time frame again. "Why did she change it?"

"Don't know, but she'd been arrested a few times as a teenager. Maybe she decided it was time to start over."

"She was in her late twenties then," Logan pointed out. "Seems a little late to be changing your name because of a troubled childhood. Any record after she became Diana Stockley?"

"No."

Logan took a moment to think. "Where's she originally from?"

"Oklahoma. Her dad left when she was young. She and her siblings ended up getting sent to live with an aunt in Des Moines."

"Anything else?"

"I've pieced together a partial employment history, but I'm still working on it."

"What do you have so far?"

He could hear the clicks of a keyboard over the phone, then Callie said, "As Diana Stockley, she's been in Braden just short of two years."

"So right after she changed her name."

"Pretty much. Before that, as Diana Baudler, she worked at a place called—"

"Let me guess. Harkin Services in El Portal, California," Logan finished for her.

"Right," she said, surprised. "How did you know?"

He told her about obtaining Diana's rental application from Mark Hackbarth.

"But her name was different. Why would she put that down?" Callie asked.

"Because she had to put something down. My guess, with the way the economy is here, she probably didn't think anyone would ever check."

"You could make a living at this if you wanted," she said, impressed.

"Yeah, *if*. What about before Harkin?"

"For about a year, she seemed to be making the rounds of bars in Reno and Carson City. Prior to that she worked in Flagstaff, Arizona, for almost four years at..." She paused. "Harkin Services."

"Again?"

"Same employer, different location."

Flagstaff was only a three-hour drive from Braden. If Diana had lived there for four years, she'd know the town pretty well. It might feel safe.

"Did you find her address in Flagstaff?"

"Hold on." More keys clicking. "Yeah, I've got it, but that was a while ago."

"I know, but give it to me anyway."

She read it off to him. As she finished, Logan's phone beeped with an incoming call.

"Just a second," he told her, and switched to the other call.

"I think they're getting ready to leave town." It was Dev.

"Why do you think that?"

"A few minutes ago, the woman and her friend came back in a hurry. The two who were chasing you met them in the parking lot. They had a conversation and then they all went into different rooms. Less than a minute ago, each came back out carrying a suitcase. They're putting them into their car now. What do you want me to do?"

"Follow them," Logan said immediately. "Let's see which way they go." He switched back to Callie. "Sorry about that. Anything else?"

"That's all I have for now," she said. "If I find more, I'll let you know."

"Hold on," he said. "I have two names you can check. Paskota and Frisk. Paskota's a female and might be a doctor. Frisk is male, no known occupation."

"First names?"

"The woman's first name might start with an E, but that's all I got. Don't have anything on the man's."

"I'll get on it."

"Thanks, Callie."

"Logan?"

"Yeah?"

"Stay safe."

TEN MINUTES LATER he got a call from Dev. "They're headed east on the interstate, just about to pass into Arizona."

Northern Arizona was a collection of small towns separated by large areas of nothing. Small towns, and one that was a bit larger than the others.

Flagstaff.

Diana had left Braden, and now her friends were heading out, too, in the direction of a town Diana had once lived in. Were they meeting up with her there? Maybe even with Sara? The possibility seemed too great to ignore.

"Stay on them," he told Dev. "I'll catch up with you."

23

SARA HAD BEEN trying the number for hours, but every single time she'd been greeted with the same message: "The caller you are trying to reach is not currently within our coverage area."

Where are you? Why aren't you answering?

Her panic had been caused by a call she'd received from Diana four and a half hours ago.

"Sara...Sara, can you hear me?"

"Yeah. You're breaking up a little, but I can hear you," she'd replied.

"Can you hear me? Sara?"

"I'm right here. I hear you."

"Oh, good. There you are."

"What's going on? Is something wrong?" They hadn't been scheduled to talk again until the next day.

"I screwed up."

Sara froze. "What...what are you talking about?"

"Have you seen anyone? Anyone at all?"

"No," Sara said. "Not since Richard came by two weeks ago. Why?"

"Stay inside. Don't go out."

"Diana, what's going on?"

"I'm taking care of it. That's all you need to know. Just hold tight."

Hold tight? "What happened?"

"I'll call you later."

"Diana! What happened?"

Dead air.

"Diana? Diana?"

Nothing.

"Dammit! Diana, can you hear me?"

It was no use. The line was dead.

Immediately she'd called Diana back. That was the first time she'd received the out-of-service-area message. She'd lost count how many more times she'd heard it since.

Movement through the window caught her eye. Panic almost choked her as she stared out at the trees that surrounded the cabin. If someone was that close already, what would she do? Run? Hide? Could she really hope she wouldn't be caught?

There it was again, a few feet above the ground.

She let out her breath and closed her eyes in relief. A deer. It was only a deer.

She quickly walked over and pulled the curtain shut, temporarily denying the existence of anything beyond the cabin walls.

Even though they had stuck to the plan, something had obviously gone wrong. It should have worked. It *had* worked to this point.

Not knowing what else to do, she tried Diana again.

"The caller you are trying to reach is not—"

She hung up, waiting five seconds, then hit redial.

24

NOT WANTING TO leave Harp and Barney without transportation, Logan arranged for a rental car through the manager at the Desert Inn, then headed east on I-40, fifty minutes behind Dev. As he passed through Kingman, Arizona, his father called.

"Hi, Dad."

"Logan? Barney and I want to go back to the hospital. You'll need to give us a ride."

"Just take the Cherokee."

Harp paused. "I thought you said we weren't supposed to drive it."

"It's fine now, Dad. The others are gone."

"Gone? Where did they go?"

"Not sure yet."

"Well, do you want to meet us for dinner?"

"I'm…um…following them. Not sure exactly when I'll be back."

"Following them? When were you going to tell me this?"

"Sorry. Had to move quickly. Didn't have time."

"Still not an excuse."

"You're right."

Harp said nothing for a moment. "What about the letter?"

Logan cringed. "I said I'd give it to you the next time I saw you. I haven't seen you yet."

"It's still with you?"

Logan could tell his father's anxiety level was rising. "It's still in the glove compartment. No one's touched it."

"It's just…okay, the next time I see you."

Logan hesitated, then said, "Do you want to talk about what's inside it?"

"You didn't look, did you?" Harp said quickly. "That's my property. You shouldn't look. You didn't, did you?"

Out of reflex, Logan said, "No, of course not."

Harp took a couple of loud breaths. "All right. Sorry. Um, if you need our help, you know where we are."

"Thanks."

An hour later Dev called.

"How far does this thing go when the needle's on empty?" he asked.

"I try not to let it get there," Logan said.

"Well, I'm about a hair's width away from it. Kept hoping they'd pull over, but their car doesn't eat as much gas as this one."

"Where are you?"

"Almost to Flagstaff."

"You still have them in sight?"

"At the moment, but I'm going to have to stop soon."

Logan frowned. "You've got probably about twenty miles. Will that get you to Flagstaff?"

"Yeah."

"Stay with them until you know if they're stopping there, or heading farther east, then fill up."

"Got it."

Logan inched the rental's speed up a few miles an hour, knowing it would never be enough to catch up with Dev in time.

Fifteen minutes passed before Dev called back.

"They got off in Flagstaff."

Logan could feel some of the tension in his shoulders easing. "You know which way they went?"

"Yeah, not that it'll do us much good. This place isn't huge, but it's big enough to get lost in. I'm filling up now. When I'm done, I'll see if I can spot them, but I'm not holding my breath."

"Don't waste your time," Logan said. "Turns out Diana used to work in Flagstaff. I have the address where she used to live. Give it a drive-by and see if there's anything interesting."

"You think that might be where she is?"

"I doubt our luck is that good, but we have to check."

"Want me to knock on the door?"

"No. Not until I get there. If you have time, try to get an address for Harkin Services. That was her employer. I should be there in forty minutes or so."

———————

AS THE LIGHTS of Flagstaff came into view, Logan checked in again with Dev, who suggested they meet at Diana's old address.

"It's not exactly what you're expecting," Dev said.

"What do you mean?"

"You'll see."

The first thing Logan spotted as he turned onto Diana's old street was the El Camino parked at the curb with Dev standing next to it on the sidewalk. As Logan got out of his rental, he checked the addresses on the buildings until he found the one Diana had used.

It wasn't a house. It wasn't even an apartment building.

It was a business called Burrage Copy Box.

He walked over and looked through the window.

"Told you it wasn't what you'd expect," Dev said, coming up behind him.

Though Copy Box was closed for the night, there were enough security lights on to see inside. The place's main features were half a dozen photocopy machines, several racks of shipping supplies, and a wall of private mailboxes, one of which had undoubtedly been used by Diana at one point.

"Just great," Logan said.

"I've got something else you'll want to see."

"What?"

Dev tossed the El Camino's keys to Logan. "Come on. I'll show you."

Following Dev's instructions, Logan drove to the end of the block, turned right, and went two more blocks.

"Park anywhere," Dev said.

"Where are we?"

As soon as they were stopped, Dev pointed at the office building beside them. In bold, white letters affixed to the brick exterior were the words HARKIN SERVICES.

"Checked out their website when I looked up their address," Dev said. "They're a contractor for the National Park Service."

"Doing what?"

"Basically running some of the parks—concessions, tours, in-park motels, that kind of thing. El Portal is right outside Yosemite. And Flagstaff is only an hour or so from—"

"The Grand Canyon," Logan finished for him.

The corner of Dev's mouth moved up a bit. "Bet she worked as a bartender at motels in both places."

Annoyed, Logan looked down the street toward where Burrage Copy Box was located. He was willing to bet a majority of the company's mail service clients were Harkin employees who worked at the Grand Canyon. A small part of him had been hoping this was Sara's hiding place. No such luck.

He got out and gave the building a once-over. Somewhere inside, either in a cabinet or on a server, would be a folder with all the information the company had on Diana Stockley—rather, Diana Baudler—including the address where she'd actually lived while working at the Grand Canyon. Maybe that would be another dead end. Still, he would love to get a look at the file.

For a second, he considered breaking in, but while he was

sure he could get through the door, he was equally positive there would be an alarm system he wouldn't be able to figure out how to deactivate in time. There were other ways to get the info, though. Perhaps Callie could help on that front.

Hearing Dev take a step behind him, he turned. "I think maybe we should—"

It wasn't Dev.

In fact, it wasn't just one person. It was two.

And both were aiming guns at his chest.

25

WITH EACH PASSING hour, Diana's sense that she'd missed her opportunity to find out what Logan and his friends were doing grew, but then the truck returned to the Desert Inn parking lot—not only with the tough guy inside, but Logan, too—and all those thoughts of failure disappeared.

After Logan got out, the other guy took off again. She didn't even consider following the El Camino. Logan was the one who'd been asking questions about Sara. That's where her focus needed to be.

She watched as he went up to the second floor and into one of the rooms. For a few seconds, she considered following him up and confronting him, but she knew that would give her no more than temporary satisfaction. If he *was* involved with whom she thought, best to just observe for now.

For a while nothing happened, then Logan exited his room carrying a duffle bag and walked downstairs. On the first floor he entered another room, came out holding a second bag, and went into the motel lobby. He stayed there until a white, generic-looking sedan pulled into the parking lot. As he exited the office, the man who'd been driving the car climbed out. The driver was wearing khakis and a bright blue golf shirt, and he was holding a tablet computer. Using a stylus, Logan wrote something on the computer screen, and the man handed him a set of keys.

A rental, she realized.

As Logan threw the bags in the trunk, Diana started her car.

Her weak point was obviously following people, but she knew if she lost him this time, she might never find him again. Given that he'd brought the bags, she guessed he was probably leaving town, and the only way to do that was via the interstate.

The freeway entrance was a straight shot down Center Street. She pulled out of the lot and headed in that direction before Logan even got behind the wheel of his car. A block shy of the overpass, she pulled into a gas station to wait.

Thirty seconds later, the rental sped by. When its blinker came on indicating it was about to make a right turn, the skin on her arms went numb.

East. He was heading east.

Sara was east of here. Could he know that?

Having no choice, Diana shifted the car out of park and took off after him.

She quickly found that freeway following was a hell of a lot easier than doing so in town, and she was able to keep Logan in sight with little trouble. As they headed through Arizona, she tried willing him to turn down US 93 to Phoenix, but he blew right past the transition, staying on the I-40.

Every mile her concern increased. When they neared the exit to Williams, she could feel her pulse pounding in her neck and arms. But Logan kept going, driving right by the off-ramp that would have taken him to the cabin where Sara was.

Could it just be a trick? Did he know she was following him, and was trying to throw her off? Having no confidence that the situation was any better than it had been, she stayed with him.

When he exited at Flagstaff, she felt her blood pressure rise again. She had a connection in this town, a connection that could possibly lead in Sara's direction. She tried to follow him into town, but once more was defeated by her lack of experience and lost him within minutes. Worse, Flagstaff was at least a dozen times bigger than Braden, so he would be much harder to find.

Her only choice was to do a methodical search for his white sedan. At least she'd been able to memorize his license plate number, making her task of spotting his amongst the hundreds of other white sedans marginally less impossible than it could have been.

When she did find the sedan within the first fifteen minutes, she didn't know if she felt lucky or horrified. It was parked in front of Burrage Copy Box. The very same Copy Box outlet she had used as a mailing address when she worked at the canyon. Oddly, Logan didn't seem to be around.

Could he have…?

With growing dread, she doused her lights, and turned down the street where her former employer's offices were located. And there, parked right in front, was the electric blue El Camino.

She pulled to the curb and reached for her phone. She had turned it off after talking to Sara, because she didn't have any answers, and had no idea what to say. It was a panic move, but now she needed to talk to Sara, tell her she was coming to pick her up tonight. She brought up Sara's number, but before she could hit SEND, she saw that there were other people on the sidewalk beside Logan and his tough friend.

Four, in fact. Two behind the friend, and two in front of Logan.

Even from a block and a half away, she could see the guns.

What the hell was this?

26

"DON'T MOVE," THE shorter of the two gunmen said.

He was the one who'd been running after Logan in Braden. The guy standing with him was his buddy who'd tried to cut Logan off at Center Street. Over at the El Camino, Logan could see the other two—the woman and her friend—holding their weapons on Dev.

The speaker stepped behind Logan and searched him, removing Logan's wallet, keys, and phone. Dev was getting the same treatment.

With a shove in the back toward the truck, the man said, "Let's go."

Three feet separated Logan from the gunman in front of him, and three and a half from the one behind. Not the best position, but there were at least four different ways he could take both of them out.

Doable, if he were alone.

While Dev was more than capable of handling the other two, *his* positioning was not as favorable. The two training their weapons on him could put a bullet in the back of his head before Logan could vanquish his two.

Escape would have to wait for a better opportunity to present itself.

When Logan and his two new buddies reached the others, the man who had searched him handed the wallet and other items to the woman—Dr. Paskota, presumably. She opened the wallet and examined the license, then compared Logan to the picture.

Once she was done, she said, "This way." She started to turn.

"Whatever you want to talk about, we can do it right here," Logan said, not moving.

"I'm sure we could, but we won't. Let's go."

The three gunmen had backed off far enough that even with a coordinated effort, Logan and Dev would have been condemning themselves to death if they tried anything. Reluctantly, Logan gave Dev a nod, and they followed the woman to the familiar gray sedan.

Six people in a car designed for no more than five meant a tight squeeze in the backseat. This could have been another opportunity, but the others weren't fools. The two who got in on either side of Logan and Dev gave their weapons to the guy in the front passenger seat—Frisk—preventing the chance one of their guns could be wrestled away. Frisk swiveled around and leaned against the dash to get a clear view of everyone in back. He made sure Logan and Dev saw the gun in his hand.

"Where are we going?" Logan asked as they drove down the street.

No one answered. He asked again a few minutes later, but received the same response.

Soon Flagstaff was behind them, and they were on a quiet, two-lane road, the forest lining each side. This part of Arizona was decidedly not desert.

For the first several miles, Logan caught glimpses of homes amongst the trees, but it wasn't long before they dwindled in number and all but disappeared as the road transitioned from asphalt to dirt.

Logan didn't like the situation at all. If it were just talk the woman wanted, they would have found a quiet spot in town. This was more an end-of-the-line kind of thing. He shared a quick look with Dev, conveying without words that they would make their move at the first chance. Dev blinked once, indicating he understood.

They hadn't gone far on the dirt road when the woman slowed and carefully scanned ahead. She took the first turn that came up. This new path wasn't so much a road as the memory of one. They weaved between the trees, going no more than a quarter mile before they stopped.

Leaving the parking lights on and the motor running, Dr. Paskota ordered everyone out.

"Put them over there," she said, pointing at a spot about fifteen feet in front of the car.

Frisk motioned for Logan and Dev to move.

The tree cover was dense, letting little of the moonlight to filter down. With the exception of the light from the car, everything was in near total darkness.

"When I make my move, head into the woods," Logan whispered as he and Dev walked in front of their escort.

For a second he wasn't sure he'd said it loudly enough for Dev to hear, but if he raised his voice, the guy behind them would have noticed.

"Uh-huh," Dev grunted.

"Right there," Frisk said.

Logan and Dev stopped.

"Now turn around."

As they followed instructions, Logan made out the silhouette of the woman leaning against the vehicle. The other two were standing to either side of him.

Frisk took a step back toward the vehicle, but Dr. Paskota said, "No. Move to the side, but stay over there in case they try anything stupid."

The escort didn't seem to be too happy about this, but he didn't protest as he moved several feet to Logan's left.

"So, Mr. Harper, you want to tell me what you were doing in my motel room?"

"I was curious."

"About what?"

"Whether it was your room, Dr. Paskota, or Mr. Frisk's here." Out of the corner of his eye, he could see Frisk flinch at the mention of his name.

"I guess we've established that you're resourceful," she said.

Logan shrugged, but remained quiet.

"You haven't answered my question," she said.

Logan smiled. "If you hadn't been following us, I wouldn't have been in your room. But since you had, I wondered why. See, I'm looking for someone, and you keeping an eye on us made me think you didn't want us to do that. The obvious reason is that you know where she is and are trying to hide her. *That's* why I was in your room."

"You mean Diana Stockley."

Logan shrugged. She knew why. She was working with Diana, after all, but if she wanted to take her time and play games, that was fine with him.

"Or was what you told that real estate agent a lie?" She smiled. "I have a feeling Diana Stockley doesn't owe you any money."

Logan kept quiet.

"I thought not. The picture, then. The one of the other woman you were showing around. That's why, right?"

"You should know," he said. "You beat up my friend because he was showing it around, too."

Off to Logan's side, Frisk had started looking at his boss every few seconds, as if he were waiting for a visual order to pull the trigger.

"Now why would we have done that?" she asked.

"Look, I know you're helping Diana and Sara, and you think that my friends and I are some kind of danger to them, but we're not here to harm them in any way."

She stared at him, the look on her face curious. After a moment, she said, "Then why *are* you here?"

Something was not right, he realized. He'd made a mistake somewhere, figured something wrong. *Can it be...?*

Beside him, Frisk was taking even longer looks at his boss, a smirk growing on his face.

"Well, Mr. Harper? Why?" she asked.

He considered his response. "Sara's a friend, that's all. We were just trying to find her."

Her look of curiosity was now one of pity. "I don't know if that's the truth or not, but I will tell you that you've been working under a misconception. I'm not *helping* Diana and Sara. I'm looking for them, just like you. The only difference is, I'm going to find them. You and your friend are a complication that has no value to me."

Logan was right, but he had no time to process the bigger picture of what that might mean. He checked Frisk again. While the man was pointing his gun at Logan, he was once more looking at Dr. Paskota.

"Are you saying you had nothing to do with the man in the hospital?" Logan asked.

"Mr. Harper, I think we're—"

Logan grunted, "Now," and dove to his left, slamming into Frisk's legs and knocking the gunman to the ground. He grabbed the man's hand that was holding the gun, wrapped his free arm around the man's waist, then rolled with him side over side quickly into the trees.

Behind him, several shots rang out.

"Let go of me, you son of a bitch!" Frisk yelled.

Logan punched him in the jaw and slammed the gun hard into the ground, catching the man's fingers between the grip and the dirt.

Out of reflex, Frisk's hand opened.

Logan immediately twisted the weapon free and whipped it into the side of the asshole's head. Frisk fell against the ground, stunned.

Staying low, Logan scrambled deeper into the darkness of the woods. When he was a good fifty yards away, he stopped and looked back.

Someone had turned on the sedan's headlights, lighting up as much of the forest as they could. He could see Frisk stumbling toward the car, but wasn't sure where the others were. What he really wanted to see was the area where he and Dev had been, but several trees blocked his sight line. He moved quietly to his right until the view opened up.

No body on the ground. *Good.* Dev had at least made it into the trees.

Logan checked the car again, searching for the remaining men. One was helping Frisk get inside the vehicle, but the other two were still nowhere to be seen.

A sound, low and soft.

An ever-so-subtle crunch.

A footstep, carefully placed on a pack of dried pine needles.

Logan waited for another one, but none came.

His eyes having adjusted as best they could to the darkness, he picked out a path that went in a large arc around the area where the car was parked, and over to the side where Dev would have gone. He needed to find his friend to make sure he was all right.

Between steps, he stopped to listen. Once he heard a twig snap, but it could have been caused by the wind in the trees. Another time he heard Frisk groan back at the car.

As he neared the top of the arc, he caught sight of a boulder just ahead. It would provide excellent cover, and perhaps there was even a crevasse or hole where Dev was hiding.

Logan came around the backside of the rock, farthest from the car. His instinct was to whisper Dev's name, but he couldn't chance it so he moved in closer. It wasn't one boulder, but several piled together on the edge of a small depression. Keeping his newly acquired gun in front of him, he checked the spaces between the rocks but saw no one there.

He glanced up. The top of the pile was about twelve feet

above him. If he could get up there, he'd be able to see where the others were. He scoped out the easiest route, then put a foot on the rock.

Almost instantly he knew it was a bad idea. Not because the rock was unstable or anything like that, but because of the gun muzzle that was suddenly resting against the base of his skull.

27

LOGAN WAS PRETTY sure he could twist out of the way and get control of the weapon without getting hit. But when it came to pistols anywhere near his head, *pretty sure* wasn't something he wanted to test.

He raised his hands, his own gun pointing at the sky.

"Set it on the rock," the person behind him whispered, the words almost like breaths. "Slowly."

As he started to comply, the muzzle came away from his head, and he could hear the person take a quick step backward.

He placed his pistol on the rock.

"To your left."

Improvising, he started to turn as he moved.

"No. Keep your eyes on the rocks."

Not seeing a choice, he complied. His gun was now a sizable lunge away.

"Far enough," the voice whispered. "Now sit."

He hesitated, confused. He had expected to be immediately marched back to the sedan.

"Sit."

This time he did so.

Silence descended. In the distance he thought he could hear another footstep.

After nearly a minute, he said, "What are we do—"

"Quiet."

From his position, the only thing Logan could see was rock. He tried not to think about anything, focusing all his energy on being ready to react at a moment's notice. Hopefully, whoever was behind him didn't know that Dev was out there, too.

A distant, angry voice broke through the stillness, and was followed moments later by the sedan's doors slamming shut. The car's engine grew loud enough to be heard, then it faded into the distance as the vehicle drove away.

What the hell?

"Who are you?" the person behind him asked. Not a whisper this time.

Surprised, he turned without even thinking about it.

"Don't!"

But it was too late. He'd seen her.

Diana Stockley was crouched next to a tree ten feet behind him. In her hand was a pistol. She looked nervous and scared, not the combination Logan wanted in a person pointing a gun at him.

"I promise I won't try anything," he said, continuing to hold up his empty palms. "Why don't you put the gun down?"

"No. Who are you?"

"I told you at your bar. My name's Logan. Logan Harper."

"That's a lie. Who are you, really?"

"That's not a lie. I'd show you my driver's license, but the others took my wallet."

"Convenient."

"If you were watching us, you know they did."

She stared at him, tight-lipped, but allowed the barrel of the gun to point a few feet to Logan's right.

"Tell them to leave her alone and not to come looking for her again," she said. "Make sure you tell them she's *not* theirs. Not now. Not ever. Understand?"

"I don't know who you think I am," Logan said. "But the last thing I want to do is hurt Sara."

The woman stared at him. "Don't you dare say her name. You don't have that right."

"I'm only here because of Sara's husband."

She looked confused. "Her husband?"

"Alan," Logan said. "And her daughter Emily, too."

Diana didn't move for a moment. Then she stood up, her pistol pointed directly at Logan's head.

"Who *are* you?"

Thirty feet behind her, Logan saw movement between the trees.

Dev. It had to be.

Logan made fists with his hands and then opened them, stretching his fingers. He hoped Dev would see it as the hold sign he meant it to be.

"I told you. I'm Logan Harper. Alan's lawyer, Callie Johnson, is a friend of mine. She asked me to help Alan find his wife. When I talked with him, I met Emily. I know she likes goldfish crackers and that sponge guy's cartoon, and I'm sure she misses her mom."

"You're lying. I don't know how you know that stuff, but you're just trying to trick me into telling you where she is."

So you do know.

As calmly as he could, he said, "I don't want to hurt anyone. I just want to talk to Sara. That's all."

"No. You want to turn her over to that woman, so she'll tell them…" She stopped herself, as if she'd just realized something important.

"Tell them what?"

"Shut up!" she said. "Shut up! Shut up! Shut up!"

"Please take your finger off the trigger, okay? I'm sure you don't want to kill anyone, and I'm not really in the mood to *be* killed."

"You don't know what I want. You don't know anything." She

seemed on the verge of hyperventilating when, with obvious reluctance, she removed her finger from the trigger. Taking another step backward, she said, "Stay away from her, and stay away from her family."

"What am I supposed to tell Alan?"

She tried to laugh. "I don't believe you ever saw Alan."

"I sat in the living room of his and Sara's house in Riverside. I saw the mural Sara painted on the wall of Emily's bedroom. I'm not lying to you."

A look of sheer terror flooded across her face as if Logan had transformed into some kind of monster. Her lips moved like she wanted to say something, but no words came out.

"I just want to talk to her," Logan tried to reassure her. "I'm here to—"

Before he could even form the next word, she ran into the woods.

"Wait! Diana, please! I'm not here to hurt her *or* you! Diana!"

But the only answer he received was the sound of her receding footsteps.

28

ERICA SEETHED SILENTLY as she drove the sedan back to Flagstaff. She would have preferred to be alone, but Markle and Clausen hadn't done anything to deserve walking back. It was Frisk who'd let Harper get the better of him, and allowed the two men to escape. She would have left him behind if he hadn't already been in the car.

Who the hell was this Harper guy? And why was he screwing things up?

For nearly two and a half years, this festering wound had nagged at Erica, intruding more and more into her thoughts. If she didn't fix it, it would come back to destroy her. She had done everything she could, wasting her own money on watchers and the associated equipment costs, spending hours going over bits and pieces of information.

Finally, *finally*, they had caught a break. Diana had been located again. Different last name, but definitely her. Erica was sure it would only be a matter of days, not weeks or months or years, before Diana led them to Sara. Everything was going to be right. Everything was going to be fine.

Then Diana disappeared and this Harper guy showed up with

his friends and everything went to shit.

Dammit!

She forced herself to take long deep breaths so she could bring herself back under control.

All was not lost, she realized. Diana was somewhere in the area, she was sure of it.

With grudging thanks to Harper, she'd received his copy of Diana's rental file from her former landlord. On the application, Diana had listed one of her previous employers as Harkin Services in El Portal, California. That set off a loud bell in Erica's head. She checked the records she'd been compiling on her computer over the past thirty months, and found that's when Diana had also worked for Harkin Services in Flagstaff, Arizona.

It was an interesting connection, but one Erica might not have done anything about if she hadn't had one of her freelance researchers hack into the transportation department for both California and Arizona, checking highway cameras for footage of Diana. The hope was her contact might be able to discover which way the woman had gone. The researcher called late that afternoon.

"Arizona," he'd said. "Early this morning."

That's when it came together for Erica. Diana would return to somewhere she knew. People always did. Flagstaff would fit that bill nicely.

Braden, Erica had decided, was a dead end. They needed to move east.

But then what happened? After driving around town and checking various addresses from Diana's file, Erica had headed over to her former employer's office and found Harper and Martin standing in front of the building.

What the hell? That's when she decided to get rid of them once and for all. *Lovely how* that *worked out*, she thought.

Her grip tightened on the steering wheel as her anger began rising again. She glanced at Frisk in the mirror. The idiot's eyelids were barely open, his skin pale.

"Do not let him throw up in here," she said.

"I think he needs a doctor," Markle said.

Erica was about to say she didn't care what he needed, but stopped. She couldn't afford the headache or the time it would take to deal with the problem if Frisk died in the car. She could just have Markle dump him on the side of the road, but that wasn't a good option, either. They were too close to town now, and there was always a chance someone would see them.

"You might want to open up a window," Clausen suggested.

Erica touched the button that automatically rolled down the window next to Frisk. As soon as the fresh air hit him, the injured man leaned toward it.

Erica found the Flagstaff Medical Center parking, and stopped where there were no other cars. She looked back at Frisk.

"Are you with us?" she said.

Frisk tried to focus on her. "Huh?"

"Can you hear me? Do you understand what I'm saying?"

"Yeah. I...understand."

She frowned. He might understand, but would he remember? "If you value your life and the life of your family at all, you will do exactly as I say. Understand?"

He tensed. "Yes, ma'am."

"As I understand, your sister just had a baby boy, isn't that correct?"

"I'll do whatever you want," he pleaded.

"I wanted you to keep an eye on the woman, but you couldn't handle that, now could you?"

"It was a mistake. It won't happen again."

"I know it won't because you know the consequences if it does." She made sure he was looking her in the eye. "This is what you will tell them inside. You were in a fight with someone you don't know. You're just passing through town, and can't remember much of anything about the evening. Got it?"

"Sure. Got it."

"Repeat it."

With some difficulty, Frisk did. It was the best Erica could hope for.

"You have any ID on you?"

He thought for a moment. "Don't think so. Should be...in my bag."

Erica looked at Markle. "Check him."

Markle shifted Frisk around, checked his pockets, then shook his head. "Nothing."

Good. At least Frisk had been smart enough not to be carrying anything with his name on it.

"Get in, get out. Don't answer any questions," she instructed the other two men.

"Yes, ma'am," Clausen said.

He and Markle helped Frisk into the emergency room. They returned just a few minutes later.

As they drove away, Erica glanced at Clausen and said, "We'll find a motel. You two get a few hours' sleep, then I want you to go back to Braden. You'll have to find your own ride. When you get there, learn all you can about that guy who got beat up outside Diana's bar. Both he and Harper were looking for the girl. Find out what their connection is and what they want her for."

"No problem," Clausen said.

Before locating rooms for the night, Erica had one quick stop to make first. At some point, Harper and Martin would find their way back to Flagstaff. The way she saw it, she had two choices: Leave either Clausen or Markle to stake out Harper's car and deal with him and his friend permanently when they returned, or see if the two interlopers could prove to be more useful. Since she'd rather not waste the manpower, the second option was more attractive.

She drove back to Harkin Services and stopped behind the El Camino.

Without a word, she popped open the trunk and got out.

In the back was the leather bag that had been waiting for her when she'd picked up the rental car. As was her habit, she had prepared for all contingencies. The bag contained some of that hardware her money had paid for, including the guns and matching sound suppressors she and the others were using. What she was interested in now was a small case with several magnet-backed trackers.

She took one out, and attached it to the inside of the El Camino's rear bumper.

As she drove away, her anger at the botched evening started to subside. They were on the right path again. She could feel it. Tomorrow she would find a new lead on Diana.

One way or another, this problem would soon be closed.

29

IF DIANA AND the Paskota woman weren't working to-gether, then the only way The Hideaway's former bartender could have been there was because she had followed the doctor's car. So that meant she'd hidden her own vehicle somewhere in the woods between where Logan and Dev stood and the main road, the op-posite direction in which she'd run. At some point, she would have to circle back.

"Come on," Logan said.

He and Dev ran along the path that Dr. Paskota had used to bring them here. They made it almost all the way back to the dirt road before Logan pulled to a stop and knelt down. Even in the darkness, he could see the eight-inch strip of compacted pine needles that led off the path. Predictably, he found a second, identical strip a few feet away.

Tire tracks.

Silently, he pointed in the direction they headed. Dev nodded.

Careful not to make a sound, the two men followed the tracks. About a hundred feet from where they began, they found a Ford sedan with California license plates, and a tag that identified it as a rental car. Though there was no one sitting inside, Logan saw that the keys were in the ignition, the car ready to go the moment the owner returned.

Dev raised a finger to his ear and tapped twice. Logan listened. Footsteps, fifty yards away and heading in their direction.

The two men immediately pulled back into the trees, hiding behind two pines close to the car. It was a whole minute before Logan saw a shadow moving through the woods on the other side of the sedan. It was Diana, of course. He'd never doubted that. She moved slowly, taking her time with each step, and probably thinking she was doing a good job of masking any noise.

Upon reaching the car, she abandoned her caution, and raced around to the driver's door. As her hand shot out and grabbed the handle, Logan silently moved in behind her, his gun in his hand.

Sensing his presence, she started to whip around, but he yanked the gun out of her hand before she could bring it even halfway up. She staggered backward and slammed against the car door, knocking it closed again. "Get away from me!"

Logan tossed her gun to Dev. "You drive. Ms. Stockley and I will sit in back."

He grabbed her arm and pulled her over to the rear door.

"Let me go!" She jerked back and forth, trying to break his grip, but succeeded in only getting him to squeeze tighter.

After Dev opened the door for them, Logan pushed Diana inside and jumped in right behind her. She immediately tried to get out the other door, but Logan was having none of it. He grabbed her again and pulled her back. "Don't waste your energy. You're not going anywhere." To Dev, he said, "Child lock."

"On it."

Dev jogged around the car, opened the door next to Diana, and engaged the child lock so that the door couldn't be opened from the inside. That done, he circled back around and got behind the wheel.

As soon as the car was moving, Logan released Diana. She pushed herself away from him, and tried the door despite the fact she'd seen Dev set the lock. When pulling on the handle did nothing, she yelled out in frustration and grabbed hold of the front passenger seat so she could climb over.

Logan clapped a hand on her shoulder and yanked her back, forcing her once more into a sitting position.

"Don't try that again," he ordered.

"I'm not going to sit here and let you kill me."

"I'm not going to kill you. I don't even want to hurt you."

"Bullshit. You're just trying to trick me, get me to tell you where Sara is. Once I do, you'll shoot me, won't you? You don't have to answer that. I know you will."

She lunged for the front seat again. This time Logan shoved her back harder.

"You don't get it," he said. "I'm not here to hurt Sara or you or anyone. I'm here because of Alan. That's all. He knows something's wrong, and he wants to help."

"I don't know where you got your information. Sara's not married. I don't know who this Alan is. It's all lies."

It was easy to see that Diana had been going over everything as she'd made her way back to her car. This was probably what she wished she'd said before. It was delivered with practiced conviction.

"Don't," he said. "You're making yourself sound stupid. You pretty much admitted you knew I was telling the truth."

"I don't know what you're talking about."

The fear in her eyes was seemed to consumer her. Logan sensed it wasn't so much for herself as for Sara, the woman she was trying to protect for some reason. He thought for a moment, then reached for his phone in his pocket. It wasn't there.

Son of a bitch. Dr. Paskota had it.

"Where's your phone?" he asked Diana.

She closed her lips tight and glared at him.

She hadn't been carrying a bag in the woods, and he could tell there was nothing in the front pockets of her jeans. He rolled her on her side so he could see the back.

"Hey!" she said.

The rear pockets were empty, too.

He let go of her.

"Is there a purse or bag up there?" he asked Dev.

Dev glanced around. "Yeah. There's something in the passenger footwell."

He stopped the car, retrieved it, and tossed it back to Logan.

"That's mine!" Diana shouted, reaching for the bag. "You have no right!"

Though he didn't want to do it, Logan raised his gun. That seemed to sober her up. She retreated to her corner, her gaze burning holes in his head.

He opened the bag and felt around until he found not one cell phone, but two. The first he pulled out was a Blackberry. He activated the screen, made sure it was getting a signal, then reached in and pulled out the second phone.

This time Diana visibly tensed.

The phone was a bare-bones model—no Web access, no email, just calls and texts. The kind of phone with prepaid minutes you'd buy at a 7-Eleven or corner shop. A throwaway phone. Anonymous.

It was off, so he powered it up, opened the menu, and found the recent-calls list. There were only a handful of calls, but all were to the same number. He looked at Diana, and back at the phone.

"Please," she whispered. "Please don't."

Sara's number?

That seemed pretty damn likely, especially given Diana's reaction. He was so tempted to hit the connect button. The only thing holding him back was the very real chance that, if it was Sara, his voice would scare her off. What he needed was Diana on his side, and *then* Sara might listen to him.

He turned off the throwaway, switched to the Blackberry, and called one of the few numbers he knew by heart.

Three rings, then a groggy, "Hello?"

"Dad, it's me," Logan said.

"What? Is something wrong? Where are you?"

He could picture Harp flipping on a light and sitting up in bed.

"Everything's okay. I just need—"

"Did you find her?" Harp asked.

"Not yet. I need Callie's cell number."

"Don't you have it?"

Logan hesitated. "Not on me."

"Hold on." There was a pause before Harp said, "Can I check a number on here without hanging up on you?"

"Yeah, all you do is hit the menu button—"

The line went dead.

Logan called back.

"Who is this?" Harp asked, once they were reconnected.

"It's me," Logan said.

"This isn't your number."

"It's the same one I just called you on."

"It is?"

"Dad, focus."

"What happened to your phone?"

"It's…broken, okay?"

"This is your new number?"

"I'm just borrowing a phone from someone."

"So I can still call you at your old number?"

"No. Don't call it, not until I tell you it's okay. Now, Dad, I really need Callie's number."

"Well, obviously I can't get it without hanging up on you."

"No. You can." He talked his father through the procedure, this time getting Callie's number without being disconnected.

"When do you think you'll be back here?" Harp asked.

"I don't know. Soon, probably. I'll call you in the morning."

"From this number?"

"I don't *know*, Dad. From *a* number. Now go back to sleep."

Once he got Harp off the line, he called Callie, but was sent to her voice mail after four rings.

"It's Logan," he said. "Call me back as soon as you get this at the number this came in on. Do *not* use my cell number."

Less than a minute later, she called back. "Sorry. I didn't recognize the caller ID or I would have picked up."

"Don't worry about it," he said. "Can you get Alan on the line right now?"

"You found her?"

"I'm getting close, but I need his help."

"Doing what?"

"Conference him in, and you can hear, too."

She was quiet for a moment, then said, "Okay."

As he was put on hold, he glanced at Diana. She stared back at him, her face a mask of defiance. But it *was* only a mask. Underneath he sensed a growing uncertainty and confusion.

It took nearly a minute for Callie to come back on.

"Okay, I think we're all here," she said. "Alan?"

"I'm here," Alan replied. "What's going on? Is she all right?"

"I don't know yet," Logan said. "But I think I have someone here who does know. Unfortunately, she doesn't trust me. She thinks I'm here to hurt Sara. I'm hoping you can help me convince her otherwise. I'm going to put you on speaker, all right?"

"Sure," Callie said.

Just as Logan hit SPEAKER, Alan said, "Wait." The rest was broadcast throughout the car. "Who are you with?"

"Her name is Diana Stockley," Logan said. He looked at Diana. "I have Callie Johnson, the lawyer I mentioned, on the line and Alan Lindley, Sara's husband."

"I don't believe you," she said.

"Who are you?" Alan asked angrily.

"She's a friend of Sara's," Logan explained. "She visited Sara in Riverside right before your trip to Tijuana."

Diana gaped at Logan. "How did you—"

"Tessie," he said.

"Tessie?" She looked both surprised and sad.

"She told me about following you. She thinks you were cheating on her."

"I…I wasn't…" she said, more to herself than to Logan.

"Hey, did you hear me?" Alan asked.

"I'm sorry, what?" Logan replied.

"Did you hear what I said?"

"No, it didn't come through."

"I said Sara doesn't *have* any friends named Diana. I would have known."

"Alan," Callie broke in. "There's obviously a lot of things about Sara none of us knew."

Logan had been about to say something similar.

Silence.

"Did she help my wife leave?" Alan asked. "Did *you* help my wife abandon her daughter and me?"

"I don't know who you are," Diana said. "But this isn't going to work. I'm not going to tell you where she is."

"I don't know who *you* are!" Alan shot back. "Sara's my wife. She's Emily's mother. Who the hell are you?"

Diana shook her head, but said nothing.

This wasn't going exactly the way Logan had planned. Alan was taking out his weeks of frustration on their only real lead.

"Everyone, just relax," he said. "I have a feeling we're all concerned about the same thing—Sara's safety."

Diana scoffed, while neither Alan nor Callie said anything.

"Alan, where do you live?" Logan asked.

"What? What do you mean?"

"What's your address?"

"Why is that important?"

"Please."

"I live in Riverside."

"The street," Logan asked, hoping the information would be the key.

A pause. "1354 Celeste Lane."

As soon as the words came over the line, a series of stuttering breaths escaped Diana's lips.

30

"I LIVE IN Riverside," the man claiming to be Sara's husband said over the phone.

"The street," Logan Harper asked.

The man didn't answer right away, but when he did...

"1354 Celeste Lane."

Oh, God.

The whole world went into a tunnel, and for several seconds Diana could see nothing but gray.

1354 Celeste Lane.

She'd driven by the house half a dozen times. Hell, she had been *in* the house with Richard, removing all the pictures while Sara was in San Diego.

It was Sara's house. *Emily's* house.

If Logan was one of them and had the address, he wouldn't need her *or* Sara anymore.

When Diana had seen the confrontation back in Flagstaff, and followed them out to the forest, she had thought it was a struggle between two groups ultimately working for the same master. In her mind, it was a game of get-to-Sara-first-and-win-the-prize.

She had wanted to hear what was being said, wanted to see the faces of the others so she'd know what everyone looked like, and could keep an eye out for them in the future. But before she could move in closer, it became apparent the others were actually going to kill Logan and his friend and get rid of their competition. That was more than enough to keep her rooted where she was.

She'd been as surprised as anyone when the two condemned men escaped. Then Logan had walked into the area where she'd hidden. That was an opportunity she couldn't ignore. She could learn what he knew, then warn him and his friends off Sara a final time.

That hadn't gone quite the way she'd expected. While she thought at first what he'd told her was a lie to get her to divulge Sara's location, soon some of what he'd said got a little too close to home.

Afraid to hear more, she'd run, coming up with a million things she could have said, *should* have said to counter his lies.

Only now…

1354 Celeste Drive.

They weren't lies.

"Diana? Diana?"

She barely heard the voice as she tried to work out how this could possibly be another trick.

"Diana?"

But she could find no path that made sense.

"Diana!"

Her eyes refocused on the dull gray tones of the car's dark interior. She lifted her head and saw that Logan was looking at her.

"What?" she whispered.

"We're just trying to help her. Can't you see that?"

"We…we don't…need your help," she said, though she knew there was no conviction in her voice.

Help was exactly what they needed. Since Sara had to stay hidden, Diana and Richard were the only ones who could do anything. And Richard…well, without Diana pointing him in the right direction, they would have long ago failed.

She'd always been the one in charge. That's how they got into this in the first place, and why now Diana would do anything to protect Sara.

She'd been the one who found the ad online. She'd been the one who'd written down the number and suggested Sara call. She'd been the one who'd pushed Sara to do it, thinking it would be the way Sara could get the real start she needed.

Though there was no way Diana could have known the truth, it was still her fault, her problem to fix.

But how could she do that with just Richard and herself?

"What's going on?" Alan asked. Alan, Sara's *husband*.

Oh, my God. What a mess.

"Diana?" Logan said.

She forced herself out of her thoughts. "I'm sorry."

There was sympathy in Logan's eyes. "I asked if you know where Sara is."

Before she even realized it, she nodded and said, "Yes."

"Thank God," Alan said. "Is she all right? Where is she? What's going on?"

"She's…she's okay," Diana said. "Just scared."

"Why? What is she scared of? Did I do something? Is it me?"

If Diana hadn't been so stunned by it all, she would have probably laughed. "No. She would have never left Emily with you if that were the case."

"Then why?" Alan pleaded.

Diana looked at Logan. This was not a question she wanted to answer.

Logan seemed to sense this. He said, "She's in trouble, we know that. Those people out in the woods, they weren't playing around."

"What people?" Alan asked.

"I'll fill you in later," Logan said, and looked back at Diana. "You need help. That's obvious." He nodded toward the driver.

"Dev and I are pretty handy to have around."

She didn't know what to say. She still wasn't completely sure she could trust them. Help would be great, but…

"I don't…I just…"

"What's the problem?" Alan asked. "If Sara's in trouble, you have to let us help. For God's sake, I'm her *husband!*"

Diana looked at the phone as if she could see through it. "Yeah, well, I'm her sister."

31

IT WAS AS if all the air had been sucked out of the world. No one breathed. No one moved. No one said a word.

Logan looked at Diana anew, trying to discern patterns in the woman's face that matched those in the less-than-perfect picture he had of Sara. There were definitely similarities—the cheeks, the lips, the curve of her jaw.

Alan was the first to break the silence. "How do we know *you're* not lying?"

Before she could respond, Logan said, "She's not."

"You knew she was Sara's sister?" Callie asked.

"No. But she's not lying. I'm sure of it."

More silence.

"I…didn't know Sara had any family," Alan said, his voice low and surprised. "She said she was an only child."

Diana looked silently out the window.

Logan deactivated the speaker function, then moved the phone to his ear. "I think it might be better if I talk to her by myself now."

"Wait," Alan said. "You can't just cut me off like that. I need to know what's going on."

"You will," Logan said.

"When?"

"When I can tell you."

"How am I supposed to live with that? Don't you see? This is ripping me apart."

"Alan," Callie broke in. "Logan's already learned more than we even got close to before. Let's let him work. If Sara's really in trouble, he'll know what to do."

Alan didn't say anything right away, then, "I just need to know she's safe."

"When she is, I'll tell you."

Logan could hear Alan breathing on the other end.

"As soon as you can," Alan said.

"I promise."

Alan hung up.

"You need anything, you let me know," Callie said before doing the same.

Logan set down Diana's phone.

"When she is what?" Diana asked.

"I'm sorry?"

"You said, 'when she is, I'll tell you.'"

Logan had to think back. "Safe. Alan wanted to know that she was safe."

"She is. For the moment."

Logan looked at her. "Sara's your sister."

Diana nodded.

"Is Sara even her name?"

"Yes."

"But everything else about her was a lie?"

Diana didn't respond.

"You need to tell me what's going on," Logan said. "It's the only way I can figure out how to help you."

"I never said we needed your help."

He leaned back. "Those people who took Dev and me out to the forest, they were in Braden, too. Who are they?"

She looked surprised. "They were in Braden?"

He nodded. "They're the ones you're really scared of, aren't they? You thought that's who we were, right?"

"Yes."

"You see now that we're not."

The look on her face said she wanted to believe that but wasn't sure.

"All right. Tell me this. Is there any possibility that they or others who might be working with them could find Sara tonight?"

"No," she said, shaking her head.

He sensed no hesitation in her answer.

Dr. Paskota, though, was obviously following a similar lead to the one Logan had, so he needed to make sure. "She's not staying someplace you used to live while you worked at the Grand Canyon, is she?"

Diana looked at him, surprised.

"It's the next logical place the others will look," Logan said. "If that's where she is, she isn't safe."

There was a pause before Diana said, "No. That's not where she is."

"But it is in the same area, isn't it?"

She said nothing.

Safe? Not safe? Until Diana trusted him more, there was just no way to know. So, how much time did they actually have? He'd have to trust she was right.

"I have a suggestion," he said. "Why don't we find someplace to get a little rest? It'll give you time to think. We can figure out what to do after that."

It was a huge gamble, but he didn't know what else to do.

She eyed him curiously, as if she were trying to decipher some hidden agenda.

"Okay," she finally said.

Since Diana's car was a rental, Logan instructed Dev to return to the El Camino. While the other two climbed in, Logan popped the hood and reached down along the engine to where his spare key was hidden.

Their first stop was the car Logan had brought up from Braden. From the trunk, he removed his and Dev's bags, and they drove off.

On the outskirts of town, they found a motel, and took a single room with two queen-sized beds. Before they went to sleep, Logan pulled an envelope out of his bag. If anything would convince Diana he was on her side, he was sure this would be it. He dropped it on the bed beside her without a word.

She gave it a casual glance, and then looked at it again, surprised.

"Alan loaned that to me," Logan said as Diana picked it up. "You're the one who left it in his trunk after you took Sara's luggage, aren't you?"

Diana stared at the envelope that contained the note from her sister to the brother-in-law she had yet to meet. "Yes," she whispered.

Logan nodded. After a moment, she stood, took a few steps toward the bathroom, then stopped.

"May I have my purse?"

"Of course," he said. He grabbed it off the dresser and handed it to her.

He wasn't naïve, but she wasn't his prisoner, so, with the exception of her gun, he couldn't justify keeping her things from her.

"Thank you," she said, and carried it into the bathroom.

32

DIANA WANTED TO trust Harper. More than anything, she wanted to believe he could actually help.

Unfortunately, the past few years had taught her the only ones she could truly trust were Sara and Richard, her sister and brother.

Anyone else was suspect.

Yet she couldn't deny that the man on the other end of the phone call had been Sara's husband. The address had been correct. Then, as if that hadn't been enough, Logan had pulled out the letter Sara had written for her husband.

She didn't know what to do.

She needed time to think it through, work it out.

She sat on the edge of the tub, and unzipped the side pocket in her purse. From it, she withdrew the photo that had been taped to the bottom of her nightstand in Braden. She looked at the kids in the photo.

Though he was only eleven at the time, Richard was already well on his way to six feet tall. Seven-year-old Sara was on his shoulders, smiling and laughing. And spraying them both with water from a hose was Diana. She'd been thirteen, and so grown-up even then. Fifteen minutes later, their aunt had come home and scolded them about making a mess in the yard, but for that precise moment, that little slice of time captured on camera by one of Diana's friends, she and Richard and Sara had been happy.

She touched the image, her finger tracing the outlines of her brother and sister, and herself.

Finally, she put the picture away, pulled out her Blackberry and sent Richard a text.

33

HARP SAT IN the chair by the window of his motel room, the book in his hands. It had been at least ten years since he'd last picked up *Lost Horizon*. Before that, the intervals were shorter, maybe every three or four years. It was the only way he knew how to reconnect with Tom.

While the story of Shangri-La, a paradise hidden in the Himalayas, had always intrigued Harp, his older brother had thought it had an almost magical quality.

"Someday I'm going to find it," Tom said once.

This confused Harp. "Isn't it just a story and not a real place?"

His brother smiled. "I don't mean the Shangri-La in the book." He tapped the side of his head. "I mean my Shangri-La. It's out there somewhere. I just gotta find it."

This did little to clear things up for Harp, but he was used to hearing Tom talk like that, spouting off ideas and dreams that seemed real only because of the way his brother spoke of them.

Until Harp's wife died, the day the telegram arrived at the farm telling Harp's parents that Tom was missing and presumed dead was the worst day in Harp's life. Still, he'd held out hope. Presumed dead wasn't *officially* dead.

Even before the war ended, Harp had concocted a story in which Tom's plane had gone down near one of the Indonesian islands. Tom had been able to get to shore, but in the wreck had hit his head and forgotten his past. Amnesia stories were big at the movies. Why couldn't it have happened with Tom? In Harp's mind, his brother had married an island girl, had spent his days fishing from canoes and playing on the beach. In a way, Harp had constructed a Shangri-La for him.

Now, nearly seventy years later, there was still a part of him that believed Tom was alive out there somewhere.

With a grunt, Barney pushed himself out of bed. "Morning," he said as he shuffled into the bathroom.

Harp finished the chapter then closed the book. Doing so reminded him of the fact that Logan still had Len's letter.

He still wasn't sure how he was going to handle it. He knew why Len had left it for him, what he wanted Harp to do. They had talked about it many times, the trip they were going to take together, the trip Len said Harp had to take, even if alone. Harp just wasn't sure he could.

As he'd done several times before, he tried to tell himself he could think about it later, but later was getting closer and closer. He would have to make a decision.

He owed it to Len, but more importantly, he owed it to Tom. *Later*, he thought again.

AS SOON AS Barney was ready, they returned to the hospital. As they walked through the lobby, the receptionist—the kind one, not the judgmental prude who was there the first day—greeted them with a big smile. "Mr. Harper, Dr. Needham, good morning."

"Morning, Myra. How are you doing today?" Harp asked.

"Just fine, thank you. I have good news for you."

The two men walked over to the counter. "Really? What news?"

"Your friend's being discharged this morning."

"Excuse me?" Harp said.

"Are you sure?" Barney asked.

As far as both men were concerned, this was *not* good news. While Pep had been improving, he was still pretty banged up.

Taken aback by their response, Myra said, "Oh...um...I was told he was cleared to go home."

"Who told you that?" Harp asked.

"Perhaps you need to speak with Dr. Groves," she said. Groves was Pep's main doctor.

"Is he in?" Barney asked.

"He's in the hospital somewhere. If he's not near your friend's room, he won't be far."

As they turned to make their way to Pep's room, they nearly ran into a young guy in a suit who'd been waiting behind them.

"Sorry," the guy said.

"It's okay," Harp told him. He and Barney then marched over to the hallway.

They found Pep already dressed in his street clothes, sitting uncomfortably in a wheelchair near the bed. Dr. Groves, however, was not present.

"Hey," Pep said.

"What's this about you being discharged?" Barney asked.

"Yeah, they're letting me leave."

"Whose idea was that?"

Pep shrugged. "The doctor came in this morning and said he saw no reason to keep me another night."

Harp and Barney shared a look then turned back to Pep.

"Have they *looked* at you?" Harp asked. "You're in no shape to leave."

"I'm going to find Dr. Groves," Barney announced, and strode out of the room.

"Honestly, Mr. Harper," Pep said. "I really don't want to stay any longer."

"Of course you don't," Harp said. "Who would? But that

doesn't mean you shouldn't stay."

"I can't help your son from a hospital bed."

"Don't even worry about that. Logan's got everything in hand."

Pep looked surprised. "Did he find her?"

"He's close, I think."

"All the more reason for me to get out of here."

Before Harp could respond, Barney returned.

"…just plain dumb," he was saying. "Whoever came up with those guidelines is an idiot."

Following right behind him was the doctor.

"I can't argue with you," Groves said. "A few more days would be great, but strictly speaking, whether he rests here or at home isn't going to make a lot of difference. And since his insurance won't cover the extra days, staying any longer would come out of his pocket."

"They'll pay if you say it's necessary," Barney argued.

"But I can't say it's necessary. If I did, I'd have to apply that standard to all our patients. And you know what will happen then? Insurance companies will stop approving treatments here, and the medical center will have to shut down. There's a bigger picture here than you're considering."

"I think you're exaggerating."

"I wish I was," the doctor said in a conciliatory tone. He turned his attention to Pep. "Mr. Pepper, I wish we could keep you longer, but the thing you need now more than anything else is rest. You can do that just as well in your own bed as here."

"It's okay, Doctor. I'm fine with it."

Groves gave him a thankful smile. "They're finishing up your paperwork. You should be good to go in fifteen minutes or so."

"Thanks."

The doctor glanced at Harp and Barney. "Gentlemen, I'm sorry about the situation, and I do agree with you, but there's nothing I can do. I have other patients I need to see, so if you'll excuse me…"

As soon as he was gone, Barney said to Pep, "When I was starting out as a doctor, you would have been in the hospital for a week, *minimum*."

"I would have also had to watch debut episodes of *I Love Lucy*," Pep said.

"What's wrong with *I Love Lucy*?" Harp asked.

A nurse entered the room, carrying a handful of documents for Pep to sign. While Barney helped him understand what was what, Harp took a walk down to the cafeteria to grab some coffee. As he was pouring his cup, the guy in the suit who'd been behind him and Barney at the reception desk walked up.

"How is it?" the man asked, nodding at the coffee maker.

"Passable," Harp told him.

"I guess passable will do."

His cup full, Harp moved to the side to add some cream and sugar.

"Sorry again about earlier," the man said as he poured his own cup.

"Our fault. We weren't paying attention."

The man smiled, and looked around. "Hate these places, know what I mean?"

"Hospitals?"

"Yeah. Give me the creeps."

"I guess they could. Don't bother me, though."

"I take it you're not a patient," the man said.

"Do I look like a patient?"

The man gave Harp a quick once-over. "Nah. Visiting someone?"

"A friend's being released in a few minutes."

"Good for him. Oh, sorry. Him or her?"

"Him."

"Well, good for him." The man took a sip of his coffee, testing it. "I'm Leon. Leon Clausen."

He held out his hand and Harp took it.

"Neal Harper."

For a split second it seemed as if Harp's name registered with the man, but the look was gone as quickly as it had appeared. "You live in Braden?" Clausen asked.

"No," Harp said, shaking his head. "Over on the coast."

"The coast?" There was surprise in the man's voice.

"Cambria. You ever heard of it?"

"No. Never."

"How about Hearst Castle?"

"That, I've heard of."

"About ten miles south of there."

"Sounds nice."

"It's beautiful," Harp said.

"I'll have to check it out."

"You should." Harp smiled. "I should get back to my friends."

"Sure, sure. You have a good day, huh?"

"You, too."

34

LOGAN DREW THE short straw and ended up being the one who had to stretch out on the floor by the window. He was sure he wouldn't be able to sleep much at all, but the next thing he knew, sunlight was spilling through the window and he could hear the TV.

He sat up with a start.

Dev was sitting on the end of the bed closest to him, watching one of the morning news shows. Logan stretched, and looked over at the other bed. It was empty.

"Where is she?" he asked.

Without looking, Dev said, "Not here."

Logan jumped to his feet. "Was she gone when you got up?"

"Yep."

"How long ago was that?"

"Thirty minutes."

"And you didn't think to wake me?"

Dev looked over at him. "Wouldn't have done any good, and I thought you could use a little more sleep."

"What do you mean, 'wouldn't have done any good'? We need to look for her. We need to find her."

He picked his pants off the floor, pulled them on, then snatched his shirt off the chair and headed for the bathroom.

"She left a note," Dev said.

Logan stopped. "Where?"

Dev nodded at the empty bed. There was a piece of paper sitting on the cover half hidden by one of the pillows. Logan walked over and grabbed it.

> I-40 West. Williams exit. Go north on State Route 64 for 30 miles. Not long after that you'll see a faded white X painted on the edge of the asphalt. Pull to the side and wait. If I'm not there by 10:30 a.m., I'm not coming.

"Think she left as soon as we fell asleep," Dev said.

Logan looked at her bed and could see his friend was right. Though he could tell she had lain there, it was otherwise undisturbed. If she had slept, then she was one of those people who never moved.

He suddenly looked toward the door. "My truck."

Before he could take more than a single step, Dev held up a hand. "It's still there. First thing I checked."

Logan looked at the note again.

"I assume we're going," Dev said.

"Absolutely."

THEIR FIRST STOP was at a mini-mart near the freeway, where they picked up a pay-by-the-minute phone similar to the one that had been in Diana's bag.

"You drive," Logan said to Dev as they left the store.

As soon as they were on the I-40, he punched in a Washington D.C. number on the cell.

"Forbus International. How may I direct your call?"

"Ruth Bobick, please."

"One moment."

He hadn't thought he would need the help of his old friend. Ruth was a busy woman, even more so these days after her recent promotion at Forbus International, the defense contractor Logan had also worked for at one time. Everything he'd needed up to this point, Callie had been able to handle. But what he wanted now was something only Ruth could do.

When Logan had worked with his late brother-in-law and best friend Carl Stone as trainers for Forbus's private security forces, Ruth had been their in-office contact. She had always been a friend, and though the company had placed the blame for Carl's death on Logan, she had never believed it. After that incident, their careers went in decidedly different directions. Ruth climbed the corporate ladder at Forbus, while Logan returned to his hometown to work in his father's garage. In her position as a vice president of a highly regarded defense contractor, she had access to information sources not available to most people. This had come in handy when Logan was trying to save Elyse Myat a few months earlier, and now could prove to be just as important to his search for Sara.

The line rang twice.

"Ruth Bobick's office. How may I help you?" Ruth's assistant asked. He sounded young and efficient, just the kind of person Ruth liked to have around.

"Tommy Shaw calling for Ruth," Logan said.

Though it wasn't public knowledge, Forbus was in the habit of recording company calls when they felt it necessary. There was no doubt in Logan's mind that if they knew he was on the line, his call would fall into the record category. He was not in good standing with the company brass, with the exception of Ruth, and he wouldn't be doing her any favors if people found out he was asking her for help. So he used a name he knew would catch her attention. Ruth had once admitted to a teenage obsession with the '70s-era band Styx, and more specifically, the band's guitar player, Tommy Shaw.

"Mrs. Bobick is on the other line at the moment. I could have her call you back."

"No. I'll hold."

"She may be on for a while, so I think it might be—"

"Tell her I'm on the line," Logan said, cutting him off.

A hesitation, then, "One moment."

Hold music replaced the assistant's voice. The wait was short.

"This is Ruth Bobick. Mr. *Shaw?*"

"Yes," Logan said, not disguising his voice. "Thank you for taking my call."

In the pause that followed, Logan knew she'd realized who he was. "Actually, Mr. Shaw, I will have to call you back."

"I see. Well, as soon as possible would be appreciated. I'm not at my normal number." He gave her the number of his temporary phone.

"Got it," she said. "Thank you."

She didn't wait for him to reply before hanging up.

Eight minutes later, she called back. By the noise in the background, he knew she'd gone outside.

"I thought we agreed you wouldn't use my office line," she said.

"Sorry. I don't have my phone at the moment, and the main number was the only one I knew from memory."

She sighed. "I'm going to regret calling you back, aren't I?"

He smiled. "Correct me if I'm wrong, but the help you gave me last time worked out pretty well for you."

Ruth had been able to use her early knowledge of what Logan had uncovered during his rescue of Elyse to bolster her position at Forbus. The information was responsible for her promotion.

"I swear to God if you hold that over my head, I will never answer the phone again."

"Yes, you will."

"I'm not going to fool myself into thinking this is a social call. So why don't you tell me what you want?"

"I need you to see if you can get locations on two cell phones."

From memory, he gave her the number to Diana's Blackberry, and the only number from the recent-calls list on her disposable cell. "If you can tell me where they are in relation to the number I'm calling from, that would be great."

"And why would I want to do this?" she asked.

"Because someone's in trouble, and I'm trying to help them."

"This is getting to be a habit. What happened to fixing cars?"

"Can you help?" he asked, ignoring her question.

She took a moment before responding. "Let me see what I can do."

Logan was about to say good-bye, but he had another thought. "Can we make that three phones?"

"Sure, why not? What's one more?" she said sarcastically. "What's the number?"

"You have it already. It's my cell."

"I'm not running a lost and found service."

"That's not why I asked. I'd just like to know where the person who has it is."

"Fine," she said, then, "Logan?"

"Yeah?"

"Are you making some sort of career change?"

"No."

"Then what are you doing?"

"Helping someone who asked."

35

ERICA WOKE STILL annoyed by the previous evening. She hated when things did not go as planned. She did everything she could to keep surprises out of her life. The work she did, the way she ran her business, even her personal decisions—they were all thought out and planned to avoid problems. Until everything returned to that norm, her frustration would continue to burn inside her.

She showered, dressed, and left, not even glancing in the direction of the room Clausen and Markle had been using. They'd be long gone by now, and hopefully reporting in with some helpful news soon.

Once she was behind the wheel of the gray sedan, she opened the specialized tracking app on her phone and touched the number tied to the GPS device she'd attached to the El Camino.

"So, Mr. Harper, did you make it back?" she said as she waited for the link to be established. "Or are you still wandering around the forest?"

A dot started glowing in the middle of an otherwise blank screen. After a few more seconds, a map appeared beneath it.

The El Camino was still in Flagstaff, but it was not in the

same place it had been.

"You made it back," she said, impressed.

She watched the dot for a moment, making sure it was stationary, then switched to her email and checked to see if she had received the other information she'd requested before she went to sleep.

There was a single message with three attachments.

> Dr. Paskota,
>
> The vehicle you provided the license number for is indeed registered to a male by the name of Logan Harper. Attached are the DMV sheet, tax info summary sheet, and military record. Please let me know if you wish further info on Mr. Harper. As of yet, I have no information on Mr. Martin, but will forward to you as soon as I do.
>
> B.L.

Military history? That could explain a lot. She opened that file first.

Harper's involvement with the military turned out to be more than just having served in the army. Once honorably discharged, he went to college then got a job with Forbus International, one of the giant US defense contractors. His job there was training private security forces—soldiers for hire. After an incident in Afghanistan that took the life of one of his colleagues, he'd been let go. Erica would have liked to know why, but that information was not provided.

She looked at the other two documents and noted that Harper lived on the central coast of California, and worked as a—

"That can't be right," she muttered.

But it didn't appear to be a typo. Harper was an auto mechanic. She'd expected something in law enforcement, even private investigator, not some grease monkey who specialized in changing oil.

So why are you even here, Mr. Harper?

Whatever that reason was, the answer wasn't in the information in front of her.

She brought the map back up and saw that Harper's car was on the move. She watched the dot until it merged onto the interstate heading west.

"And where are we going this morning?"

Shifting into reverse, she pulled out of her parking spot and headed for the freeway.

Fifteen minutes after she hit the interstate, Clausen called.

"You're going to find this interesting."

"What's that?" Erica asked.

"The guy who got beat up was just released from the hospital."

"Were you able to talk to him?"

"Not yet. But that's not the interesting part."

Erica frowned. She didn't like games. "Then what is?"

"One of the two men who picked him up is named Neal Harper."

Her mind flashed onto Harper's military history. His next of kin—wasn't it a Neal Harper? Yes, it was.

"Did you hear me?" Clausen asked.

"Sorry. I did. Older? Younger?"

"Older, definitely. I'd say seventysomething."

Logan Harper's dad?

"So how would you like us to proceed?" Clausen asked.

Erica thought for a moment, then smiled, and told him *exactly* what she wanted them to do.

36

LOGAN AND DEV reached the Williams turnoff just before nine thirty a.m. They followed Diana's instructions and headed north on State Route 64. Logan had been hoping to hear back from Ruth by now, but she hadn't called.

Around the twenty-minute mark, Dev started glancing at the odometer. Finally he said, "That's twenty-eight miles."

Logan focused on the edge of the road, looking for the white X, but there was only a solid white line, three feet from where the asphalt ended.

"Twenty-nine," Dev said, slowing some more.

Still nothing.

"Twenty-nine and a half."

White line.

"Twenty-nine point seven…point eight…point nine…and here comes—"

"There it is," Logan said, spotting the marker.

"—thirty," Dev finished. He pulled the El Camino to the side of the road.

Logan had seen similar Xs on roads before, and knew precisely a mile ahead they'd find a second one. The Xs were markers highway patrol helicopters could use to gauge a car's speed.

Logan looked around. The area was covered with low shrubs for as far as he could see. In the distance, hills and mountains sporadically jutted up from the ground, altering what would have been an otherwise flat horizon.

Logan checked his watch. It was a few minutes shy of ten a.m., more than thirty minutes left on Diana's deadline. He'd been hoping she was waiting for them, but unlike in Flagstaff where the forest surrounded the road, there was nowhere here for anyone to hide. Logan and Dev were the only ones around.

Logan opened the door and got out to stretch. Though he couldn't see it from here, not too much farther to the north was the Grand Canyon. The only real indication of this was the constant traffic on the road.

He looked at his watch again and then chastised himself. Checking the time wouldn't bring Diana here any faster.

If she's coming at all.

He gritted his teeth and tried to push that thought away, but it wouldn't disappear completely. He walked several feet into the brush and considered giving his dad a call. He did owe Harp an update, but his pay-as-you-go phone didn't come with call waiting or voice mail and he didn't want to chance missing Ruth. He looked back at the unevenly spaced traffic on the road, each car merely another blob of paint and metal racing by.

"Come on, Diana. Where are you?"

37

"ARE YOU HUNGRY?" Barney asked.

He and Harp had brought Pep back to the Desert Inn, and given him one of the beds in their room.

"I'm fine," Pep said.

He carefully lifted his legs one at a time onto the mattress, then leaned against the headboard, his arm wrapped around his damaged ribs.

Barney grimaced. "I still can't believe they let you go."

"Don't worry about it. They kept waking me up at the hospital. At least here I might be able to get some sleep."

Though Barney didn't want to admit it, it was a fair point.

"I could use some water," Pep said.

"Let me," Harp offered.

While he disappeared into the back sink area where they were storing the bottled water they'd bought, Barney picked up the TV remote from the nightstand and held it out to Pep.

"Feel free to watch whatever you want," he said.

Pep smiled. "Thanks."

As the TV came on, Harp reentered the room holding two bottles.

"This is all we have left," he said. He gave one to Pep and tossed the other to Barney. "Why don't I go over to that store across the street and get some more?"

Barney reached for his wallet. "You need some money?"

Waving him off, Harp said, "I got it." As had become his habit anytime he left the room, he tucked the copy of *Lost Horizon* under his arm before opening the door.

"Oh," Barney said as Harp stepped outside. "Get some Gatorade, too. That'll be good for him."

"Anything else?" Harp asked.

Barney and Pep shook their heads.

"Okay. I'll be right back."

As soon as the door closed, Barney stretched out on the other bed and made himself comfortable. On the TV, the images flew by as Pep flipped through the channels, searching for something to watch. He ended up stopping on *Judge Judy*.

"Really?" Barney asked.

Pep chuckled. "These people are all idiots. I love watching them make fools of themselves."

It was definitely not the show Barney would have chosen, but Pep was the patient, and the patient got what he wanted. Barney leaned back and closed his eyes, figuring he'd catch a few minutes' rest before Harp got back.

When he opened them again, he felt like his body was covered in molasses. It took extra effort to sit up. He always felt this way if he slept for more than fifteen minutes.

On the other bed, Pep was snoring, the remote moving up and down on his chest. A gunshot rang out from the TV, causing Barney to look over. Though the channel number was the same as before, *Judge Judy* was gone and a rerun of some cop show was playing.

He checked his watch, and thought perhaps it was broken. He glanced at the digital clock on the nightstand. It said the same thing—12:07 p.m. When Barney lay down, it had only been a little after eleven.

"Harp?" he said, holding his voice down so he wouldn't wake Pep.

There was no answer.

He got to his feet and walked to the bathroom.

"Harp?"

No one was there.

Must have gone back out when he saw we were asleep.

But if that was the case, where was the water or the Gatorade?

Barney slipped on his shoes, grabbed his phone, and went outside. From the walkway he could see the store where Harp was headed, but Harp was nowhere in sight.

With growing anxiety, he called Harp's phone.

Two rings, then voice mail.

"Hey, where are you?" Barney asked once the beep sounded. "Thought you were coming right back. Just…well…call me."

Of course, he realized. What probably happened was, the mini-market didn't have the Gatorade he'd asked for, so Harp must have taken it upon himself to find it elsewhere. That sounded just like him.

Barney slipped his phone into his pocket and turned to go back inside, but he paused before grabbing the knob.

Yes, it did make sense, but…better to check, right?

He went down the stairs, peeked into the motel office in case Harp was in there, then walked across the street and into the market.

The cashier was sitting on a stool behind the counter, reading a copy of *Entertainment Weekly*. Instead of bothering him, Barney did a quick search through the store.

Harp wasn't there, and there was plenty of Gatorade in the refrigerated section.

"Excuse me," he said to the clerk when he got back up front.

The guy looked up, startled, and jumped off his stool. "Sorry. Find everything you need?"

"Actually, I'm wondering if a man came in here about forty-five minutes ago and bought some water and Gatorade. He'd be about my age, an inch or two shorter than me, but with more hair."

"No, not that I can remember."

"You're sure?"

The guy shrugged. "The only people in here during the last hour were a couple of my friends, and a woman with two kids. No older guy. And I haven't sold any Gatorade all day."

"Okay. Thank you."

I must have gotten the store wrong, Barney thought as he went back outside.

He looked up and down the block. There was a gas station with a little store attached on the neighboring corner, and another about a block down. Barney tried both, but no one had seen Harp.

No longer just a little worried, he called the hospital, but no one had been admitted all morning. He then tried the police, who'd had no reports involving an elderly gentleman.

Hurrying back to their motel room, he hoped that somehow they'd crossed paths without realizing it, but when he opened the door, everything was the same as it had been when he left.

Harp, where are you?

He did the only other thing he could think of and called Logan, but like with the call to Harp, he was put through to voice mail.

"Logan, it's Barney. Call me as soon as you get this. I don't know, but I think something might have happened to your dad. I can't find him. Call me. Please."

38

THE BUZZ SOUNDED like it was coming from under Erica's seat. It was rhythmic—on, off, on, off—and after the fourth buzz, it stopped.

She thought maybe something had gotten stuck beneath the car, vibrated against the undercarriage, and finally fallen free.

But then there were two more, both the buzzes and the gaps between shorter this time.

She pulled to the side of State Route 64, climbed out of the car, and checked to see if she could find the source.

Her first instinct had been right. It had been wedged beneath her seat. A cell phone.

Harper's or Martin's.

She tried to activate the display but the cell was password protected. Not a big deal. There were ways of getting around that if need be.

She opened the back door. On the floor were the other phone and the men's wallets and keys. She grabbed the second cell and put both of them on the front passenger seat. If they rang again, she wanted to see who was calling. That might come in handy.

She decided to check the tracking device before she pulled

back onto the road, and was glad she did. Harper's car was stopped about seven miles ahead. She watched it, waiting to see if it moved again, but it didn't.

Ever since they'd turned off the interstate, Erica had known she'd made the right choice to follow them. If last night's events had scared off Harper and his friend, they would still be on I-40, heading back to California. But a detour toward the Grand Canyon, the park where Diana had once worked? To her, that had to mean they were still on Sara's trail.

She checked the monitor again. Harper's car had not moved. Were they waiting for something? Perhaps Sara herself? There was no way she'd learn that from the device in her hand. She needed to see with her own eyes.

She pulled back onto the road, nearly cutting off a camper. The other driver laid on his horn and shouted silently at her through the window, but he disappeared as Erica sped away.

Every few seconds, she would glance at the monitor. When the dot was only a mile and a half away, she gazed ahead, trying to pick out the El Camino in the distance. But though the view was clear, there were enough dips and turns in the road to make it impossible to see the other vehicle. The terrain caused another problem, too. Once she was close enough to see the truck, she wouldn't be able to pull over without the men noticing. Hell, just driving by would be taking a chance, but that was one thing she couldn't avoid. She needed to know what was going on.

She sped up so that she was tucked in close to the car in front of her. Hopefully that would provide the shield she needed.

It wasn't until she was half a mile away that the El Camino finally came into view, its blue exterior standing out in sharp contrast to the browns and tans and greens of the plain.

She hunched down in an effort to change her profile but it was unnecessary. Harper and Martin were sitting in the cab of the truck, talking.

And they were alone.

Damn. She'd been hoping the girl was with them. She could

have then simply neutralized the situation, and walked away with the woman. Even if it had been Diana and not Sara, it would have been worth the risk.

What the hell are they doing?

She kept going for two miles, then turned down a dirt road and stopped. She grabbed her phone and called Clausen.

"Update?" she asked.

"We're on our way."

Good. "How far are you from Williams?"

"About an hour and a half away."

"Cut it to an hour, but call me before you get there and I'll tell you exactly where to go."

"Yes, ma'am."

"Were you able to learn anything new?"

"He's definitely the guy's father."

"You're sure?"

"Absolutely."

"Get anything else out of him?"

"No," Clausen said, his voice lowering to a whisper. "He's not being very cooperative. I could try something…more aggressive."

Erica considered the idea. "No. Not yet." She paused before adding, "But that doesn't mean you can't make the threat."

She hung up, switched to the monitoring screen, and waited for the dot to move again.

39

HARP HAD NEVER had a gun pointed at him in his life, at least not until he reached the bottom of the staircase at the Desert Inn Motel.

"You open your mouth even to breathe and I pull the trigger. Understand?"

The man standing in front of Harp was the same one he'd talked to in the hospital cafeteria just a little while earlier. Harp nodded.

"Good. We're going to walk to my car and go for a ride. You first."

Harp remained riveted to the bottom step. "I'm not getting in your—"

"I said, don't open your mouth. That's your only warning. Let's go."

Harp knew he had no choice. Even if he'd been younger, he'd have been no match for the man. Unlike his son, Harp had never had any military training, and the only real fight he'd ever been in was in fifth grade. That had ended quickly with him on the ground and Donald Yeager standing over him, laughing.

The car turned out to be a dark blue sedan. A second man

was sitting behind the wheel, his face blank as Harp climbed reluctantly into the backseat. The gunman followed and shut the door.

"Let me see that," the man said.

He reached out and grabbed the copy of *Lost Horizon* from Harp's hands.

"No!" Harp said, trying to get it back.

The man frowned at him. "Sit back."

As their car pulled away, he leafed through the book and then tossed it on the floor.

"Please, can I just hold it?" Harp asked.

"So you can try to hit me with it later? I don't think so."

"I won't. I promise."

"Shut up."

No one said anything else as they drove through town before getting on the interstate heading east.

The silence continued until they reached Arizona, when the gunman looked over and said, "So, Mr. Harper, perhaps you should tell us what you were doing in Braden."

Harp's initial fear had ebbed. Now he felt a surge of anger. "This is kidnapping," he said. "And across state lines. Do you realize what kind of trouble you two are in?"

"Seems to me you're the only one in trouble here." The man adjusted his hand holding the gun. "What were you doing in Braden?"

"None of your business."

"What about Logan?"

"Logan? You leave him alone!"

The man paused. "Why did your…son leave town?"

"He had to take care of some business."

The man smiled as if Harp had just told him something important. "Why is he interested in Diana Stockley?"

"I don't know who you're talking about. I've never heard of her."

"I highly doubt that."

"I've got nothing to say to you," Harp replied.

"What were you doing in Braden?"

Harp repeated his previous statement, and kept repeating it with each successive question, no matter what it was. How long this went on, Harp had no idea, but it seemed like forever. Finally the gunman told the driver to pull over.

They took an exit that led to a deserted road in the middle of nowhere, and stopped along the side.

"Watch him," the gunman said. He got out of the car and raised a phone to his ear.

The driver turned so he could see into the backseat. He grinned as he reached under his jacket and pulled out a gun, aiming it at Harp.

It was overkill as far as Harp was concerned. As much as he would have liked to run, there was nowhere for him to go. And that was if he was able to run. He was almost eighty, for God's sake. The best he could manage was a medium-paced walk. The others wouldn't even break a sweat catching him.

He glanced at the floor. Could he at least chance grabbing Tom's book? He wanted to more than anything, but he doubted the driver would be too receptive if he tried.

Outside, the gunman paced until he finished his call. "Let's go," he said as he climbed back in.

They reentered the freeway.

"Mr. Harper," the gunman said. "Let's try this again. What were you doing in Braden?"

"I've got nothing to say to you."

The gunman gave him his now familiar grin. "That phone call was an update from one of our colleagues. I thought perhaps you'd like to know what's being done to your son."

"What?" Harp said, confused.

"Logan is being as uncooperative as you've been so far. So it looks like our friend will be forced to use stronger methods."

"What do you mean? He'd better not hurt him!"

"Or what?"

Harp hesitated, then said, "I don't believe you. Logan wouldn't let himself get caught."

"I don't think anyone ever plans on getting caught, but your son and his friend…what was his name? Martin? Things didn't turn out the way they anticipated."

Harp's skin grew cold as blood rushed to his heart. *Oh God, no!*

"So, I guess it's up to you. You cooperate and everyone will be fine. You don't? Well, I'm sure you can imagine." He paused. "What were you doing in Braden?"

Harp stared at the back of the seat in front of him. He wasn't dumb enough to think that just because he cooperated, nothing would happen to Logan and Dev, but he knew for certain something would if he didn't. Two choices, neither of them good.

"We're…we're helping a friend."

"To do what?"

Harp let out a defeated breath. "To find his wife."

40

"IT'S TEN FORTY," Dev said.

Logan stared out at the road heading toward the canyon. "I know."

Diana's message had said if she wasn't there by ten thirty, she wasn't coming.

"Five more minutes," he said.

"Okay."

The question of, "And then what?" hung in the air between them, but Logan didn't have an answer for that yet.

He checked the rearview mirror. The line of cars and vans and RVs continued. The problem was, he wasn't sure if she would be coming from the Williams end or the Grand Canyon end. Or if she was coming at all.

Two more minutes passed, three, then—

The cell phone rang in a loud, inane tune that someone at the manufacturer had deemed appropriate. Since this was the first call Logan had received on it, adjusting the settings to vibrate hadn't occurred to him.

He hit the green button, cutting off the noise. "Hello."

"You're playing some kind of joke on me, right?" Ruth asked.

"What are you talking about?"

"The phone numbers you asked me to locate."

"What about them?"

"I'm looking at a live map right now. I've got the phone you're using right in the center. I see you're taking a little vacation to the Grand Canyon."

"Did you locate the others?"

"You're kidding, right?"

"Ruth, what are you talking about?"

"Seriously?" she asked.

Keeping his calm, Logan said, "I appreciate your help, and I know I've asked a lot. But if you know where the other phones are, please just tell me."

"Well, you should know where one of them is right about now."

He started to ask if *she* was joking with *him* when Dev's voice cut him off.

"Logan."

Logan looked over just in time to see a ten-year-old Pontiac Grand Prix pull abreast of the El Camino's driver's side window. Sitting behind the wheel was a man Logan didn't recognize, but in the passenger seat was Diana.

"I thought you didn't have a phone," she said, leaning through her window and staring past Dev at Logan.

"You're late," he told her.

"You're lucky I came at all."

"You believe us now?"

She pulled back inside her car. "Follow us, or don't. It's up to you."

Dirt shot up from under the back tires as the other car took off.

Without having to be told, Dev started the engine and headed after them.

"Are you still there?" Logan said into the phone.

"Yes. Logan, you're about to pass the second phone."

"What?"

"About a mile ahead of you, on the right side of the road."

"Which phone?" he asked, thinking Sara might be closer than he'd realized.

"Yours. Your original one, that is."

He paused, then put his hand over the phone and said to Dev, "Dr. Paskota's less than a mile ahead on the right."

Dev looked surprised. "How did she find us?"

"I don't know." Logan brought the phone back up. "And the last phone?"

"It's about twenty miles from your position. Off the main road, though. In fact, the map I'm looking at shows no roads within a mile of its location. You want the GPS coordinates?"

Logan opened the glove compartment, cringing a bit when he saw his dad's letter, and rummaged around for a pen and scrap paper. Once he had them, he said, "Give them to me."

As he was writing, Dev said, "Don't look, but there she is."

"You're sure?"

"Definitely. Same gray car. Same profile."

Dev switched his gaze to the rearview mirror.

"What's she doing?" Logan asked.

"Nothing yet."

To Ruth, Logan said, "Can you hold on for a few minutes? I want to see what the car we just passed does."

"Logan, I have—"

"Please," he said.

"Fine."

For the next two miles, no one spoke. Then Ruth said, "He's moving."

"She," Logan corrected her.

"Okay, *she's* moving."

"Which way?"

"After you."

"Fast?" Logan asked, figuring the woman would want to get them in visual range.

"No. She's going about the same speed you are."

The same speed? Did she feel safe leaving that much room between them because, for the moment anyway, there wasn't really anywhere to turn off the road? But how would she know how fast they were going?

"I want to try something," Logan said so that both Dev and Ruth could hear him. "Ruth, don't hang up. Dev, get Diana's attention and get them to pull over to the side."

Dev flashed the Grand Prix with the El Camino's lights several times, and flipped on the right turn signal. At first, the other car did nothing. Then, after Dev repeated the whole process, it slowed and angled onto the shoulder, where it stopped. Dev eased the El Camino in behind it.

"Anything happen?" Logan asked Ruth.

"No. She's still coming your—" She stopped herself. "Hold on. She just pulled to the side of the road."

"How far back?"

"A mile and a half."

"Son of a bitch. Hang on." He looked at Dev. "Check the car. She's got us bugged somehow."

He put the phone on the dash, hopped out, and ran over to the Grand Prix. Diana looked at him through the window for a moment before rolling it down.

"What?" she asked.

"There's a problem."

"What kind of problem?"

"One of the people from last night is following us."

Her sense of detached self-control disappeared. "What?"

"We're out of here," the guy behind the wheel said as he reached for the gearshift.

"Hold on," Logan told him. "Just give me a few minutes, okay?"

"No way," the guy said.

Logan locked eyes with Diana. "Just a few minutes."

"If he's following us, won't he be here any second?"

"Diana, don't listen to him," the driver said.

She shot him a look. "Richard. I'll handle this."

He didn't look very happy.

Diana returned her attention to Logan, waiting for an answer. "She won't be."

"She?"

"Yes."

Diana looked apprehensive. "How do you know?"

"I do, okay?"

Neither of them spoke for several seconds.

"Two minutes," she said. "That's it."

He nodded his thanks and ran back to the El Camino. Dev was on the ground halfway under the car on the passenger side.

"Anything?" Logan asked.

"I checked my side," Dev said. "And around the front. I didn't see anything."

Logan looked into the bed of the truck, but with the exception of his and Dev's bags, there was nothing there that could have hidden a tracking device.

Dev scooted out from under the car. "Nothing there, either. Maybe there isn't anything. What if they have two cars? Someone we don't know in the other one, keeping tabs on us?"

Logan looked out at the road. That was a possibility, but if there was someone else, they weren't in sight at the moment.

He leaned down and felt around the wheel well on the back passenger side. Having basically rebuilt the El Camino himself, there wasn't an inch of its surface that he didn't know. The well was clean.

Moving quickly, he ran his hand along the inside bottom of the fender all the way to the back, then got down on his knees and moved his hand along the inside bottom of the rear bumper.

He almost missed it.

As it was, he had to go back a second time to make sure there was something there. It was small, and wasn't right on the bottom, but up the side a bit. The only reason he found it was because it brushed against his knuckle.

Carefully, he grabbed it between his fingers and pulled. There was some resistance at first that made him wonder if it had been glued in place, but then it popped free.

He frowned. He'd seen one of these before, albeit a military-grade model. It had been developed and manufactured by one of Forbus International's competitors.

He wrapped his fingers around it, and had to hold himself back from chucking it as far into the brush as he could.

"What the hell's going on?" Diana called out.

She was looking back at him, her head and shoulders sticking out the window.

As he jogged toward her, he said to Dev, "Get back in the car."

When he reached the Grand Prix, he showed Diana the tracking bug. "Who *are* these people?" he asked.

"What is that?"

"This is a Fitzer."

"Fitzer?"

"FT3-ZR, a GPS-enabled tracking chip with a magnetic mount. It's expensive, so not something your normal asshole is going to be walking around with. So who are they?"

Before she even tried to answer, her companion dropped the Grand Prix into gear and hit the gas. Logan jumped back and barely avoided being hit by the rear fender as the car turned onto the highway.

As he raced to the El Camino, Dev leaned over and threw open the passenger door. Once Logan was inside, Dev hit the accelerator.

"What happened?" Dev asked.

"I don't think her friend likes me very much."

Dev glanced at Logan's clenched hand. "You just going to keep that?"

Logan opened his palm and glanced at the tracking chip. Until he got rid of it, Dr. Paskota could continue to track them.

Which, if they played it right, was something they could use to their advantage.

He snatched up the phone, but the line was dead. He redialed Ruth's number.

"Sorry," Ruth said when she answered. "Had better things to do than hang on the phone and wait for you. Figured you'd call back."

"My fault. What about our friend?"

"Following you again. Two miles back."

"Figured. She put a hitchhiker on my bumper. A Fitzer."

There was a pause on the other end. "Really?"

"Yeah."

"Logan, what have you gotten yourself involved in?"

"I'm not sure yet. Is there any way to track where this thing came from?"

"I might be able to get it back as far as the retailer. After that, it would depend on if they tracked who bought individual pieces," she said, sounding unsure. "How was it connected?"

"Magnetic mount."

"You'll have to get that off. On the underside will be the serial number."

"Okay. Hold on. Let me try."

He set the phone down and took a closer look at the device. The mount was affixed to the tracker via a tiny frame that fit around the edges of the square. Using the pen he'd written down the GPS coordinates with, he worked one of the edges loose and pried it down. The chip slipped easily out.

He picked up the phone, and turned the chip over.

"Dammit," he said.

"What?"

"The serial number's been scratched off."

"Then there's not much I can do."

"Yeah, figured."

As Logan hung up, Dev said, "Looks like our friends are playing nice again."

They had caught up to the Grand Prix, the driver now keeping it at a steady pace and not trying to lose them.

Logan nodded.

Let's hope it lasts.

41

TREES ONCE MORE began to appear along the side of the road, short and scattered at first, then growing in both height and density.

So far, while there had been several opportunities for Diana and her friend to speed off and try to lose them, they hadn't. Logan wasn't ready to take that as a sign they fully trusted him yet, but it was a start.

"We're going to have to get rid of that at some point," Dev said, glancing at the GPS tracker.

Logan was still holding it, absently turning it over and over in his hand. He nodded, but said nothing.

Several minutes later they passed a sign indicating the town of Tusayan was only a couple miles ahead, and that the entrance to Grand Canyon National Park was just beyond it. Several ideas had been playing through Logan's mind, some more far-fetched than others. He finally settled on the one that had the best chance of improving their situation, and punched in Diana's number on his phone.

When she answered, she was silent at first, then, "Who is this?"

"It's Logan," he said.

He could see her twist around and look back at him.

"Stop in the first gas station in Tusayan," he told her.

"You're not in charge."

"You know the area better than I do, but isn't this the last town before the park? Wouldn't it be a good idea to top off our tanks so we don't run out later?"

He could hear her breathing on the other end, and then the line went dead.

The town turned out to be basically a half-mile strip of motels, restaurants, touristy stores, and not much else. The Grand Prix sped right past the first place to get gas without even slowing.

Logan brought up Diana's number again, ready to hit redial, but then the Grand Prix's brake lights flashed, and it turned into a station right across the street from the National Geographic Grand Canyon visitor's center.

A needless power play, he knew, meant to show him they were the ones in charge. Diana and her friend stopped beside one of the pumps, and Dev pulled the El Camino in behind it.

Dev started to get out to fill the tank.

"Wait," Logan said.

His friend looked back at him.

"I'm going to leave this with you." Logan put the Fitzer on the dash.

"Where are you going?"

"With them," Logan said, nodding at the other vehicle.

"Are you sure they're going to like that?"

"I don't care. What I want you to do is drive into the park. Our shadow will follow you. Once you're there, park somewhere there's a lot of other cars, and keep an eye out for her. I'll check in with you later to make sure she's out of our way."

"Okay, but one problem," Dev said. "No phone, remember?"

"I'm going to take care of that right now. Fill it up. I'll be right back."

Logan got out of the El Camino and walked over to Diana's

car. Her big companion was standing by the pump, filling up their tank. He glared at Logan, making it clear he was not nearly as convinced of Logan's good intentions as Diana was.

Being the first time Logan was able to get a good look at the man, he noticed something beyond the glare—the nose, the cheeks, the set of the man's jaw. They were nearly identical to Diana's.

And Sara's, too.

Diana lowered the passenger window as Logan walked up.

"I need your Blackberry," he said.

"I don't think so."

He quickly laid out his plan.

"You didn't get rid of that thing already?" she asked, shocked.

"That would have only made her come for us sooner. This way, she won't think anything's up."

She shot a glance at the street, then back at him. "She could be driving by us right now."

"She could be, but she won't."

"How do you know for sure?"

"I don't, but it wouldn't make any sense. She knows where we are. She also knows that Dev and I know what she looks like. She won't chance that exposure. We can use her trust in her equipment against her."

He watched as Diana processed this, the tension in her face easing only slightly once she realized he was right. "Who *are* you?"

He smiled. "Can I have your phone now?"

She handed him her cell.

Back at the El Camino, he gave it to Dev. "Be careful."

"Don't worry about me," Dev said, looking at Diana's friend. "You're the one who needs to be careful. He might be a problem."

"I'll be fine."

Logan retrieved the small canvas bag he kept behind the El Camino's bench seat, and shoved in the pistol he'd obtained the night before. By the time he walked back to the Grand Prix, the big guy was already behind the wheel. He looked back in surprise as Logan opened the rear door and climbed in.

"What are you doing?" he said.

"He's coming with us," Diana told him.

"Hell, no, he's not!" He looked back at Logan. "Get out of the car!"

"We're wasting time," Logan replied, his eyes locked on the man. "Let's go get your sister."

There was a full second's delay before both Diana and her brother realized what Logan had said.

The man gaped at him. "How did—"

"Richard," Diana said. "Just go."

The brother—Richard—continued to stare at Logan. "I told you we couldn't trust this guy. He already knows too much. It's just a trick. He's playing us to get to her!"

"Think about it," Diana said. "He *knows* where Emily is. If he's with them, he doesn't need Sara anymore."

Richard still seemed less than convinced.

Diana looked at Logan, and back at her brother. "*I* trust him."

Richard narrowed his eyes and said to Logan, "You make one wrong move, and I will kill you."

"You could try," Logan said, staring back. "Now, are we going to just sit here? Or are we going to go help keep your sister alive?"

42

SOMETHING WAS GOING to happen soon. It had to. They were running out of road. According to the map, not far ahead was the town of Tusayan, and then the Grand Canyon. There *was* a road that traveled along the southern rim to the east that eventually ran into another highway, but Erica couldn't imagine them going that way. South on that highway would take them back to Flagstaff. It would have been considerably easier for them to take that route originally instead of the interstate to Williams then north to the park on the state highway.

No. Wherever they were headed, they were getting close. She was sure of it.

As she was about to check the monitor again, her phone rang. "Yes?" she said.

It was Clausen.

By the time the call was done, Erica was smiling more broadly than she had in months.

43

INSTEAD OF TURNING right and continuing in the direction they'd been headed, Richard went left out of the gas station parking lot, up one block, then left again onto a deserted side road. Within a minute, the town was behind them as they headed east.

Though the road had been paved, it was obvious that maintaining it had not been a huge priority. Mix that with the snow and summer rains and it was almost a wonder there was still any asphalt left at all.

"Where are we going?" Logan asked.

Richard glanced at him in the mirror and then refocused on the road.

As Diana opened her mouth to respond, her brother said, "Don't."

She looked at him, exasperated. "Richard, just drive. Let *me* do the thinking."

It was clear this wasn't the first time Richard had been similarly rebuked by Diana. He looked annoyed and uncomfortable, but he said nothing.

Diana turned to Logan. "A cabin. Belongs to a friend I knew

when I used to work around here. He moved back east so he doesn't get this way very much anymore. Impossible to tie it to me, so not a chance anyone would look for Sara there."

Logan wasn't sure it was impossible, but it was better than using a place Diana had lived in before.

"You still haven't told me who these people are."

"Does it really matter? I'll let you talk to Sara, see that she's all right. Then you can tell her husband to forget about her."

"Whoa. I thought I was here to help."

"And I never said we needed it, did I?"

He paused, glancing out the window. The day was dimming as a mass of gray clouds began to cover the sky. "You really think Alan can forget about her?"

"He has to."

"Why? Why does he have to?"

She shook her head. "It's better if he doesn't know that."

After a moment, Logan said, "I'll know where she is."

"No, you won't," Diana told him. "When we leave today, we'll all go together. We'll drop you in Tusayan and your friend can pick you up. Sara's already been here long enough. Time for her to move on."

"To where?"

She looked at him, snorted a laugh, and turned away.

Soon the road got really rough and became more dirt than blacktop. After a mile of this, they turned down another road that was no more than two well-worn tire paths.

Richard dropped their speed to a crawl, carefully navigating the dips and rises so that the bottom of the car didn't scrape against the mound between the ruts. The road finally ended in a small clearing. It was just big enough so Richard could turn the car around and park it so that it faced the way they'd come.

Logan scanned their new surroundings. "Where's the cabin?"

Diana pointed at the trees behind the car and climbed out. Logan removed his pistol from his bag and joined her. As Richard was coming around the back to where they were standing, he suddenly stopped, raised the gun he was holding, and pointed it at Logan.

"I told you we couldn't trust him!"

His gaze flicked to Logan's pistol.

"Are you kidding me?" Logan asked. "These people who are after Sara tried to kill me last night. Until this is over, I'm armed. Got it?"

Richard didn't lower his gun. "As soon as you know where the cabin is, you'll put a bullet in the back of our heads and then go after Sara. Plain as day, Diana. You've got to see that now."

Logan couldn't help but feel a bit of sympathy for Richard. The guy might have been lacking a little in the smarts department, but he more than made up for it with his sense of loyalty.

Logan crouched down, set his gun on the ground, then stood and took three quick steps until the barrel of Richard's gun was only a foot in front of his chest.

"Happy?" he asked.

He concentrated on Richard's face, seeing the man's anger and confusion and stubbornness mixing together.

Richard opened his mouth. "I—"

In a single, fluid motion, Logan's hands shot up, twisting the gun free as he pivoted to Richard's side and dropped him straight to the ground. By the time Richard could have reacted, Logan had a knee on his back, and the man's own gun pointed at his head.

In the darkening sky, a thunderclap rolled over them.

"I could put a bullet in you right now. That would solve a lot of problems. But I am not your enemy. Got it?"

He stared down at Richard for a moment before tossing the gun several feet away and pushing himself up.

"Ready?" he asked Diana after he retrieved his own gun.

She looked as stunned as her brother had been, but she finally nodded. "Yeah."

Logan looked back at Richard. "Are you coming?"

44

FIRST THE THUNDER, then the rain.

Only this time, the storm didn't take Sara's mind off her troubles. If anything, it made it worst. It had been a day since she'd last heard from Diana. All she could think about was one of the last things her sister had said to her.

I screwed up.

Screwed up what? Was that the reason she hadn't called back? Had Diana been caught? Worse?

She had told herself she would give it another three hours and then she'd hike out. There was a backup plan—there was *always* a backup plan—so she knew what she needed to do, but what if Diana and Richard were in trouble? They had done so much for her. Could she just turn her back on them?

Emily.

That's who this was really about. She had to remember that. No matter what was going on with her brother and sister, she had to stay alive and hidden for her little girl.

Though the storm looked like it might become one of the most intense yet, it was surprisingly easy for her to ignore it as she rechecked the pack with her emergency supplies, and made herself eat something to help her stamina on the potential journey ahead.

As she took a bite of the peanut butter sandwich, she looked at the map again. Diana had marked the best route for her to hike into the park, where she could mingle with the tourists and catch a ride on one of the dozens of buses that visited the canyon every day. They had even walked the trail partway together the day Diana brought her out here.

She didn't know where she'd be without her sister and brother. Actually, she did know. Dead, and no longer able to protect her daughter.

She knew Diana felt a tremendous guilt, blaming herself for Sara's problems, but Sara never held her at fault.

After she finished the sandwich, she poured herself a glass of water, took a few sips, then folded the map and carried it back over to the pack. Just as she was sticking it back in the pocket, lightning struck. She glanced out the window as the bolt lit up a portion of the trail she and Diana had walked. It ran along a ridge about a quarter mile away.

Sara froze.

There were three figures on the path. She rushed over to her pack, retrieved the binoculars, and focused them on the ridge.

Too late. Whoever had been there was gone.

Two things she knew for sure: they were coming this way, and since there were three people, they couldn't be just her sister and brother.

Storm or no storm, she had to leave now.

45

THE RAIN SOAKED Logan, Diana, and Richard to the skin, and turned the dirt trail into a slick slurry of mud and pine needles. More than once, Logan found himself skidding across the surface, fighting to keep his balance.

They had been walking for five minutes when the storm struck, and had traveled for another ten so far in the downpour.

"How much farther?" Logan asked.

"There's a ridge right up there," Diana said, pointing ahead. "We go along that, then down the other side. Less than ten minutes."

He nodded and fell back behind her.

As they crossed the treeless ridge, a bolt of lightning hit the ground about three hundred yards away. For a second it was brighter than day. Though Logan had been in a lot of storms, that was the closest he remembered ever being to a lightning strike, and he hoped it stayed that way.

"Come on!" Diana urged. "We need to get back under cover."

They jogged along the path and down into a flatter area where they were back amongst the trees. The ground was a bit firmer here so they picked up their pace, and soon reached the edge of a small field. In the center was a solidly built wood cabin. Together, they ran across the open space to the shelter of the covered entrance.

Diana pounded on the door. "Sara! It's me! Open up!"

Nothing happened.

She knocked again. "Sara? Open the door! We're getting soaked!"

Still no response.

Moving over to the window, she looked in. "Sara?"

She leaned back, confused, then ran to the corner of the cabin and disappeared around it. Logan and Richard quickly followed. When they reached the back, they found the door open and Diana inside, yelling Sara's name. Logan rushed in just as Diana went through a doorway on the far wall. She reappeared a few seconds later.

"She's not here."

"Where else would she be?" Richard asked, his panic even greater than hers.

"I don't know! I just know she's not here."

A book on the kitchen counter caught Logan's attention. It was lying flat, its black cover open. A sketchbook. There was a pencil stuck between two pages about three quarters of the way through. Drawn there were the beginnings of a face. He flipped back through and saw page after page of more faces. Rather, page after page of only two faces—Emily's and Alan's.

Sara couldn't get her family out of her mind.

As he looked up from the book, he noticed some food pushed to the back by the sink. A loaf of bread and an open jar of peanut butter.

"She hasn't been gone long," he said.

"How do you know that?" Richard asked.

Logan lifted the bag containing the bread. "It's open, but the bread's still fresh, not dried out."

Richard sneered. "Still could have been hours."

Logan pointed at the nearly full glass of water.

"That could have been there even longer."

Shaking his head, Logan ran his finger along the top of the glass. "Rim's still wet."

Diana's eyes grew wide. She darted to a closet at the end of the kitchen and pulled the door open. "Her pack's gone." She looked back at the two men. "She must be heading for the canyon."

"Why would she leave?" Richard asked.

"I don't know. I told her to hold tight."

"Doesn't matter why," Logan said, heading for the door. "Which way did she go?"

A second later, they were back in the rain, running into the woods north of the cabin.

46

SARA KNEW THE others had to have reached the cabin by now, which meant they knew she was gone. The question was, would they guess where she was headed?

Don't worry about that. Just keep going!

But that was becoming a problem. When Diana had shown her the path, it was almost noon on a bright sunny day. Now, with the low gray clouds and relentless rain, she just couldn't be sure she was going the right way. For the first five minutes, it had all been recognizable, but after that she was having a hard time spotting the landmarks she'd been told to look for.

Wiping the water from her face, she paused and turned in a circle, scanning her surroundings.

There. That rock. Isn't it the one Diana had called "bear rock"?

The angle was wrong, but the basic bear-like shape was there. Seeing no other options, she headed toward it.

Bear rock, then the forked tree, then the hill and the field and the rotting tree…

She repeated the order like a mantra that would magically make each marker appear.

It *was* bear rock. She wasn't lost.

"Thank you, God!" she said.

Everything was going to be—

"…ara…"

A voice in the distance. Male? Female? It was impossible to tell. But one thing Sara knew for sure, it was coming from somewhere between the cabin and where she was now.

Without wasting another second, she picked up her pace.

The forked tree, then the hill, then the field and the rotting tree and the pile of rocks.

The forked tree, then the hill, then the field and the rotting tree and the pile of rocks.

The forked tree, then the hill, then the—

Not more than fifty yards behind her, Sara heard a branch snap.

47

"THE PATH ARCS through these trees, then past a couple of large rocks, one on top of another," Diana said. "After that, it's almost a straight line into the park."

They'd been moving as quickly as they could through the woods, but whatever tracks Sara might have left behind had been filled with muddy water.

"We should spread out," Logan suggested. "In this weather she could be thirty or forty feet on either side of us and we'd never see her."

"I don't think that's a good idea," Richard argued.

"Stop it, Richard. He's right," Diana said. She pointed into the forest beside her. "You go that way about twenty yards. Logan, you do the same on the left."

Logan tucked his gun into the waistband of his pants at the small of his back, and headed into the woods.

"Sara!" Diana called out.

"Sara!" Richard echoed.

Logan wanted to yell, too, but Sara wouldn't know his voice, and if she heard him, she might run instead of stop. He plunged between the trees, his head swiveling back and forth, scanning as wide a range as he could. Every few seconds, he glanced at the ground, hoping to find some sign of her passage.

It wasn't long before he realized he was moving faster than the others. Their voices fell farther and farther behind him, but he didn't slow his pace.

Every few steps he wiped his forehead, the water flying off to the side. Though the tree cover did shelter him from some of the rain, it didn't really matter. He was as soaked as if he'd just climbed out of a swimming pool.

Somewhere ahead were the two stacked rocks Diana had talked about. Once he reached them, he'd have to wait for her so he'd know which direction to go next.

As he stepped around another tree, his foot landed on an old branch and snapped it in two. He stumbled, but quickly regained his footing. As he looked up, he saw a flash of movement ahead.

Even with the reduced visibility, he knew it wasn't a deer or some other animal living in the forest. It was a person.

Sara.

He started to run.

48

AT FIRST SARA thought she was just hearing her heart pounding in her chest, but the rhythm was wrong, and she soon realized the sound was feet running through the woods, heading in her direction.

She rounded bear rock without even stopping.

The forked tree. The forked tree. Next is the forked tree.

But which direction was it?

More to the right. No, no! To the left. More to the left.

As she corrected her path, she slipped and went down, her knees and elbows slapping into the mud. Grimacing in pain, she forced herself back to her feet.

She knew the person chasing her had to be one of them. She couldn't let them catch her. She couldn't let them know where Emily was. She began running again, but the footsteps behind her were closer now.

"I don't want to hurt you!" a voice called out.

Right, she thought.

There, just ahead, the forked tree. *When I reach that, then it's up the hill, then—*

"Sara! Please stop!"

She chanced a look over her shoulder. The man behind her was as drenched as she was. He seemed to be alone at the moment, but she knew there were at least two others out there. She'd seen them on the ridge. Her pursuer was lean and strong. No way was she ever going to be able to outrun him. She had only one chance.

As she ran on, she pulled her left arm out of the strap to her backpack, and swung the bag around so she could get at it. Fastened to the side was a twelve-gauge shotgun. She retrieved a couple shells from the side pocket, then pulled the gun loose and dropped the bag to the mud.

The forked tree. Get to the forked tree.

It was just ahead, big enough so she could hide behind it and use the fork to safely take aim at the man.

She loaded the shells and sprinted the rest of the way to the tree. She leaned against the trunk, catching her breath as she listened to the man approach. Once it sounded like he was no more than fifty or sixty feet away, she slid into place, and propped the barrel of the gun in the fork. She chambered the shell, the distinctive *clack-clack* cutting through the storm.

The man could not help but hear it, too. He stopped in his tracks, but instead of going for cover, he raised his hands in the air.

"I'm not here to hurt you," he repeated as his gaze found her in the break of the tree.

"I'll shoot if you come any closer!" she shouted.

"Sara, I'm a friend. I came here with Diana and Richard."

"Liar!" She was suddenly sure her sister and brother were both dead. *It's my fault! My fault!*

Her finger tightened on the trigger.

"I'm not lying. I'm here because of your family," he said. "I'm here because of Alan and Emily."

So overcome by her own despair, she almost didn't hear the names. Once she realized what he'd said, she froze. Then a whole new level of anxiety kicked in.

He knows about Alan and Emily. They *know about Alan and Emily!*

A scream flew from her lips as her finger jerked the trigger.

49

THE SHOTGUN BLAST echoed through the woods.

Logan, flat on his stomach, felt the pelts fly through the air where he'd been standing seconds before.

He'd been watching her eyes, and knew she didn't believe anything he said. A split second before she screamed, her face scrunched up in rage. That's when Logan dove left and hit the ground.

The moment the pelt had flown past, he scrambled to the cover of an old pine. A second blast hit the trunk, but nothing touched him.

Back in the direction of the two stacked rocks, he heard someone running. Then Diana called out, "Sara! Sara! Are you okay?"

"Sara!" Richard joined in.

"Diana?" Sara said, her voice low and uncertain. "Richard?"

"Sara! Where are you?" Diana yelled.

"Diana?" Sara called out more loudly this time. "Is that you?"

"Yes. Are you okay?"

"They're here. One of them was chasing me! Be careful. He's behind a tree in your direction."

"I'm not one of them!" Logan shouted. "Diana, tell her!"

He could see Diana and Richard making their way through the trees now.

"He knows about Alan and Emily!" Sara yelled. "We have to stop—"

"Sara," Diana shouted back. "He's not with them! He's with us!"

Silence, then a disbelieving "What?" from Sara.

Logan waved a hand, getting Diana and Richard's attention.

"He's not with them," Diana said, no longer needing to talk as loudly. "Alan sent him."

"Alan? Wha...what do you mean? Why?"

"Honey, it's okay. Just come on out, all right?"

Diana walked past Logan into full view of the mangled tree Sara was hiding behind. With a frown, Richard held out his hand and helped Logan to his feet. The two men then moved out behind Diana, Logan more cautiously than Richard.

Another clap of thunder, this one farther away than before.

Diana walked steadily toward the tree. "Come on out, Sara. It's okay. Everything's fine."

Sara still stood on the other side of the V created by some long-ago accident inflicted on the tree. The barrel of the gun had tilted upward, pointing at the clouds. Then both the gun and Sara disappeared.

For half a second, Logan wondered if she'd run off again, but then she emerged from around the side of the tree and ran into her sister's arms. Richard joined them, putting a hand on Sara's back, and whispered something in her ear.

Logan could see that weeks of stress and fear had taken their toll on Alan's wife. Even as she hugged her siblings, she shot worried glances in Logan's direction, as if she'd bolt if he so much as moved an inch in her direction. She was all survival and fear and determination.

Finally, Diana pulled back and said something to her sister that Logan couldn't make out. Sara asked a few questions, each time looking at Logan. Finally, the three siblings walked over to him.

"Sara, this is Logan Harper," Diana said.

Logan held out his hand, but Sara didn't take it. "You say you're a friend of Alan's but I don't know you."

"No. I never said that. I said I'm here because of Alan. I *am* a friend of his lawyer, Callie Johnson."

"Callie? You know her?"

"I've known Callie all my life. She used to babysit me."

This odd detail seemed to soften Sara a bit. "I don't understand how you're involved."

"She asked me to help," he said. He gave her a quick version of how Alan had been looking for her, had enlisted Callie's help, and how she had found out that Sara didn't exist.

"I still don't understand why they involved you," she said.

"Because I'm a friend, and she knew she could trust me."

She looked at him, clearly not satisfied with his response.

He shrugged. "And I know how to get things done."

"Like what?" Sara asked, growing tense again. "What needs to be *done* about me?"

Logan paused. "At first, I think Alan just wanted to know what happened to you, for himself, and also for Emily, so when she grows up she'd understand why her mom went away."

"You said 'at first.'"

"When they realized you weren't who you said you were, Alan became concerned."

Richard jutted out his chin. "He thinks she cheated on him or something?"

Logan could see that Sara didn't believe that at all. "No," he said. "He became concerned that your sister was in trouble, and he wanted to help. He *is* her husband, after all."

"Oh, and you're that help?" Richard scoffed.

Sara touched her brother's arm. Richard's previous tough demeanor cracked a little, and he whispered to her, "Sorry."

She looked at Logan. "I am in trouble, but there's nothing

Alan or you can do. The fewer people involved, the better."

"But Alan's your husband. Emily's your daughter," Logan said. "They're your family."

"Don't you see? They're the reason I had to leave. The people after me, they don't want me. They want…"

"Emily," Logan said, knowing that was what she was going to tell him.

She nodded.

"But why?" he asked.

She took a moment, then said, "Because they believe she's their property."

"What do you mean, 'property'?"

She looked at the ground. "Go back to Alan, tell him…tell him that I love them both, but it's better if they just forget me."

Logan was about to ask another question, but Diana cut him off. "Okay. I've brought you to her. You've talked. Now you can go back to her husband and set his mind at ease."

"Exactly how am I supposed to do that when you haven't told me why Sara's on the run?"

Ignoring his question, she said, "We're done. We'll drive you out and drop you off in Tusayan."

She put an arm around Sara, and started walking back to the cabin. Richard followed them.

"Dev's still got your phone," Logan said, joining them.

"I'll get a new one."

The intensity of the rain began to ease.

"Where will you go?" he asked.

"Better if you didn't know."

"You're making a mistake."

"What mistake?"

"You all can't run forever."

Diana looked back at him. "We don't need to run forever. Just…long enough."

50

WHEN DEV PAID the entrance fee to the park, he was given a map and told the best place to start out was Grand Canyon Village. From there, the ranger said he could get pretty much anywhere using the free shuttle bus system.

Dev didn't care about park transportation. He just wanted somewhere with a lot of cars where he could leave the El Camino, then walk a little ways away and watch without being observed. The village turned out to be perfect for this. It was a mixture of rustic-looking motels, restaurants, tourist shops, and tiny cabins for the seasonal workers.

He found a spot in a parking lot next to a gift shop called Hopi House. On the other side of the building was a wide sidewalk, then the canyon itself. Dev had been to the park a few times when he was younger, but the intensity of the view and the sheer scale of the canyon were just as breathtaking now as they had been then.

He was able to find a spot along the walkway near the rim of the canyon from where he could still see Logan's truck. The place was crawling with tourists, so there was no chance he'd be spotted.

As he settled in to wait for Dr. Paskota to drive by, he noticed gray clouds moving in and threatening to blot out the otherwise blue sky. Looking around, he saw that several of the other canyon visitors were carrying umbrellas. He didn't have one, but was getting the feeling it was something he might need very soon.

Just inside the back entrance to Hopi House, he saw a display of umbrellas. He checked the road, saw no sign of the woman, and dashed inside. He made a quick purchase, and was back out in less than a minute. He was confident that even if she had driven by while he was inside, she would have still been around, trying to figure out where Logan and Dev had gone.

Five minutes after he exited Hopi House, it began to rain, proving his timing had been good. It was a light rain at first, but then it got heavier and heavier. As the intensity grew, lightning started striking closer and closer. Park rangers quickly moved along the walkway, advising everyone to find cover inside one of the buildings. Dev joined the crowd on the covered porch of the El Tovar Hotel.

An hour passed with no sign of the gray sedan. He thought the woman must have been cautious. Maybe she'd even parked somewhere else and was watching the El Camino on foot just like Dev was.

Doing nothing to draw attention to himself, Dev looked around and indentified all the locations someone could covertly watch the truck from. Then, keeping his exposure to the open sky to a minimum, he visited each one by one. No Dr. Paskota, not even one of the men who'd been with her.

Confused, Dev looked out at the road that led toward the entrance.

Where the hell are you?

51

ONCE THEY WERE back in the car and had reached the partially blacktopped road, Logan called Dev.

"Hey," Dev answered. "Everything okay?

"Well, I guess. Yeah," Logan said.

"Did you find her?"

"Uh-huh."

"And?"

Instead of answering, Logan asked, "What happened there?"

"Nothing happened here."

"What do you mean, 'nothing'?"

"She hasn't shown up."

"At all?"

"Haven't seen her or her car."

That was definitely not what Logan had expected. He took a moment, then said, "Head back to Tusayan. Same gas station as before. I'll be waiting there. But keep your eyes open. Maybe she's just been waiting for you to come back out."

"You going to be there *alone*?"

"Undetermined at this point."

"All right. See you in a bit," Dev said.

As soon as the line went dead, Logan called Ruth.

"I've got someone in my office," she said quickly before Logan could speak.

"Anyone I know?"

"As a matter of fact."

"Oh, God, it's Jon, isn't it?" Jon Jordan was the head of Forbus International, and the man responsible for blaming Carl's death on Logan.

"Yes. That's correct."

"Well, please don't tell him hi for me."

"I think that's a sound plan."

Before she could say good-bye, he said, "Ruth, I need you to check on that cell phone that was in the car following me earlier. I have to know where it is."

"That might be a little difficult."

"Please, Ruth."

"I'll tell you what. Let me finish up here, and I'll give you a call back."

"How long?"

"Oh, I wouldn't worry. Talk to you soon." She hung up.

Logan set the phone in his lap and looked out the window, his mind willing Ruth to hurry.

"Something wrong?" Diana asked. She was sitting in back with him while Sara sat up front with Richard.

"I'm...not sure."

"Not sure about what?"

"It's probably nothing."

"Oh, I see. Now you don't want to share."

He was tempted to remind her she wasn't sharing, either, but instead he said, "The woman who was following us. My friend never saw her."

She became instantly concerned. "You don't think she could have followed us to the cabin, do you?"

"If she had, she'd have probably tried to take us by now, don't you think?"

"What woman are you guys talking about?" Sara asked, looking back.

"There are four people, actually," Logan explained. "Three men and a woman. They tried to kill my friend and me last night. The woman seems to be the one in charge."

"What's she look like?"

The fear Logan had seen on Sara's face back in the woods had returned, only it seemed even more intense now.

"She's maybe forty. Short blonde hair. Fit."

Sara stopped breathing.

"We don't know if it's her," Diana said, trying to calm her sister down. She glanced at Logan. "It'll be better if we drop you outside of town. Shouldn't take you more than ten minutes to walk to the gas station."

Logan wanted to ask who it was they thought the woman might be, but his phone rang. Ruth.

"Well, that was almost awkward," Ruth said.

"How's Jon?"

"The same."

"Still a dick, then."

"Pretty much."

"Can you tell me where the other phone is?"

"I'm pulling it up now."

He waited.

"Whoa," she said. "Um, okay. I'm looking at the phone you're calling on and the other three on the map. I see the one that was out on its own is with you now."

"Yeah, that's not the one I'm interested in."

"The other one's heading south from the canyon."

"You mean the one that was following me?"

"No. That one's clear back on I-40, heading west."

Logan was surprised. "Toward California?"

"Not there yet, but that direction."

"Okay, thanks." He disconnected the call.

Why had Dr. Paskota backed off? It didn't make sense. If

Logan had been in her place, he would have stuck with the tracking device, knowing it was his best lead to find Diana or Sara. In fact, the *only* reason that could have gotten him to back off was if either woman had been located elsewhere. But they were here, with Logan.

Wait. There was one other possibility.

Emily.

If Dr. Paskota knew where she was, then she wouldn't need Diana or Sara.

"Are you going to tell us what's going or not?" Diana asked.

Ignoring her, he called information, and had them connect him to Callie's law firm. A few seconds later, he was put through to her office.

"Logan, where have you been?" she asked, her voice full of concern.

"Sorry, I'll explain later," he said quickly. "Right now, I need you to have Alan and Emily—"

"Logan," she cut in. "Harp's missing."

He thought he hadn't heard her correctly. "I'm sorry?"

"Your father is missing."

"What happened?"

"You need to call Barney. He can give you the details. Do you need his number?"

"Please."

She read it off to him, then asked, "What was that about Alan?"

"Get them out of Riverside. Someplace safe that only you know about. Don't tell anyone."

"My God, what's going on?"

"Maybe nothing. I'm probably being overly cautious. Just do it, okay?"

He hung up, and immediately started dialing Barney's number.

"You think Alan and Emily are in trouble?" Sara asked.

Logan held up a finger. "Give me a minute." He put the

phone up to his ear and listened to it ring.

A click, and then Barney said, "Hello?"

"It's Logan. What's going on?"

"Oh, Logan. Finally," Barney said. He told him what had happened.

"You checked everywhere?"

"Yes. He's not here."

"Stay by your phone."

One of Logan's strongest points was his calm in the face of chaos and danger, but he'd never been in a situation like this that involved his father. He had to force the pounding in his head to relax, and cage his emotions so they wouldn't overtake him.

He called Ruth back, and had her do a similar check on Harp's phone. It was sixty miles east of Braden, seemingly stationary, just off the interstate. But that wasn't the worst part.

The phone in Paskota's car—Logan's phone—was traveling down the freeway off-ramp at the very same exit where Harp's phone was located.

52

"NO," RICHARD SAID. "There's no way to know that for sure. We stick to the plan, leave him here, and get you someplace safe."

"But what if he's right?" Sara asked.

They were parked behind the Grand Canyon Camper Village at the north end of Tusayan. Dev had pulled up several minutes earlier, but sat waiting in the El Camino. Logan had spent the time laying out what he had in mind. Now it was up to them to decide. He already knew what he would have to do, one way or another.

"And what if he's wrong?" Sara's brother retorted. "Or maybe it's a trap just to get you."

"Richard! *I'm* not the point, remember? Emily is. They're not going to use her to get to me." She paused before speaking in a softer voice. "If he's wrong, then we'll know soon enough, and we can still disappear."

Richard clenched his jaw. "I don't like it." He looked at Diana. "You don't like it, either, do you?"

Diana closed her eyes and massaged her right temple. When she opened them again, she gave her brother a halfhearted smile.

"It doesn't matter what we think. It's up to Sara. But if it were my call, I'd probably say we have no choice."

"To get out of here," Richard stated.

She shook her head. "No."

"But—"

"Richard, our family is bigger than the three of us now. Remember that. There's Emily and Alan, too."

He grimaced. "Alan's not—"

"Yes, he is," Sara said. "He's my husband. Your brother-in-law."

She stared at Richard, challenging him to contradict her. As much as he looked like he wanted to, he didn't.

"So?" Logan asked.

"Yes," Sara said.

Logan nodded. "Give me a minute." He got out of the car and stepped over to the El Camino.

Dev rolled down the window. "Well?"

"Follow us out of here," Logan told him. "Once you're on the interstate, I want you to push it, go as fast as you dare. If you get pulled over, that's fine. But if you don't, you'll be able to get there fast. We'll be coming behind you, but will stay at traffic speed. I can't afford to have us both delayed by cops. Here." He handed Dev a piece of paper with a number on it. "That's Barney's cell. Call him, and tell him and Pep to be ready to leave in the next thirty minutes. Tell them I'll call when it's time. I'm going to keep tabs with Ruth. If possible, I want to time things so that Pep and Barney get on the road just ahead of the doctor and her people. She'll probably be traveling pretty fast and will overtake them at some point. When that happens, they need to try to stay with her."

"Pep should drive."

"I agree," Logan said. "If they've forced my father to tell them where Alan is, they'll be heading straight to Riverside. We'll know that soon enough. Callie's getting Alan and Emily out of town as we speak, which means the house will be empty. I'm hoping we can trap the woman there, and get my dad away from her."

"And then what? Call the police?"

Logan looked back at the Grand Prix. "If I can convince them of that."

53

HARP KEPT HIS eyes closed, hoping the others would think he was asleep. It wasn't that he had some elaborate plan for escape. That was something his son might think up, not him. He just didn't want to talk anymore.

It wasn't fair. He was a nearly eighty-year-old man, whose son was the only family he had left. Once threats were made about Logan, Harp hadn't stood a chance, and he'd talked. He hated himself for it, but what else could he do? He couldn't run. He couldn't fight. He couldn't call anyone even if they hadn't taken his phone away.

Harp could hear other vehicles entering and leaving the truck stop. Most sounded like regular, family-sized cars, but every so often there were low rumbles and vibrations of big rigs pulling in to fill up.

Once he'd tried to signal a passerby, but his interrogator had simply reached over and slapped his hand down. If he tried again, he was pretty sure he'd get more than a slap.

As soon as they had stopped, the driver had made a call, told the person on the other end their location, and hung up. The two men then took turns going into the station to use the facilities.

Harp, though, was not offered the same opportunity.

Finally, his mind started to drift. His body, on edge since the moment he'd been taken, felt suddenly drained and useless. If he were lucky, soon he wouldn't just be pretending to sleep.

A phone rang, loud and jarring.

Harp's eyes sprang open, his breath catching in his throat, as whatever adrenaline he had left shot through his system.

"Hello?" the driver said into his cell. He listened, nodding, and hung up without saying anything else.

"Well?" the man in back asked. He was the one who'd introduced himself as Leon Clausen at the hospital cafeteria.

"Almost."

They fell into silence again.

Almost what? Harp wondered.

He didn't have long to wait for his answer. Only a few minutes went by before a gray sedan with a blonde woman behind the wheel pulled up next to theirs and stopped.

"We're switching to the other car," Clausen said to Harp. "Don't do anything dumb."

Dumb was getting out of bed that morning. Dumb was offering to get water for Pep by himself. Dumb was telling the men where Alan and Emily lived. Trying to get away from men with guns would be colossally idiotic.

Harp moved over into the gray sedan without a fight. The man who'd been driving took over the same duties in the new vehicle, and soon they were back on the interstate.

Once they had settled into a steady speed, the woman twisted around in the front passenger seat and looked at Harp, studying him.

"I see the resemblance," she said. "Your son has your eyes, and your...ears, I think." Her smile sent a chill through Harp. "But I'm glad to hear his stubbornness didn't come from you."

Harp said nothing.

"I advise you to continue to be cooperative, Mr. Harper. If I get the feeling that you're not, you become unnecessary, and I don't keep anything unnecessary around."

54

DR. PASKOTA AND her men had over a two-hour lead on Logan and the others. They might be able to close the gap some, but it wouldn't be by much. The question was, would the woman blaze into Riverside and go straight after Alan and Emily? Or would she take a little time to evaluate the situation first?

That really depended on why the woman was after the girl.

"If I'm going to help you, *really* help you, then you need to tell me exactly what's going on," he said.

"No," Richard said. "All you need to know is that those people are trying to hurt my sister and her family. That's it. That's all you need. That's all you get."

"Those people also happen to have my father. He's not a young man. There's not a lot he can do to protect himself. I *need* to know what's going on!"

"I'm sorry about your dad," Richard shot back. "But I don't give a shit. If you hadn't come nosing around in the first place, he wouldn't be in trouble."

All Logan had to do was grab the back of Richard's head and slam it into the steering wheel. That would be that. Of course, they'd all be dead, but at least he'd have a little satisfaction.

His hands remained at his side.

"I'm going to ignore that last part, because I know you're trying to protect your sister. That's admirable. I also know that you're not very smart. There's nothing you can do about that."

Richard's face balled up into a reddening mass of fury. "You son of a—"

"Richard!" Diana yelled. "Just drive!"

"I'm pulling over and we're kicking him out."

"No, we're not," she said. "Keep going."

"Go to hell, Diana! Sometimes *I'm* right. Sometimes we do what *I* say!"

"Richard," Sara said, her voice calmer than the others. "Logan's right. We all know you're doing your best to help me. I love you more for that than I can ever express. But Logan's not the problem here." She pointed out the front window at some imaginary point in the distance. "She is. Logan's involved in this now whether you want him to be or not. Which means he needs to know the truth. Please. Keep driving."

A whole minute passed, then two, as if the air in the car needed to calm first before anyone spoke. Then Sara started talking.

55

"DIANA AND RICHARD had it harder than me," Sara said. Diana shook her head. "That's not true."

"It is. We all had the same mother, but Diana and Richard had a different father than me. Didn't really matter, though. Their dad, my dad, neither of them stuck around. Mom was…not picky, you know what I mean? There were different men all the time."

"Until Jerry," Diana said.

"Yeah," Sara agreed.

When neither of them said anything more, Logan asked, "What happened?"

"Richard and I came home from school one day," Diana said, picking up the story. "Sara was four at the time, and was sitting in the living room watching TV. That usually meant Mom was busy with one of her boyfriends in back, but when I went to my room, I noticed her door was open, and she was stretched across the bed. There was something odd on her pillow, so I tiptoed in to see it, thinking she was asleep." Diana paused. "It was blood, and there was more on the sheets. Her face was bruised and swollen. Turned out Jerry beat her into a coma at some point during the day, then gave Sara a sandwich, put her in front of the TV, and left. They caught him a week later. Mom never came out of the coma. She lasted three months before she died, and six weeks after that Jerry went to prison."

Sara said, "We were sent to live with our aunt and uncle in Iowa. Unfortunately, they weren't particularly big fans of our mom. They tolerated us at best. Diana and Aunt Jill didn't see eye to eye at all, so Diana left when she was a junior in high school. Richard and I both made it through our senior years before we got out."

"I knew they weren't going to help me out when I left," Diana said, "but I thought they'd give Richard or at least Sara a hand. But no, once they were out of high school, it was out the door, have a good life. Which meant the only thing we had was the only thing we'd always had—each other.

"I was bartending before I could even legally drink. My bosses didn't know that, but a job's a job. When Richard moved out, I'd get him work bussing tables, sometimes security, that kind of thing. I did the same for Sara—waitress, hostess, whatever. It always killed me, though. Sara's the smartest of us. She should have gone to college. Of the three of us, she's the one who could make something of her life."

"She's giving me too much credit," Sara said. "Diana's the smart one. I always wanted to be like her."

Diana reached out and squeezed her sister's hand. "Shut up," she said, smiling.

"It's true."

"Anyway," Diana said. "I kept looking for ways for Sara to get a better life. I was constantly checking online for something that might get her on the right track. My dream was finding her a job that might even pay for her education at some point. Anything better than where she was would have been great, you know?"

Logan nodded, sympathizing with Diana's desire to help her sister.

"Three years ago I spotted something that I thought would be perfect. It wasn't a job, per se, but the money she could have gotten would have paid for college. The ad said accepted applicants could earn up to fifty thousand dollars and continue working at their current job. All Sara had to do was…"

"Get pregnant," Logan said, already knowing the answer.

Diana nodded.

"I didn't want to do it at first," Sara told him. "A child growing in my body? How was I supposed to give that up? I was told the baby wouldn't be related to me, that I'd just be a surrogate, but it just seemed wrong."

"I talked her into applying anyway," Diana jumped in. "I told her she could back out whenever she wanted, but to at least hear what they had to say, and find out how much she could make. I even took her to the interview."

"From the moment we walked in," Sara explained, "the nurses and the staff were so nice, so concerned about…me. Even when Dr. Paskota came in, she seemed—"

"Hold on," Logan said. "Dr. Paskota?"

Sara looked at him. "It's her, isn't it? In the other car? The woman?"

"Yes."

She closed her eyes and looked like she was fighting off a wave of pain.

"Are you sure?" Diana asked him.

"It's what the others called her. When I did, too, she didn't correct me."

"I knew it," Sara said, her eyes still closed.

"Maybe…maybe this isn't a good idea," Diana said.

"No," Sara said, looking at her sister now. "It was going to happen at some point."

"We could still run."

"But Emily…"

"We get her, then disappear. We've done it before. We can do it again."

"I can't keep running."

For several seconds, there was only the sound of the tires on the road.

Sara turned back to Logan. "We ended up spending four hours at the clinic that first day. When we were done, the doctor had answered most of my concerns, and had actually made me feel good about the process. I mean, I was possibly going to help a couple who couldn't have kids on their own become parents. That was actually pretty cool. While I was there, they ran a few tests, and told me they'd call me later to let me know how much I would be paid if I chose to sign up."

"I assume they called," Logan said.

She nodded. "That evening. They said I was in particularly good health, and that I fit a specific profile one of their clients had been looking for. The offer was for sixty-five thousand dollars. A month or two prep before the pregnancy, the pregnancy itself, and the birth. That was it. *Sixty-five thousand dollars* for maybe eleven months total, *and* I could still work."

"I couldn't believe it," Diana said in a low voice, as if she were caught in the memory. "It was more than we could have hoped for. Sara could use that money to go to school and get a degree. She was going to do something better. Exactly what I'd wanted."

"Something obviously wasn't right, or we wouldn't be here," Logan said.

"Everything went fine until the fifth month," Sara explained. "I was visiting Dr. Paskota. She told me an irregularity had popped up on one of the tests. Nothing to be worried about, but she wanted to do an amniocentesis as a precaution."

Diana said, "Sara was worried about the baby, but I was worried about the money. She'd only get a small portion if something happened with the pregnancy. I don't mean that to sound cold-blooded, but Sara was my concern."

"It was several days before I got the call," Sara said. "I was a wreck by then, worried that the baby was having problems I could do nothing about. It didn't matter that she wasn't mine. I cared about her. So much. The caller wasn't Dr. Paskota, but a woman who said she was one of her nurses. She told me the doctor wanted her to call as soon as they got the results back. She said that everything was fine. I've never felt so relieved in my life. But then she told me something else. 'I didn't realize you were also the egg donor.' I thought I misheard her so I asked her to repeat what she said. That's when I found out that I wasn't just a surrogate. I was the actual mother. When it became clear to her that I had no idea, she said, 'That's what I thought. We need to talk.' I was confused and scared, but I agreed to meet a few hours later, and took Diana with me."

"The woman told us to call her Brenda. When I said I didn't remember seeing her at the doctor's office, she said that was because she didn't really work there. We almost left right then, thinking she was just some crazy person trying to scare us. But Brenda said enough for us to hear her out." Sara paused. "She said she worked in the lab that handled the tests, and took it on herself to run a DNA match between the baby and myself. I was definitely the mother."

"She didn't just happen to work at that lab, though," Diana clarified. "She said she'd purposefully gotten herself hired there."

"Right."

"Why would she do that?" Logan asked.

"Because they handled all of Dr. Paskota's tests," Diana said.

Sara nodded. "Brenda told us she had a cousin who'd been recruited by Dr. Paskota. After a while, Ruby—that's what Brenda called her—began to get suspicious that something wasn't right. She talked to Brenda, who *was* actually a lab tech at a hospital across town, and said she was going to start asking some questions she should have asked a long time ago. Two days later, her car was broadsided by a truck that had lost its brakes. Brenda didn't like it, not at all, so she started digging."

A baby mill, Logan thought. There were no barren families, at least not those who were looking for surrogates. The doctor was creating the product, and undoubtedly selling them to the highest bidder. Though he was sure that had to be it, he said, "So what did she find?"

Sara looked too distressed to continue, so Diana took up the story. "Dr. Paskota had set up a program that has one purpose—to insure the health of its clients."

"Insure? Like insurance?" he asked.

Diana shook her head. "Not in the way you're thinking of. Something a bit more tangible."

How does selling babies insure health? "I'm not following."

"It's a long-term plan," she said. "People. Genetically matched people."

He stared at her, still not getting it.

"If you're rich enough and still relatively young," she said, "why not hedge your bets against the future? Thanks to Dr. Paskota, somewhere there's a person, your offspring, just waiting in case you need...anything."

Logan's lips parted in horror. "I hope I'm misunderstanding what you're saying."

"I doubt it," Sara said. "Heart, lungs, kidneys, liver, whatever—perfectly matched to you, just hanging around in case you ever needed them."

He hadn't misunderstood. It was...inhuman.

"Do you have proof?" he asked.

"The fact that they have your father isn't proof enough?" Richard said.

Again, Sara put a hand on her brother to calm him down, then said, "That's what Brenda had been collecting. We made plans to take what she had to the FBI. I was going to be the final piece of evidence, an actual person still in the process. Only she didn't show up when she was supposed to, and on the news that night, there was a report about a woman who had been murdered while getting money from an ATM, a lab technician named Monique Pond. The picture they showed was Brenda's. I immediately called Diana."

"If Dr. Paskota knew about Brenda, she probably also knew that Sara had been talking to her," Diana said. "Hell, I was concerned someone was waiting outside Sara's apartment to mug her, too. I told her to pack only what she really needed, then sent Richard to pick her up. I was right. Someone was waiting. The doctor and one of her men."

"They tried to grab me when I came down," Sara said. "Dr. Paskota said I was going with them someplace where they could keep an eye on me until the baby was born. Whatever kindness I'd seen in her was gone."

Her brother grinned. "They weren't expecting me, though. Dislocated the guy's shoulder and broke his leg. The doctor I only knocked to the ground so she'd get out of our way."

Quite a family, Logan thought.

"We've been hiding Sara ever since," Diana said.

"Hold on," he said. "What if you'd never found out and had Emily there? Then what?"

"They would have paid me and I would have gone on my way," Sara answered.

"And Emily? What would Dr. Paskota have done about her? She can't just stick all these babies in a room until they're needed."

"She doesn't have to. This isn't the only thing Dr. Paskota does, though there's no doubt it makes her a ton more money than anything else. See, the other thing she does is help match newborns with families wanting to adopt. It's the perfect cover. When one of her special cases comes up, she can just add the baby to the mix, and carefully track them as they grow up. Once a special child reaches sixteen, he or she becomes viable. If the client associated with that child ever needs a kidney or, say, a heart, the child is simply snatched and…harvested. The doctor makes money on both ends—the clients who are buying the insurance in case they have a need someday, and the parents who think they've just adopted their dream child."

"Has that happened?"

Sara shook her head. "From what Brenda could learn, Dr. Paskota had only been doing this special service for about twelve years, which means about fifteen now. Those first kids will soon become viable, and then it becomes a waiting game."

"They may never be used, though. Not everyone's going to need a transplant."

"True, but remember, to the ones who've paid for these kids' existence, the cost is minimal so it's worth the risk. Most of the children will probably live full lives, but not all. No way was I going to risk Emily's life like that."

So horrifying, yet so simple. Logan wondered if there were others doing something similar.

"Why didn't you go to the FBI on your own?"

"We didn't have Brenda's proof," Diana said. "Why would they believe us? The three of us with our less-than-stellar family history versus the good Dr. Paskota? A woman who's helped hundreds of deserving families get matched with 'needy' children? Not only would all the adoptive parents come to her defense, but her wealthy special clients wouldn't want their involvement in her program exposed. They would do anything to help her keep things quiet. The FBI would never listen to us."

"There's another reason," Sara said. "One of those clients is Emily's father. What if he got custody of her? What would I do then?"

Though unsure what he would have done in similar circumstances, he understood their reasoning.

"Why did you marry Alan? Wasn't that taking a chance?" he asked, wanting to fill in the holes so he could have the full picture.

"I didn't set out to meet him, and I certainly didn't mean to fall in love," Sara said defensively. "After we started seeing each other, I can't tell you how many times I almost disappeared. And when he asked me to marry him? Oh, God. I wanted to so bad, but how could I?"

"I'm the one who encouraged her to say yes," Diana said. "I'm the one who came up with the plan that if something happened, she could leave Emily with him. That way she would be safe."

"So what triggered you to run again?"

"I have people I talk to," Diana said. "Friends who think I'm on the run from a bad relationship. They keep their eyes open and let me know if anyone's asking around about me or Richard or Sara. About three months ago I started getting calls, and knew it wasn't going to be long before they figured out my new last name and tracked me down. Once they did that, they'd try to use me to get to Sara. So I knew it was time for her to disappear."

"But *you* didn't," Logan said. "You stayed in Braden."

"I wanted to be sure. If they didn't show up, then perhaps we were in the clear, and if they did, I'd just sneak away. I thought your friend the other night was one of them. Hell, I thought you were, too." She paused. "Sorry about your friend. That was…a mistake."

Logan looked at Richard for a second, then back at Diana. He'd already figured Richard was the one who'd attacked Pep.

"Don't blame him," she said. "I was the one in charge. It was my mistake."

Logan glanced out the window. They were in the desert again, the vast brown landscape seeming to go on forever.

There was so much to think about, to process. He'd seen enough of the bad in the world to know that people like Dr. Paskota existed. He just didn't want to believe it. Unfortunately, that wasn't a choice.

"Now you know why we had to run," Diana said, breaking the silence. "And why we'll need to continue running once we have Emily. What other choice do we have?"

Logan couldn't think of one.

261

56

"HERE COMES ANOTHER one," Pep said, checking the rearview mirror of Dev's Cherokee.

Barney watched the car go by on their left. "No, not them."

The two men had left Braden forty-five minutes earlier. Barney had made it clear he was less than keen on the idea of Pep driving. In his opinion, Pep should have stayed at the motel. Barney had said he could do this on his own, but Pep wasn't about to let that happen.

"Maybe we left too late," Barney said, worried.

"We didn't," Pep said. He'd been the one who talked to Logan right before they hit the road, and knew that Logan was somehow able to track the other car.

When he was given the go signal, the other car apparently had been fifteen minutes behind them. Keeping their speed just below the sixty-five-miles-per-hour limit, Pep figured that the others would probably pass him and Barney somewhere in the next fifteen to twenty minutes.

He'd made sure Barney started checking early in case his calculation was wrong, and so that Barney could get some practice at not being obvious when he looked at the other cars. The old doc was getting better at it, but he still needed to refine his method.

"Act like you're talking to me," Pep suggested.

"That's what I'm doing," Barney said.

"Then actually do it. Say something." Pep glanced at the mirror again. A blue minivan was pulling out to go around them. "Try it on this one."

Barney shifted once more in his seat. "So, um, it's...pretty... hot outside." As soon as the van passed, he added, "Not them." He turned back to the front.

"You know what?" Pep said. "Just keep looking at me even if there aren't any cars. It'll seem more natural that way. We can talk about whatever you want."

"I don't want to talk about anything. I want to find Harp."

"Let's talk about that, then."

"What's there to talk about?" Barney said. He looked at Pep, exasperated. "He's gone. If I hadn't fallen asleep, maybe none of this would have happened."

"And how, exactly, would your staying awake have kept him from being taken?"

"I...I...I would have known sooner. Maybe we could have done something."

"Like what?" Pep checked the mirror. Two more cars were coming.

"I don't know!"

"Exactly. We're doing everything we can to—"

"Harp!" Barney shouted.

He started to raise his hand to point, but Pep quickly grabbed it and pushed it back down.

"Which car?" Pep asked.

"The second one. The gray one. See? That's him in the back on the left. I'd recognize his hair anywhere."

Pep let the other car pull ahead, then he started to gradually increase the Cherokee's speed. It was okay if the sedan pulled away a little. He knew which one it was now and would catch up.

"I counted four people inside," Pep said. "How about you?"

"Yes, four. Two in front, two in back." Barney leaned forward anxiously. "Hurry up, we're going to lose them."

"No, we're not." Pep grabbed his phone, put it on speaker, and conferenced in both Logan and Dev. "They just went by us."

"Did you see my dad?" Logan asked.

"Yeah, he's in the backseat."

"Did he look okay?"

"He was sitting up, but staring out the other window. I couldn't see his face very well," Barney said.

"Were his eyes at least open?"

"I think so."

"Okay, where are you guys?"

"About fifty miles west of Braden," Pep said.

"How about you, Dev?" Logan asked.

"I should hit Braden in about fifteen minutes," Dev announced. "Making pretty good time so far."

"We're about ten minutes behind you," Logan said. "Stay on them, Pep. Don't let them out of your sight."

57

"IS THAT IT?" Erica asked.

The old man looked out the window at the house they were driving slowly past.

"Mr. Harper, is that it?" she repeated.

"I…I don't know. I think so. I wasn't driving so I wasn't paying attention."

She scowled, and turned back around.

It didn't really matter if the man didn't recognize it. According to the address her researcher had found, this was the house where Sara's husband was supposed to live.

A tricycle was parked along the driveway so a young child did live there, one who would be around the same age as the baby girl Sara had.

"Doesn't look like anyone is home," Clausen said.

"He's probably still at work," she said.

"What do you want me to do?" Markle asked from behind the wheel.

"Go around the block one more time. Let's see if we can find a quiet place where we can wait."

58

"THEY JUST PARKED at a school," Pep said into the phone.

"It's in the same neighborhood where Alan lives," Barney chimed in, his voice louder than it needed to be.

"They're just sitting there?" Logan asked.

"They were a moment ago," Pep said. "There was no good place to watch them from so we're a few blocks away."

"Okay. Let me think for a second."

The line went silent.

"We need to get Harp," Barney said to Pep, his voice lower now.

"We will," Pep whispered back.

"Maybe we can distra—"

"Okay," Logan said, coming back on. "Here's what I want you to do. Find someplace to park near Alan's but not in direct sight. Then, if you feel up to it, Pep, I want the two of you to stroll around. It's not likely they'll recognize either of you, so you should be able to keep an eye on things. Barney, show him exactly where Alan's house is."

"Should we try to see if we can get Harp out, too?" Barney

asked.

"No! It's too dangerous for just the two of you. Promise me you won't do anything stupid."

"I'll make sure he doesn't," Pep said.

"Okay, good. Call me the moment anything happens."

59

"WHY?" ALAN HAD asked.

"I don't have all the details," Callie had told him. "Only that we were right. Sara *is* in trouble. But it's more than just her. The people who are after her want Emily, too."

"Emily? Why would they want Emily?"

Callie hadn't had the answer for that, either. "I have a cabin in Big Bear. Take her up there. Don't call anyone. Don't tell anyone. I'll have the management company I use leave a key under the mat."

Since Sara had left, Alan had felt useless. Even though he didn't admit it to himself at the time, he knew right after he read her note that she needed help. Later, when he really thought about it, he realized he should have known even before then.

It had been little things, moments when he'd caught her off guard, staring at the wall or the ground or nothing at all, a look of despair on her face. He knew it wasn't him, that it couldn't be him. She loved him so much. She told him that every day, not just in words, but in each touch and smile and glance. These were enough for him to dismiss her half-hidden anguish and moments of panic.

He was Sara's husband, dammit. He should have pushed to find out what was wrong. He should have done everything in his power to help her *before* she left, not after. But he'd failed her, and now, if he made a mistake, he would fail Emily, too.

He should have...should have...should—

"Daddy, go Macee Donal?"

Alan looked around.

My God. How did we get here so fast?

They were on the freeway already. He didn't even remember taking the on-ramp.

"Daddy. Macee Donal! Macee Donal!"

He glanced in back. Strapped in her car seat, Emily was shaking her hand at the window.

"Macee Donal!"

At the exit just ahead, a McDonald's sign was raised high in the air so travelers, especially two-year-old girls, wouldn't miss it.

"Want friend fry, Daddy. Want friend fry!"

"Not right now, sweetie. We don't have time."

"Daddy, Daddy, pease!" She started to cry.

He felt a tug on his heart. "Okay," he said, moving quickly over to the right lane. The least he could do was try to keep his daughter happy. "We'll get some fries, all right?"

"Thank you, Daddy." She sang his name in a way he always loved. "Soda?"

"How about milk?"

"Toclate milk!" she said with enthusiasm.

"Fine. Chocolate milk."

She giggled, and began repeating, "Friend fry, toclate milk. Friend fry, toclate milk."

Instead of using the drive-through, Alan decided they'd go inside. He needed to calm down and get control of himself. If he stayed on the road like he was, they were going to get into an accident.

He purchased the fries and chocolate milk for Emily and a coffee for himself. They found a booth along the wall.

An older Latina walked by and smiled at Emily. "Oh, so cute," the woman said.

Alan had to do everything in his power not to reach out and put a protective arm in front of his daughter. Who was this woman? Why was she looking at Emily? Was she here to try and take her?

"Thanks," he said.

The woman must have sensed his strain, her smile not as bright as she moved on.

Emily was in her own happy world, gingerly dipping one fry at a time into the dollop of ketchup Alan had squeezed onto the tray liner. She held one out to him.

"You, Daddy."

"Thank you, sweetie," he said, taking it.

As he watched her, he couldn't help thinking he had to do something more than just hide. Whatever problems Sara was having, they were his problems, too. That's what being married meant. Problems were something he dealt with every day. *He* had the experience in that area, so he needed to be involved in the solution.

He looked at Emily again. "How would you like to visit Aunt Rachel?"

She nodded as she put another fry in her mouth.

He could get to his sister's and back in three hours. He'd tell her he had some emergency business he had to deal with. Chances were, Rachel would offer to keep Emily overnight. That would probably be best.

"Hurry up, sweetie. We need to get back on the road."

"No," she said. "Finish first."

"Okay. Finish first."

60

THE LONG SUMMER day was finally turning to night. Twice more since they'd arrived, Erica and her men had driven by Alan Lindley's home, but each time the driveway was empty, and there was no other sign of anyone being home. It was after eight o'clock now. Surely a man with a young daughter couldn't still be out.

"Check again," she ordered.

Markle started up the car.

61

THE THREE-HOUR round trip to Alan's sister's house turned into over five.

First Emily had not wanted Alan to leave, so he stayed and played with her, wearing her down until she took a late afternoon nap. Then Rachel had become concerned, saying he was acting strange, and wanting to know what was going on. That wasted another twenty minutes, spent reassuring her that everything was fine and that he was just a little stressed from work. He knew she didn't completely buy it, but he was able to finally get out of there without further questions.

Unfortunately, this meant he left smack in the middle of rush hour. At one point it got so unbearable, he'd exited the free-way and tried to find a surface-street way around the mess. That turned out to be a horrible idea. Not only was there almost as much traffic off the freeway as on, he didn't know the area and soon found himself lost. It took him over fifteen minutes just to locate the freeway again, and when he did, he stayed on it this time, not exiting until he reached Riverside just after eight p.m.

62

LOGAN'S PHONE BUZZED. It was Pep.

"Someone just pulled into Alan's driveway."

Logan sat up. "Who? Paskota?"

"No. It looks like just one guy. Hold on. He's getting out."

Logan glanced out the window. They had just passed Victorville and were about to hit the Cajon Pass, putting them no more than forty minutes away from Riverside.

There was movement on the other end of the line.

"Logan?" It was Barney. "It's Alan. He's come back."

"What? Are you sure?"

Both Sara and Diana looked at Logan, concerned by his outburst.

"I'm positive. The light came on in the garage after he drove in, so I got a quick look at his face."

"What's he doing there?"

Though Logan meant the question for himself, Barney seemed to think he wanted an answer. "You want us to find out?"

"What's who doing where?" Sara asked.

Logan looked at her. "Alan. He's at your house."

"I thought he was supposed to leave. Where's Emily?"

He had been wondering the same thing. "Is Emily with him?" he asked Barney.

"I...I don't think so," Barney said. "He drove into the garage, then just went straight into the house. Didn't even look back into the car."

Why was Alan there? Callie had assured Logan he was taking Emily someplace safe.

"Okay," he said. "You need to get him out of the house and—"

More movement from the other end, and Pep came back on the line. "The others are coming back up the street."

Dammit! Logan closed his eyes. This was exactly what he'd been trying to avoid.

"What is it?" Sara asked.

Ignoring her, Logan said, "Can you get to the house?"

"Not without being seen."

No way could he send a retired doctor and a recuperating sixty-year-old vet into harm's way. They wouldn't have a chance. Not that Alan had much of one, either. "Is the garage door still open?"

"No. He closed it."

"What about lights? Can you see any from the garage or the house?"

"No."

"Okay, hold your position. If it looks like before, they shouldn't stop."

"Here's hoping."

63

ERICA SCOWLED. EVEN from down the street, she could tell the house looked dark and unoccupied.

Where *was* this guy? Maybe they didn't have the right address. She glanced back at Logan's father. "Is this the street or not?"

"I told you. I'm not sure. I don't do directions well. It could be. I don't know."

The poor-old-guy routine was wearing thin. She suspected that the elder Harper knew more than he was saying. Not the most trustworthy family, those Harpers. When she finally secured the girl, she'd have to clean up this mess. The two Harpers would be at the top of the list.

Markle kept their speed at a nice, slow neighborhood level. Most of the houses they passed had lights on, families settling in for the night. In one yard, two kids were playing catch under a particularly bright porch light. Another house had its garage door open, a man inside doing something at a workbench. And farther down the block, past the target house and on the opposite sidewalk, the old man from earlier was out walking again with the guy Erica guessed was his son.

The house Sara and the girl had lived in was three away, then two, then one.

She turned toward it as they drove past, its dark silhouette taunting her.

Then, just as the driveway began to recede behind them, the porch light flicked on.

64

"OH, CRAP."

Logan's grip on his phone tightened. "What is it?"

"The porch light. He turned on the damn porch light," Pep said.

"Did they see it?"

"Hell yes, they saw it. They were just driving by. I think they were going to keep going, but the moment that light came on, they hit the brakes. They're pulling into the driveway right now."

The ramifications of involving the authorities no longer mattered. "Call the cops. Tell them anything, just get them there now!"

"Got it."

Logan hung up.

"What happened?" Sara asked.

He told her.

"No. No!" She turned to her brother. "You've got to go faster."

"Any faster and we'll get pulled over."

"I don't care!" she yelled. "They're going to hurt him! He didn't do *anything*!"

"Sara, stop," Diana said. "Everyone's doing the best they can."

Sara looked back, her eyes blazing with anger. "It's not enough!" To her brother, she said, "Please. As fast as you can."

65

ALAN WAS JUST finishing up in the bathroom when the doorbell rang.

It had to be Logan. Callie had said he was on the way. Surely that meant he'd get there in time to deal with the others.

As he walked through the house, his sense of determination to find out what the hell was going on grew to the point that when he opened the door, he was already asking his first question.

"I want you to tell me right now—"

That was as far as he got before he saw the gun in the hand of a man standing on his porch. Beside him, unarmed, was a blonde woman.

"Mr. Lindley?" she asked.

A good businessman knew when it was time to contemplate a decision and when it was time to just react. This called for the latter.

Alan shoved the door closed, and ran toward the sliding glass door that led out onto the back deck. If he could get there, he could go around the house and get out to the street.

Behind him, a dull thud was accompanied by the shattering of wood. He knew at that moment he would never make it outside in time. His head whipped around, looking for anything he could use as a weapon. But each item his gaze landed on seemed pitifully inadequate. The man had a *gun*. For all he knew, the woman had one, too. What good would a palm-sized brass Buddha do?

He cut around the sofa, and headed for the kitchen. The door to the garage was there. If he could get through that, maybe he could jump in his car and get away.

"Mr. Lindley," the woman called out. "Our problem isn't with you. If you'll just cooperate, everything will be fine."

Alan yanked open the garage door, and rushed through. He took a few seconds to look around for anything he could use to jam the door closed but quickly gave up, knowing he was wasting time. On the wall was the switch that opened the garage door. He slapped it, ran over to his car, and got in.

As the engine roared to life, the door to the kitchen opened. He flinched, thinking he was about to get shot, but neither the man nor the woman raised a gun. They merely stood just inside the doorway, smiling at him.

Not stopping to figure out what the hell they were doing, he turned so he could look out the back window to see if the door was high enough for him to leave.

It was, but he wasn't going anywhere.

There was a car sitting right in the middle of the driveway with two more men inside.

A tap on the glass made him jump. He turned and saw the woman standing just on the other side of the door.

"You have two choices, Mr. Lindley. Come out on your own, or my friend here shoots you somewhere that won't kill you, and we pull you out. I guarantee you the glass won't offer any protection."

The man behind her held up his gun and grinned. The barrel was longer than a normal pistol, like something had been added on the end.

A silencer. That's what they called it in the movies, right?

If they did shoot him, no one would hear.

He opened the door.

"Good choice," the woman said, helping him climb out.

"Who are you?"

"Your wife never told you about me? I'm an old friend. In fact, I was hoping to meet her daughter. Where is she?"

Feeling his anger well again, Alan said, "Fuck you!"

The woman smiled. With a speed Alan would have never expected, she slapped him hard on the side of his head.

He fell against the car, his ear ringing.

"Search the house," she said to her companion.

The guy nodded and went inside. He was gone less than a minute before reappearing. "Not here."

"I'll ask again, Mr. Lindley. Where's the child?"

"My daughter is no concern of yours!"

"*Your* daughter?" The woman nodded at Alan's car. "Check it," she said to the gunman.

In the distance, they could hear sirens, but as much as Alan wished they were heading his way, the near constant sound of emergency vehicles was part of living in the big city.

"No girl," the man said. "But there is a portable GPS."

"Bring it."

Alan could feel the blood drain from his face. The little box kept records of his travel.

At the top of the list would be his trip to Rachel's.

66

THE SIRENS COULDN"T have been more than a half-mile away, but Pep knew they weren't close enough.

The other car—now with the addition of Alan Lindley—was pulling out of the driveway. They'd be blocks away before the police arrived.

"Hurry, hurry," Pep urged Barney.

They had stayed where they could see what was going on as long as they could. Now they needed to get back to their car. If they weren't moving in the next thirty seconds, they'd lose the others for sure. Logan might be able to track them down again using his friend, but Pep didn't want to count on that. He *had* to keep the others in sight.

The Jeep was parked right around the corner. Pep jumped in, fired up the engine, then leaned across the seat and opened the passenger door. As soon as Barney's butt hit the seat cover, Pep jammed down the accelerator.

"Whoa!" Barney said, reaching out and pulling closed the door. "I'm not even fastened in yet."

Keeping his tone calm, Pep said, "We're kind of in a hurry, Barney."

"You're right, you're right. Sorry."

They turned onto Alan's street just in time to see the taillights of the other car at the far end of the block. Pep had to restrain himself from pressing the gas all the way to the floor. They were in a neighborhood, and it was still early enough that someone might step out in front of them.

The other car turned right onto the street that led to a main road. Pep reached the intersection and saw the other car turn onto another road. This time he had no choice but to increase their speed and hope to God no one was around. When they arrived at the stop sign, he barely paused before making the turn. The first thing he saw was a police car speeding down the street in their direction. Pep jerked the Jeep to the curb, and stopped. As soon as the police cruiser passed, he pulled out again. A quick glance in the mirror confirmed what he thought. The cops were turning onto the road he'd just been on.

"A little late, guys," he said under his breath.

"Maybe we should go get them," Barney suggested.

Pep could see the other car a block down, its progress also slowed by the police. "We can't," he said. He tossed his phone to Barney. "Get Logan. We need to let him know what happened."

Barney put the call on speaker.

"They got away before the police could get there," he said.

"What about Alan?" Logan asked.

"They have him."

Logan said nothing for a moment, then, "Do you know which way they went?"

"We're following them right now," Pep said.

They could hear Logan take a breath. "Okay. Stay on them."

"Where could they be going?" Barney asked.

"I'm not sure. Perhaps—"

"Ah, Logan," Pep said.

"Yes?"

"Looks like they're getting on the freeway."

67

"LOOKS LIKE THEY'RE getting on the freeway," Pep said.

Logan shot a look at Sara. "How well do you know Riverside?"

She shrugged. "Okay, I guess. I was only there for about a year and a half."

"Dr. Paskota has Alan."

Her face tensed, but she didn't look surprised, obviously having worked that out from hearing his side of the phone conversation.

"They're getting onto the freeway," he said.

"Which one?"

"Which freeway?" Logan asked Pep.

"Two fifteen," Pep replied. "North."

"The 215 North."

She frowned. "The 215 takes a sharp right in the middle of town where it intersects with the 60 and the…uh…91."

"So which way are they going?"

She shrugged. "They could be going anywhere. If they stay on the 215, they'll be headed right at us."

Logan turned back to the phone. "Stay with them," he said.

"I'll call you back in a minute."

Though he knew who they were headed toward, he didn't know where. He called Callie.

"I've been dying here," she said. "What happened?"

"It's not over yet. Alan went back to the house this evening before we could get there."

"What?" She sounded even more surprised than Logan did when he first heard. "He promised me he was going to get Emily out of there."

"Emily wasn't with him."

"She wasn't? Where is she?"

"I was hoping you could tell me that."

"I told him to take her to Big Bear," she said. "I have a cabin up there."

"If you were going to Big Bear from Alan's house, would you take the 215 North?"

"Sure. Up to the I-10, then east to Highway 38."

"Is there anyone in Big Bear he could have left Emily with?"

"I don't know. I'm not sure if he knows anyone up there."

"Okay. Thanks."

As he hung up, he asked Sara, "Did you guys have friends in Big Bear?"

"No. Well, I didn't. Alan never mentioned anyone, either. Is that where Emily is?"

"That's where Callie told him to go."

"Alan would never leave Emily with just anyone. It would have to be someone he trusted."

Having more questions than answers, Logan called Pep back to get an update.

"I was just about to call you," Pep said.

"Why?"

"We're not on the 215 anymore."

"Where are you?"

"On the 60 Freeway, heading west."

Logan put a hand over the phone. "They're on the 60 West."

"Sixty? That's not the way to Big Bear," Sara said.

"Maybe Alan's misdirecting them," Diana suggested.

"Yeah. That must be it," Sara agreed, nodding.

Logan wasn't ready to buy that yet. "You said your husband would only leave Emily with someone he trusts. Who would those people be?"

Sara thought for a moment. "Um…we have some friends. The Carters. They'd watch Emily for us in a pinch."

"Anyone else?"

She shook her head. "We didn't leave Emily alone much."

Logan knew of one time they had. "What about when you and Alan went on your trip to San Diego and Tijuana?"

At the mention of the trip, she looked embarrassed. Then she froze. "Oh…oh, no…Alan's sister. Rachel."

"She's in Riverside, too?"

She shook her head. "Simi Valley."

Simi Valley was way on the other side of the San Fernando Valley, just northwest of Los Angeles.

"When we go to Rachel's, we'd always take the 60 West part of the way."

68

"I DON'T REMEMBER her number," Sara said.

"You don't?" Logan asked, surprised.

"I made sure I didn't memorize anyone's number. And I got rid of my old phone when I left."

Of course. Sara had done everything she could to create a protective wall between herself and her daughter.

"It's okay. Callie will have it," he said. He was right. Once he had the number, he punched it in and handed the phone to Sara. "Just hit SEND."

He could tell the moment the call was answered. Sara pulled back, her eyes focusing downward.

"Hi, may I speak to Rachel?" She put a hand over the phone and whispered, "Kurt answered. Her husband." Suddenly her attention was back on her call. "Rachel? It's…it's Sara…Rachel?… Yes, it's me…I promise I'll tell you later, but I need to—" She paused. "I know that. I didn't mean to hurt anyone. It was the only thing I could do…Please, you have to believe me…Rachel, Rachel, hold on. Just let me—" Her head drooped and she nodded, listening. Finally, she said, "I understand, and I know you're angry. I would be, too, but I need to ask you something…Is Emily with you?...No, I'm not going to try to take her. I just need to know if you have her...Rachel, please...Okay, okay, you don't have to tell me. But if she *is* with you, you and Kurt have to get out of the house right now...Because there are some bad—" She cocked her head. "Rachel?....Rachel, are you there?" She looked at Logan. "She hung up."

"Try again."

She did, then shook her head. "She's not picking up."

"So what do you think? Is Emily there?"

"If she wasn't, I think Rachel would have just said so."

Logan agreed. He made a quick call to Dev, rerouting him to Simi Valley, and handed the phone back to Sara.

"Keep trying," he said.

"Richard," Diana said. She was looking at an old paper map she had fished out of the glove compartment. "The 210 West is coming up in a mile or two. That'll be quickest. We might even gain a little time."

"If we can do that, it'll be the first thing that's gone right today," Logan said.

Ahead, the sign for the 210 Freeway loomed over the lanes. Barring a traffic jam, they'd reach Simi Valley in less than sixty minutes.

He checked his watch then looked back at the road, hoping that wouldn't be too late.

69

THERE WAS A part of Erica that leaned heavily toward disposing of their two passengers before they retrieved the girl. They cut her manpower by half, forcing her to leave someone with them whenever she got out of the car.

If it had just been the old man, there would have been no question. They'd already extracted everything they needed from him, and any leverage they might have had over the man's son by holding on to him no longer mattered. Logan Harper was undoubtedly still fooling around in Arizona, thinking he'd outsmarted her. Maybe he'd even found Sara. All the better if he did. When this part of the operation was over, she would have Clausen and Markle make the younger Harper tell them where Sara was before they silenced the bastard. The information would most likely net them not only Sara, but her bitch of a sister and oaf of a brother. Then they would be gone and everything would be perfect.

But since it wasn't just the old man, it made more sense for them to take care of him when they took care of Sara's husband, and they couldn't do that until they had the girl. Once she was in Erica's possession, Clausen and Markle would dispose of the two

EVERY PRECIOUS THING |

men while she flew with the girl back to the program's offices and arrange a suitable family for her. It would be harder than usual, given the girl's age, but not impossible.

She checked out the road ahead. Thankfully traffic was moving at a pretty good clip, unlike the irritating crawl they'd had to suffer downtown. According to Clausen, they were currently in the San Fernando Valley and Simi Valley was just over the next pass.

Just a few more miles and the girl would be secured.

And this annoying aberration in her well-run program would be erased.

70

SARA LEANED FORWARD and pointed at a sign ahead. "That's it. Tapo Canyon Road. Take that exit and go right."

Richard eased the car into the slow lane.

According to Logan's last conversation with Ruth, Dr. Paskota had been delayed as she passed through downtown, so they had actually arrived in Simi Valley first with a five-to-ten-minute lead. He hoped to God that was enough.

Once they were off the freeway, Sara guided them to another street that took them up the gentle slope of a hill and past a middle school. After that, they zigzagged through a well-kept, middle-class neighborhood until they reached Summit Avenue.

"This is it," Sara said. "About halfway down and on the left."

As Richard slowed the car, Logan's phone beeped with a message from Ruth.

EXITING TAPO CANYON

"They're only a few minutes behind us," Logan said.

"I thought we had more than that," Sara said.

He did, too. "We don't."

"Which one?" Richard asked.

Sara turned back around, studied the homes, then pointed. "There. That one."

As they neared, Richard made like he was going to pull into the driveway.

"Don't," Logan said. "If they see your car parked there, they'll ask Alan if it belongs. Even if he lies and says yes, they'll see through him."

Richard looked at him in the mirror, unconvinced, but Diana nodded.

"On the street," she ordered.

Her brother rolled his eyes, but did as she said.

As they climbed out of the car, Sara asked, "What if they don't open the door?"

"They will," Logan said.

"But what if they won't?"

"It's not going to be an issue."

They crossed to the other side, and walked up to the porch. Sara was closest to the door, while Logan stayed in back. She stood there, doing nothing.

"Sara, you're wasting time we don't have," Logan said.

She nodded, hesitated a second longer, then knocked.

They could hear footsteps on the other side, and the porch light flicked on. The door, however, remained closed. The dim light that had been visible through the peephole turned black.

There was nothing for a moment, then, "What do you want?"

"Rachel, please open the door," Sara said.

"You can't just come in here and take her."

"That's not why I'm here. Please, just let me in."

"Who are those people with you?"

Sara glanced behind her. "My sister and brother, and—"

"Your what? Since when do you have a sister and brother?"

"I'm sorry. I never talked about them, but—"

"There is *no way* I'm letting you in."

Logan knew she meant it. "Keep her talking," he whispered. He moved off to the left, along the front of the house.

Behind him, the conversation faded as he slipped around the corner into the side yard. Halfway down was a cinder-block fence walling off the back. He didn't even bother trying the wooden gate built into it. He simply scaled the fence and hopped down on the other side.

The section of the yard he landed in had been set up as a dog pen. There was a wire fence continuing out from where the house ended, making a squared-off area of about ten feet by ten feet. The dog it was meant for was nowhere to be seen.

Logan passed through the open gate, prepared for the animal appearing at any second, but when he peeked into the main part of the backyard, he was happy to see it was unoccupied. The dog must have been inside for the night.

Like most California homes, there was a sliding glass door, this one opening onto a small brick patio. The screen was closed, but the door was open a few feet, letting in the pleasant evening air.

Logan stopped at the edge of the door and listened. Rachel was saying something, but it didn't sound like she was talking to Sara.

Then a male voice said, "Just ignore her. She'll go away."

Kurt the husband, Logan figured.

"I'm going to call Alan."

"He's going to tell you the same thing."

Logan chanced a look. Just inside was a brightly lit family room. The TV was on, and there was a bowl of chips on a table in front of the couch. A fat, old golden Lab lay sleeping on the sofa. Beyond the room, Logan could see a portion of the entryway at the far side of the house. While the sister was hidden from view, the back of the man was visible. Kurt was short, maybe five six or five seven, but he carried the weight of a man a foot taller.

Logan frowned. He wished he could do this a different way, but there wasn't time. He pulled out his gun, and quietly slid open the screen. The dog didn't even stir.

He crossed through the family room, and stopped ten feet

behind Rachel and Kurt.

Leaving the gun at his side, but visible, he said, "Open the door, please."

For half a second, he thought he'd given the man a heart attack. While both of them had turned around in surprise, Kurt had actually grabbed his chest and fallen against the wall with a thud.

"What do you want?" he said. "How did you—"

"I want you to open the door," Logan replied.

As Rachel fumbled with the lock, Logan heard the dog roll off the couch and walk slowly into the foray.

"Get in!" Logan told Sara and the others the moment he saw them.

They rushed in. As soon as the door was closed again, the dog began roaming between the visitors, sniffing their hand.

"Reggie, don't do that," Kurt said.

The dog glanced at him, and continued what it was doing.

"No, Reggie. Go lie down."

Reggie ignored him.

Logan focused on Rachel. "Where's Emily?"

She shot an accusing glance at Sara. "You *did* come to take her."

"No. We came to save her, and you," Sara said.

"I don't know what you're talking about."

"That's something we'll discuss later," Logan said. "Where's Emily?"

Rachel shook her head. "You can't have her."

"If you stay here even a few minutes longer, there's a good chance you're going to die," Logan said.

Both Rachel and Kurt couldn't help but look at his gun.

71

"*I'M* NOT GOING to kill you," Logan said.

Sara wasn't about to stand there any longer. She raced toward the hallway.

"Hey!" Rachel called out. "You leave her alone."

Sara heard someone running after her. She glanced over her shoulder, thinking it might be Rachel trying to stop her, but it was Diana.

"Hurry," her sister said.

Rachel and Kurt's house was a single story with three bedrooms. They had two sons, both away at college, so Sara guessed Emily would be using one of their rooms. The first was Troy's, but it was empty. The second was Cory's.

Sara stopped in the doorway, frozen in place by the sight of the small form sleeping on the bed.

Emily.

She had almost convinced herself she'd never see her daughter again, but there she was, peacefully asleep. Sara could even hear her breathe. It was like music.

"Did you find her?" Diana asked, stopping behind her.

Sara pulled herself out of her trance and raced into the room.

She pulled back the covers, put her arms under her daughter, and lifted Emily from the bed. The girl rolled against Sara's chest, then seemed to realize something was different.

Her eyelids fluttered, and opened. She stared at her mother for a full second. Then her eyes grew wider than Sara had ever seen them, and she threw open her arms and wrapped them around Sara's neck.

"Mommy, Mommy, Mommy!"

Sara hugged her daughter tight. "It's me, sweetie. It's me."

"We gotta go," Diana said.

Sara remained motionless, wanting to remember this moment for the rest of her life. Then she nodded, and carried Emily out the door.

72

AS SARA AND Diana ran from the room, Logan checked his watch. They were almost out of time.

He nodded at Rachel and Kurt, and said to Richard, "Keep an eye on them."

He made a quick circuit of the formal living room, dining room, and family room, turning off all the lights and the TV. Reggie, apparently deciding to be his shadow, followed happily behind.

"Why are you doing that?" Kurt called out.

"He's trying to save your life," Richard said.

Ignoring both men, Logan stepped over to a window that faced the street and pulled back the curtain. At the moment, it was quiet, no cars in either direction as far as he could see, but he knew that wouldn't last long.

He heard footsteps and turned to see Sara and Diana walk back into the entryway. Emily was in Sara's arms, hugging her.

"Can I see her?" Richard asked.

Logan realized this must have been the first time Sara's brother ever laid eyes on his niece. Diana, he knew, had seen her earlier that summer when she visited Sara in Riverside. But as wonderful as that moment should be, this wasn't the time.

"You need to go, now!" Logan ordered.

Richard looked annoyed, but he turned from his sisters and opened the front door.

As the others moved to follow him, Rachel reached out to grab Emily from Sara. "You're not taking her anywhere."

"You *all* go!" Logan yelled.

Emily started to cry.

"It's okay, sweetie," Sara said. "It's okay."

"Go, go!" Logan said.

"Go where?" Kurt asked.

"I don't care," Logan said. "Away."

"Why?"

Both Richard and Diana had already disappeared outside, but just as suddenly, they came running back in.

"Car," Diana said as Richard shut the door.

Logan moved back to the window.

A car was heading down the road toward the house.

"Keep going," he whispered. "Keep going."

But his mojo wasn't working this time, and the vehicle started to slow.

"Out the back," he said quickly. "Go over the fence to the next yard!"

"What are you taking about?" Kurt said. "I'm not going over any fence. You're going to tell us what's going on, and you're going to tell us now."

"Go, dammit, go!" Logan said. He pulled out his phone and dialed Dev.

No one seemed to move. Instead everyone started arguing.

Outside, the car was only half a block away, its speed at a near crawl now.

"Logan?" Dev said.

"Where are you?"

"I'm in Simi. Maybe five minutes away."

Five minutes was too long. "I'm in the house. It appears the others are just pulling up."

"I'll get there as quickly as I can."

Logan hung up, and looked back. Everyone was still there.

"Do you all not get it? There is only one person in this house the people who just got here want alive, and it's not any of you, or me." He glanced at Emily, then scanned the others. "Get the hell out of here *now!*"

They started to move. Even Rachel's husband seemed shaken enough not to put up a fight.

Logan returned his attention to the street. The car was only one house away now, angling for a section of the curb directly behind the car Logan and the others had arrived in. As soon as it parked, its lights went out, but the doors remained closed.

Logan looked down the street, wondering if they might be waiting for reinforcements, but, as of now, there were no other cars heading this way.

He heard one of the sedan's doors open, and looked back at it.

Not one door, but two. Dr. Paskota exited the front passenger side, while one of her goons climbed out of the backseat. Logan could see three shadowy forms still inside—Alan and Harp in the back, and a final man still behind the wheel.

Logan clearly saw what he needed to do. Divide and conquer.

He stepped over to the front door. Leaving the deadbolt undone, he turned the knob lock just enough so that it was partially engaged, then looked through the peephole to be sure the woman and her friend were definitely heading his way.

They were.

Logan moved quietly through the house, with Reggie lumbering slowly behind him.

"Scoot, scoot," he said to the dog, pushing him through the open sliding glass door, and following right behind.

As soon as they were outside, he shut the door and took a quick look at the back fence. Richard was trying to help Kurt get over the wall, but it was obviously a struggle. The others were gone.

"You guys need to hurry," Logan whispered. He patted Reggie on the head. "Come on."

With a hand on the dog's collar, he guided Reggie along the back of the house into his pen, and closed the wire gate.

"Be a good boy and stay quiet, okay?"

Reggie licked his hand and chuffed once.

"No, no. Quiet," Logan said, holding his finger to his mouth. This time the dog sat down.

"Good boy. We'll be back for you soon."

Hoping he was right, he stepped to the fence and eased himself over the top.

73

AS HARP WATCHED the woman and Clausen walk across the street toward the house, he'd never felt so hopeless and frustrated in his life. There had to be something he could do. If they could just overpower the guy who'd been left with them—Clausen called him Markle—then maybe they could get help, but he wouldn't be able to do that alone, and Alan was barely holding it together. He kept looking at the house, then out the front window, then back at the house, his hands shaking as if he were freezing to death.

Paskota and Clausen were at the door of the house now. The place was dark. Harp hoped that meant no one was home, but knew it was just as likely whoever lived there had gone to bed early. He couldn't hear if they knocked or not, but after a few moments, the door eased open, and they stepped inside.

Harp turned his head just enough so he could see out the back window. No cars coming. Not that he would have known what to do even if one headed their way.

He gave Alan a nudge and smiled, trying to convey that it would all be okay. Alan wasn't buying it. Quite frankly, Harp wouldn't have, either, in his shoes.

For God's sake, there *had* to be something he could do. Anything. He must—

The driver's door flew open. As Markle turned, a hand reached in, grabbed his arm, and yanked him outside.

Something metallic clattered to the ground, then—

Swack. Swack.

Swack.

Alan looked at Harp, his eyes wide. Harp couldn't see his own face, but knew he was wearing a similar expression.

Something scraped along the road, rounding the car.

Then silence.

74

LOGAN KNEW HE couldn't count on Dr. Paskota and the man with her staying in the house for more than two minutes.

Keeping as close to the neighboring home as possible, he jogged to the sidewalk, went down a couple of houses before crossing the street, and worked his way back to the car his father and Alan were being held in.

He was only one house away when the shadow of a man passed around the back of the car and walked up to the driver's door.

Logan ducked down, thinking that the reinforcements he'd worried about had arrived.

Then suddenly the shadow pulled the door open and hauled out the man sitting behind the wheel. The driver's arms flailed as he tried to bring his gun around, but his assailant wrenched it away and tossed it to the ground.

Two quick punches, then a third, and the driver slumped motionless on the asphalt. The shadow immediately grabbed the guy by the shoulders and hauled him around the back of the car. As he yanked him up onto the grass that lined the curb, a second shadow peeled away from the hedge in front of the nearby house and joined him.

Kneeling beside the unconscious man, the face of one of the shadows moved into the bit of dome light filtering through the car's window.

Dev.

Logan extracted himself from his hiding place, ran out and picked up the suppressor-enhanced gun off the street.

As he joined the others at the curb, Dev looked at him and smiled. "Figured that was you," he whispered.

"Hey, Logan." The second shadow was Pep.

"Where'd you guys come from?" he asked.

"Found them parked just up the street around the corner," Dev whispered. "Thought we'd take advantage of the other two going inside. Guess you had the same idea. Where's everyone else?"

"Safe," Logan said. "I hope."

"Is this the son of a bitch who ambushed me?" Pep asked, looking down at the driver.

"Um, we'll have to talk about that later." Logan looked at the car and saw that Harp and Alan were still inside, looking around nervously. "Didn't you tell them to get out?"

"I didn't really have time to say anything," Dev said.

75

SOMEONE WAS APPROACHING the car again. Harp had no idea what was going on, so he braced himself, preparing for the worst. The door next to Alan opened.

"You guys just going to stay there? Or are you coming out?"

It was Logan.

Without another thought, Harp pushed Alan out the back and crawled out after him, pausing only long enough to pick up the copy of *Lost Horizon* that had been pushed partway under the front passenger seat. The book had gone to war, come home with Len, hung around for another sixty-plus years, and it had been damaged more in the last few days than in any of that time before. It hurt him to see it so, but he was glad to be holding it again.

He was even gladder to see his son, and gave him a big hug.

"Not a lot of time right now, Dad," Logan said.

Harp pulled back. "I thought you were still in Arizona."

Logan ushered both of them onto the sidewalk. "I heard the real action was in Simi Valley."

"Evening, Mr. Harper," Pep said.

"Hey, Harp," Dev chimed in.

"Dev. Pep," Harp said, his surprise continuing. Then he noticed Markle's body on the ground. "Is he dead?" He turned to his son. "Did you kill him?"

"What makes you think *I* did it?" Logan asked. He pointed at Dev.

"Still alive," Dev said.

Alan shook himself, his eyes refocusing. He looked at Logan and Harp, then turned and headed for the house.

Logan reached out and grabbed him. "Where do you think you're going?"

"They're inside getting Emily. I've got to stop them."

"They may be inside, but they're not getting Emily."

"What?"

"She's not there."

"Where is she?"

"With your sister and Sara."

"Sara?" Alan all but shouted.

"Quiet!" Logan said. He pointed up the street. "I need you two to go get Barney. He's in Dev's Jeep around the corner. Dad, when you get there, call Callie. Tell her to call the Simi Valley Police and that FBI contact of hers she mentioned when she told us about Alan. Get them here now. Once you've done that, come back here and the three of you watch this guy. I don't want him wandering off. But be careful. Don't let anyone else see you."

"What are you going to do?"

"What do you think?"

Harp frowned but said nothing.

"I'm coming with you," Alan said.

"No, you're not. You'll get us killed."

"I won't."

"You will. Trust me. Now get going!"

Harp grabbed Alan by the arm. "Come on. They know what they're doing."

Alan didn't look happy, but he finally allowed himself to be led away.

When they reached the corner, Harp looked back. Logan and the others were gone.

76

ERICA WATCHED AS Clausen pulled out a set of lock picks and set to work on the door.

"Forgot to lock their deadbolt," Clausen whispered with a smile. He worked the bottom lock for a few seconds before it gave in. "Too much faith in crappy hardware."

He eased open the door wide enough for them to enter, then drew his gun and stepped inside. Erica followed.

There was a smell in the air, something musty, but not old. Like a...dog. Yes, that was it. The smell of a dog. That could be a problem. If the animal sensed their presence, it could start barking and expose them, making their job harder. Erica put a hand on Clausen's back.

"Hold on," she mouthed.

They held their position for half a minute, but the sound of claws running across the floor never materialized. With any luck, the dog was asleep in one of the bedrooms, or, God willing, outside.

They did quick checks of the living room, kitchen, and family room, noting dishes in the sink from a meal eaten not too long ago. Of special interest was the child's sippy cup. It wasn't proof that the girl was still here, but in Erica's mind, there was no doubt now that this was where she had been hiding.

They approached the hallway that led to the bedrooms, stopping just outside it to listen.

All quiet. Too quiet.

Was no one at home? Where would they have gone? They'd obviously eaten dinner here, and if they were at all responsible, they wouldn't be out too late with a two-year-old.

She looked into the hallway. It had a hardwood floor, partially covered by a carpet runner down the middle. The hall veered to the left, then made a ninety-degree right turn, disappearing from view. The only door visible led to a bathroom a few feet down.

Stepping all the way onto the runner, she carefully transferred her weight to minimize any sound of creaking floorboards. She repeated the process step by step down the hallway and around the corner.

There were three doors along the new section. When she reached the first, she looked in. Bedroom. It looked like a boy's room, though clean and tidy, as if the kid who used it hadn't been home for a while.

The bedroom at the end of the hall was clearly the master. Even the small portion Erica could see was nearly twice as wide as the room she'd just checked. If the girl *was* here, her bet was that she was in the room across the hall and down a little ways from where Erica was standing.

She motioned for Clausen to check the master while she checked the other room. With a nod, he moved past her down the hall.

The curtains of the last bedroom were closed, so as Erica walked in, it was hard to see much of anything. She activated the screen of her phone and swept it across the room like a flashlight.

There was a bed, a dresser, and some toys on the floor. Though the bed was unoccupied, its covers were pulled back. It was apparent from how the blankets were disturbed that whoever had been in the bed had not been very tall. A toddler, at best.

She put her hand on the sheet covering the mattress. Warm, but it was a warm night, so that didn't necessarily mean anything.

Clausen appeared in the doorway. "Empty," he said, not bothering to even whisper. "No one's home."

"Then where the hell are they?" she asked.

"Movies, maybe. Out to dinner."

"They had dinner." Erica checked her watch. It was going on eight thirty. "And I doubt they would have taken a kid that age out to a movie at this time of night."

Clausen shrugged. "Maybe they just went for some ice cream or something."

"Maybe." Wherever they'd gone, she was confident they'd return soon. "We'll wait."

Though the ultimate satisfaction of closing this problem was delayed, Erica was actually feeling pretty good. The girl was close. Soon she'd have possession of her, and it would all be over.

"Go get Markle and our guests, and bring them in," she ordered. "We can tie up the two and lock them in the hallway bathroom for now."

If I can think of a way to stage it, maybe we could even get rid of them here.

As Clausen started to turn down the hallway, there was thud in the backyard, followed almost instantly by a low groan and what sounded like a hushed voice.

"Wait," Erica whispered.

She went to the window and carefully moved the curtain just enough so she could see out, but spotted nothing unusual.

"The dog?" Clausen suggested.

If it had only been the thud and the groan, perhaps, but Erica was sure she'd heard a human voice, too.

She let the curtain fall back into place. "We need to check."

77

"HARP!" BARNEY JUMPED out of the Jeep as Harp and Alan walked up.

Barney held out his hand, but Harp, being in a hugging mood, wrapped his arms around his old friend.

"I...wasn't sure we'd see you again," Barney said once they'd separated.

"Yeah. I wasn't sure you would, either," Harp confessed.

"What happened? How did they get you?"

"I'll tell you in a minute. I need your phone first."

"Uh, sure." Barney ducked back in and retrieved his cell from the car.

Before he could hand it over, Harp said, "You have Callie's number, right?"

"Yeah. Is that who you want to call?"

Harp nodded.

Barney fiddled with the buttons for a moment, then gave the phone to Harp. "It's ringing."

Harp listened as it rang for a second time.

"Hello?"

"Callie? It's Harp."

She drew in a quick breath. "Are you okay?"

"I'm fine. I'm with Barney now."

"And Logan?"

"I saw him a minute ago."

"So what's happening?"

"Logan wanted me to tell you to call the police and your friend at the FBI, and have them get here as quickly as they can."

"All right," she said quickly.

"Wait!"

"What is it?"

"You might want to send an ambulance, too." At the very least, they'd need it for the jerk on the curb, but he thought it best to be prepared for the worst.

"Oh, God," Callie said, and clicked off.

"What was that all about?" Barney asked.

"Come on," Harp said, handing the phone back to Barney. "The three of us have something to do." He turned to include Alan in the conversation, but Alan wasn't there. "Where'd he go?"

Barney looked around. "I don't know. He was here just a moment ago."

"Alan?" Harp called out as loudly as he dared.

No answer.

"Maybe he went back to the other car," Harp said. "That's where we're supposed to go." He took a step toward the curb, then stopped and looked back. "I want to get something out of the back of the Jeep first."

78

NOW THAT HARP and Alan were free, and Emily was out of harm's way, Logan's only goal was to keep Dr. Paskota and the man with her at the house until the authorities arrived—something he knew would be a hell of a lot easier said than done.

If it hadn't happened already, the doctor would soon discover no one was home. Once that happened, there were two possibilities—either she would stay in the house and wait, thinking that Rachel and Kurt would return with Emily soon, or she would leave.

If it was the first, great; there was little Logan would have to do. So he concentrated on the second possibility. Better to be prepared than not.

The choke point was the front door. That was the way they'd gone in, and the most logical way they'd come out. So the primary goal would be to keep her from using it.

"Set up in the bushes on either side of the porch," Logan whispered to Dev and Pep as they ran across the street. "If they try to leave, you make sure they understand that's not an option. I'll find a spot in the backyard to make sure they don't go out that way, either."

Logan handed Dev his own gun, keeping the one with the suppressor for himself.

He looked at Pep. "Sorry, I only have the two."

"Don't worry about it. I'll get 'em if they run."

Logan hoped it wouldn't come to that. Pep might have been mentally prepared to chase the others down, but his broken ribs would have something to say about it.

They crossed the lawn and paused just shy of the porch.

"The idea is not to kill them, but to detain," Logan whispered.

"At all costs? Or only if possible?" Dev asked.

"If possible. I'm going to—"

A muffled *thup-thup* came from either the other side of the front door or beyond the house. Though it was difficult to pinpoint, it was a sound Logan had heard before—bullets passing through a silencer. Two, in this case.

He whirled back around.

"Who are they shooting at?" Dev asked.

Logan shook his head. "I have no idea."

Thup.

A cry of pain.

79

ERICA AND CLAUSEN exited via the sliding glass door and split up, Clausen going left while she went right.

Scanning the darkness, she looked for any sign of movement. There were no places for anyone to hide against the house or the back of the garage, with the grass running right up to the foundation. Closer to the back of the property, though, along the cinder-block wall that served as the fence, was a metal gardening shed, and beyond it, across the rear of the lot, was a wide section full of bushes and trees and plants.

She headed for the shed first, pausing a few feet away to listen.

Breathing. Faint, either coming from inside the shed or out further in the bushes.

She moved over to the door, but immediately saw the sound couldn't have been coming from within. The door was padlocked.

Whoever was hiding had to be in the bushes.

She glanced at the other side of the yard. Clausen had headed straight for the planted area on his half, and was working along it in the opposite direction.

Erica clicked her tongue once against the top of her mouth.

Clausen turned, and she motioned to the section of the brush area where she thought the voice had originated. With a nod, Clausen switched directions so they were closing in on the area like a vise.

As Erica inched forward, she looked specifically for any pattern in the shadowy vegetation that didn't fit.

Movement, subtle at first, then a rush of leaves slapping against each other.

"Don't shoot, don't shoot!" a man said, popping out of the brush, his hands above his head.

He was large, not tall but fat.

"Who the hell are you?" she asked.

"Please don't hurt me. I haven't done anything."

"Answer my question."

The man hesitated. "Kurt. Kurt Abbott."

"That name means nothing to me."

"This…this is my house."

"Oh, it is, is it? Then tell me, Kurt Abbott, where's the girl?"

"I don't know what you're talking about."

Abbott wasn't a very good liar.

"Step out of the bushes," Erica said. "Slowly."

Abbott didn't move. "Why?"

"I just want to talk to you."

"Please. Just go. I won't call the cops or anything."

Erica's face hardened. "Get your ass out here. Now."

As Abbott was about to take a step forward, another man erupted out of a bush just to the right.

Erica and Clausen swung their guns around and pulled their triggers, but both fired in surprise, their shots going wide.

Clausen fired again.

With a cry of pain, the man went down.

"Holy shit," Abbott said.

The guy on the ground was also big, but in the muscular-and-tall way.

Erica used her foot to roll him over, while Clausen kept an

eye on Abbott. The injured man winced in pain. His arm hugged his gut, the shirt beneath turning dark with blood.

Most times, Erica liked to leave the gun work to others, but after the two days of frustration, and now this, she was pissed off. "Who the hell are you?"

"Go to hell, Dr. Paskota," the man grunted. Then he smiled. "You're too late. She's gone."

Erica's eyes narrowed, her sense that everything was working out slipping away. She put her foot on back of the hand the injured man was pressing against his wound, and shifted her weight onto it.

The man cried out.

"Who *are* you?"

80

THE FIRST THING Harp saw as he and Barney neared the other car was that Alan was not there. Unfortunately, he didn't have time to worry about that at the moment, because the second thing he noticed was Markle pushing himself off the ground.

"Oh, no, you don't," Harp said, rushing forward.

He raised the tire iron he'd taken out of the back of the Cherokee.

"Go to hell, old man," Markle said. He started to stand, not taking the threat seriously.

Harp clenched his jaw, hesitated a second, then swung.

The tire iron slapped the side of the man's head. He twisted toward Harp, dazed, his eyes trying to focus on his former captive before he dropped to the ground.

"Harp!" Barney said.

"What?"

"You hit him!"

"Yeah, I did."

"You…you might have killed him." Ever the doctor, Barney dropped to his knees and checked the man's pulse.

"Well, he and his friends wouldn't have hesitated to kill me."

"He's alive," Barney said, relief in his voice. He looked back at Harp and smiled. "Good thing you're not so strong, huh?"

"'Good thing you're not so strong,'" Harp shot back like a sixth-grader. He thrust the tire iron into Barney's hands. "Take it."

"Why?"

"Next time it's your turn."

"I can't hit him. My oath."

"Oh, good Lord. Give it back."

81

AS LOGAN REACHED the sliding glass door, he heard another cry of pain.

Dr. Paskota was standing over someone on the ground, her foot pushing down on the person. Her companion had a gun trained on a man standing in the bushes.

Rachel's husband, Logan realized. Which meant the man on the ground had to be Richard.

Dammit. Why hadn't they gotten out of here?

"Who *are* you?" the doctor demanded.

The time for stealth was over. Logan raised his gun and fired through the open door from inside the house. Though he was a good marksman, it was dark and the weapon was an unfamiliar one, hindered by the suppressor. The bullet went left of its intended target, clipping Dr. Paskota in the arm instead of hitting her in the shoulder like he'd intended.

She jerked sideways and dropped to the ground, facing the house.

Clausen hit the grass, too.

"Who's in there?" the doctor yelled.

Logan stepped to the side, out of direct line of the guns. He pointed at the window on the other side of the door. Dev nodded, dropped into a crouch, and snuck over to it.

Staying in the darkness, Logan edged back out just enough so he could see the woman.

"The next shot takes you down," Logan yelled.

Thup-thup. Thup-thup.

Bullets flew into the house, but hit only wall.

"You want to try again?" Logan asked.

"Harper?" Dr. Paskota said.

"Right on the first try, Doctor."

There was a pause. "How about we make a deal? We walk away, and you can come out and help your friends."

Dev whispered, "The other one's sneaking up to the house."

That wasn't a surprise. Logan hadn't believed the woman for a second.

"How about you put your guns down and we don't kill you?" Logan countered.

"I don't think so. Tell me, is the woman with you?"

"Not anymore. Right now she's with her husband and baby. Oh, and my dad, too."

"I guess I misjudged you, huh?"

"I guess so."

Dev looked over. "Can't see him anymore."

Logan stepped back so he could no longer see what was going on.

"So tell me, Dr. Paskota, what are your clients going to say when the FBI shows up at their homes and starts asking about these babies you've created for them?"

"You don't know what you're talking about."

"I know enough to know that creating children just so they could provide parts for a biological parent is probably going to get you quite a few years in prison."

Silence, then, "That's not going to happen. Once we take care of you, I'll find the girl, and this will all just be a bad memory."

Logan was about to agree with the last part, but before he

could say anything, someone shouted, "No!"

Then Reggie barked.

82

ALAN WASN'T ABOUT to just stand around and wait. As soon as Mr. Harper was on the phone, he quickly made his way back to the corner.

He was only halfway to his sister's house when he heard several dull thuds coming from somewhere near her place. He picked up his speed.

The front door was open, but he was smart enough to not rush through it. Instead, he decided the best idea would be to circle around the house. That way, he might be in a position to surprise the people who were trying to hurt his wife.

With effort, he climbed the fence and let himself down gently on the other side. Reggie was in the pen. When he saw that his visitor was Alan, he struggled to his feet, loped over, and began licking Alan's hand.

"No, Reggie," Alan whispered, petting the dog on the head.

He moved over to the gate of the pen and slipped his hand through the wire, undoing the latch. Suddenly there were more of the thuds. This time they were accompanied by voices—a woman and Logan Harper.

It was clear the woman was one of the people after his wife

and daughter. All the anger and emotions that had plagued him since his wife left suddenly had focus.

This woman. She was the problem.

He tried to focus on what was being said, but was having a hard time making some of the connections. Logan was saying something about creating children and biological parents and prison, but it didn't fully make sense.

What he heard next did.

"That's not going to happen," the woman said. "Once we take care of you, I'll find the girl, and this will all just be a bad memory."

Emily. She meant Emily.

No. No. No!

Without even realizing it, he was running through the gate.

"No!"

83

"IT'S ALAN," DEV said, his view on that part of the yard better than Logan's.

Immediately they both raced for the door.

"She's not yours!" Alan yelled.

Thup.

Logan sent a bullet toward Paskota. He twisted to the side as he raced out the doorway, and fired twice at the man along the wall. As Logan's bullet caught him in the shoulder, the man spun and reflexively pulled his own trigger.

Alan, who had just rounded the corner, yelped as he fell to the ground.

"Watch him!" Logan said to Dev, with a quick nod at the guy he'd just shot. He whipped back around to cover the doctor, but Dr. Paskota wasn't there anymore.

If she had gone into the bushes, Logan would have heard that. So the only place she could be was along the side of the garden shed.

"It's over, Dr. Paskota," Logan yelled. "You know it is."

As soon as the last word was out of his mouth, he raced quietly across the grass to the shed.

"You're a dead man, Harper," the woman said.

84

"IT'S OVER, DR. Paskota," Harper yelled. "You know it is."

Erica's mind raced. There had to be some way out of this. She was Dr. Erica Paskota! She was the one who called the shots. She was the one in charge. Things couldn't be this fucked up. They just couldn't!

She winced as pain radiated out of her wound. Her *wound!* She'd been *shot!* She never thought in her entire life a bullet would ever touch her skin. This was wrong, all wrong!

"You're a dead man, Harper," she yelled.

This should have been simple. She should have already been on the way back with the girl.

Done.

Done, done, done.

But she'd been shot. And it was that son of a bitch Harper's fault. He shouldn't have even been involved at all.

I've got to get out of here. I've got to get out of here.

But even as the words repeated in her mind, they began to sound hollow.

"Dr. Paskota, put your gun down, and come out," Harper said.

He was only a few feet away, just around the front of the shed.

I'm not *getting out of here, am I?*

The thought actually relaxed her for the first time in…years.

Harper had said she would be going to prison, but he was wrong.

She unscrewed the suppressor from her gun, and slipped the barrel into her mouth without hesitation.

85

AS MUCH AS Logan hoped she would come out peacefully, he knew she wouldn't. Her arrogance wouldn't allow that. He would just have to keep her there until the police arrived. They could figure out how to get her out.

He heard the faint squeak of something being unscrewed.

What the—

With sudden realization, Logan raced around the corner.

Dr. Paskota had the muzzle of her gun in her mouth. She was opting for the coward's way out, but he couldn't let that happen. He dove, his hand knocking into the weapon just as she pulled the trigger. The blast was so loud that Logan didn't even hear himself hit the ground. He did, however, feel her gun fall on his back and roll to the ground. He flipped around, intending to grab the weapon before she could get it again, but he needn't have bothered.

Dr. Paskota was lying on the ground, unmoving.

"No, no, no!" Logan said as he pulled himself to his knees.

"You all right?" Dev called out, his voice sounding tinny and far away.

"I'm fine."

Logan put a hand on the woman's neck, sure she was dead, but there was a pulse. It wasn't very strong, but it didn't seem to be in danger of stopping.

He flipped her over, and saw what had happened.

He hadn't hit the gun in time to pull it out of her mouth before it fired, but he had moved it enough so that the bullet ripped through the doctor's cheek instead of the back of her head, leaving a nasty hole that was now covered with dirt.

But she was alive, and she *would* answer for what she'd done.

He ripped the sleeve off his shirt and tore it into several pieces. He used a strip to wipe the dirt away from her facial wound, and stuck another over the hole. A third he used to tie off the wound on her arm. He then grabbed her by the shoulders and pulled her out from behind the shed and into the yard.

He checked the others. Of all the injured, Richard had it worst. Gut shots were never good, and his only chance was to get to a hospital soon.

Logan looked over at Kurt, who had yet to move from where he'd been standing. "Come here."

Kurt mouthed something, but Logan couldn't hear it.

"What?"

"I'm fine where I am," Kurt said, his voice barely audible to Logan.

"Come here and keep pressure on this," Logan told him, his hand pushing down on the makeshift bandage over Richard's wound. "He tried to save your life, for God's sake."

That got Kurt moving. He took over for Logan, who then joined Dev next to Alan. The bullet had caught Sara's husband in the meaty part of the thigh.

"Don't think it hit the bone," Dev said. "And it's not bleeding *too* bad, so no artery."

Logan glanced at Alan, wanting to ask what he thought he'd been doing, but the pain in the man's eyes stopped him. The truth was, Logan knew what Alan had been trying to do.

"Where the hell are the cops?" he asked Dev.

His friend gave him an odd look. "They're like a block away. Can't you hear them?"

Logan shook his head. "Ever had a gun fired right next to your head?"

His friend grinned. "Once or twice."

The police rushed in a few minutes later, shouting at everyone to get on the ground. Of course, everyone was already on the ground, either injured or tending to them.

Once the cops secured all the weapons and confirmed the danger had passed, the EMTs were allowed to come in and assess the wounded.

Richard, as Logan expected, was the first out the door. Dr. Paskota went next, then Alan and Dr. Paskota's companion.

Logan and Dev were ordered to sit at the patio table and wait with an officer assigned to watch them.

A thought suddenly occurred to Logan. "There's another one," he said to the cop. "He's across the street, on the other side of one of the sedans parked there."

"You mean the one the two old guys with the tire iron were watching?" the officer said.

That answered that.

Fifty minutes after the police stormed the house, FBI Special Agent Kara Sanchez arrived. She didn't look much older than Logan, and had her dark hair pulled back into a tight ponytail.

"You're Logan Harper?" she asked.

"Yes."

"What the hell were you thinking? Do you know how many people could have been killed here?"

"I do. Do you know how many people *were* killed?"

She narrowed her eyes. "You've created one giant mess here, my friend, and I don't envy you."

Logan looked past her, making it clear he was checking to see if anyone else was around. "Really?" he said. "What I thought I had here was a case that could make an FBI agent's career."

"Oh, is that so?" she said, her attitude unchanged.

"It is."

She looked at him for a moment, and he saw what he knew he would—a subtle shift in her eyes.

86

LOGAN WAS IN the middle of his story when Callie arrived. As soon as she had made the calls to the police and Special Agent Sanchez, she'd left Riverside. Now, as Logan went on, she confirmed many of the points he told Sanchez, and soon they were all heading to the hospital.

Though Sanchez wanted them all to travel together, Logan insisted on taking his own car. He had a very important reason for this, a promise he had yet to keep. So, after Callie gave Sanchez her personal assurances that Logan wouldn't bolt, they headed over separately—Callie with the agent and Dev with Logan.

Logan and Dev arrived first and found Harp and Barney sitting in the lobby. Barney had insisted that Harp be taken by one of the ambulances so he could be checked out after his hostage ordeal.

"What did the doctor say?" Logan asked.

"About me?" Harp said, surprised.

"Yeah, Dad. About you."

"Said for a man my age, I seem to be in perfect health."

Logan looked at him skeptically, but Barney nodded.

"Yeah. If I hadn't been there, I wouldn't have believed it,

either."

"Means I'm going to be around for a while still, so you should remember that," Harp said.

"Great," Logan replied, rolling his eyes in mock disgust. "I hear you're pretty handy with a tire iron."

"As a matter of fact, I am."

"You should have seen him," Barney said, swinging his arm through the air. "He didn't even think about it. He just did it."

Beaming, Harp said, "See? I can be useful."

"Of course you can, Dad. I've always known that." Logan paused, then said, "I have something for you."

Harp raised an eyebrow, curious. "What?"

Logan pulled the envelope from Len out of his pocket, and held it out. "Just a little late on my promise."

Harp lit up. "Thank you. I…I appreciate it."

The outside door opened and Sanchez and Callie came in.

"When we have a little time," Logan said to his dad, "we're going to talk about what's inside."

"I thought you said you didn't look," Harp said.

"I did. Sorry, Dad."

"Oh."

"But I didn't read it."

Harp hesitated, then nodded. "Okay. We'll talk."

"Mr. Harper? Mr. Martin?" Sanchez called out. "Are you coming with us?"

They proceeded into the emergency room, where they learned that both Richard and Alan were in surgery. They found Sara, Diana, Rachel, and Kurt in a private room waiting for news of their loved ones. Emily was there, too, wide awake and clinging to her mother.

There was a happy moment of reunion as Logan and the others walked in.

"Boy, was I wrong about you," Diana said.

Logan shrugged. "Maybe a little."

"Thank you," Sara told him. "Is…Dr. Paskota…"

"Probably in surgery right now," Logan said. "And under arrest. It's over."

Judging by the look on her face, she didn't agree. He knew she was thinking about the client still out there who'd paid for Emily's existence.

He looked over at Rachel and Kurt. "Do you mind giving us a few minutes alone? We need to talk to Sara and Diana."

Rachel nodded. "We'll be in the cafeteria."

Once they were gone, Logan turned his attention back to Sara and Diana. "I know you're still worried, but this can be over if you want it to be." He glanced at the other two women in the room. "Sara, you already know Callie. The person with her is Special Agent Sanchez with the FBI. I think you all have a lot to talk about."

87

ALAN SLOWLY OPENED his eyes, finally waking from his surgery. His head was still a bit cloudy, but the searing pain in his leg seemed to be gone. He knew that was just temporary, the drugs he'd been given dulling his senses.

He closed his eyes again, trying to piece the evening back together, and wondering what had happened. After several seconds he realized something was pressing against his hand. He forced his lids open and glanced down.

"So you are awake."

He froze. Despite the words, he thought he might still be sleeping, lost in a dream.

Using what strength he had, he forced himself to look to his right.

"Hi," Sara said.

It was really her. She was sitting in a chair beside his bed, holding his hand.

"Hi," he managed.

"The doctor says you're going to be okay. A little sore for a while, but okay."

He stared at her, unable to form any words.

She smiled. "You will have to stay here for another couple days, though."

"Oh," he said, suddenly tense. "Emily. Where is she?"

"Rachel has her. They wouldn't let me bring her in."

"Is she all right?"

"She's fine. She just wants to see her dad." She hesitated. "I'm...I'm sorry. I didn't mean to hurt you. It was never about you. It was...my past."

"Don't," he said.

"I've never loved anyone like I love you."

He watched her for a moment. "Are you going to disappear again?"

"Never. I promise."

He could see the pain and the truth and the love in her eyes.

He squeezed her hand. "If you do, I'll send Logan to find you again."

She laughed, and after a second, he did, too.

88

Three Weeks Later
Manila, The Philippines

LOGAN MET HIS father in the lobby of the hotel.

"You ready?" he asked.

Harp looked nervous, but he nodded and tried to smile.

Logan guided him out the front door to the car waiting for them at the curb. Harp climbed in first, sliding over so that Logan could get in behind him. Moments later, their driver was navigating them through the notorious Manila traffic.

It took nearly an hour to reach their destination southeast of downtown, near Aquino International Airport. The sign out front read:

MANILA AMERICAN CEMETERY AND MEMORIAL

They passed through an open gate in a gray, barred fence, but had to stop just on the other side for a guard. The driver rolled down his window and the guard stuck his head in.

When he saw Harp and Logan in the back, he said, "American?"

"Yes," Logan said.

"Okay. Park over there." He pointed at a white building off to the right with the word VISITORS etched in the stone at the top of a small portico.

Suddenly, it was like they were in a different world. The chaos of Manila disappeared, replaced by an empty road running up a tranquil, grass-covered hill. At the apex of the gentle slope, Logan could see their destination.

"I can ask if it's okay to drive up there," Logan said to his father. The road did go all the way up.

"I'd rather walk."

They exited the car and headed up the road. On either side of them was a well-kept expanse of grass, lined with row after row of white stone grave markers, crosses, and Stars of David. These were soldiers and sailors and marines who had died in World War II, but Harp and Logan weren't there to see one of those tombstones.

As they neared the end of the road, the monument came into full view. Two arcs, each half of a circle separated enough so that a wide stone walkway ran through the openings at either end. The arcs, constructed of a similar stone, were maybe fifteen feet high, the curving roofs held in place by dozens of walls set up like dominos in side-by-side pairs.

These were what the two Harper men came to see. Carved on both sides of the walls were names, nearly forty thousand in all. These were the ones who had never been able to receive a grave like their fellow servicemen buried nearby. There was nothing of these men to bury, for they were the missing in action.

"Just a second," Harp said as they reached the steps that led up to the arcs.

"Sure, Dad." Logan was actually glad to rest a moment.

As a former soldier himself, he couldn't help but think about those he'd served with who had never come home. Those he was surrounded by here were as much his brothers and sisters as the ones back in Afghanistan had been. A wave of sadness and loss threatened to overwhelm him. Feeling his eyes grow moist, he turned away from his father and took a few deep breaths.

When he was finally back in control, he said, "Whenever you're ready, Dad."

Harp waited a few more seconds, then nodded.

They found the wall they were looking for about halfway down the arc on the right. Logan spotted the name first.

HARPER THOMAS J AVN ORDNANCEMAN 2C USN
KANSAS

Harp let out a gasp when he saw it. He reached out and touched the letters, gently brushing against them as if they might vanish if he pushed too hard.

For nearly five minutes, neither of them said a word.

Then Harp pulled Len's envelope from his pocket and removed the one that was inside, the letter he had sent to his brother, Tom.

Harp had finally told Logan this was the trip he and Len had talked about so many years ago, the one Len was never able to make, the one he wanted to make sure Harp didn't miss, too. Logan had immediately booked the flight, and now here they were.

Harp broke the seal, but seemed unable to pull out the letter.

Logan leaned over and carefully removed the paper from inside.

"Here, Dad," he said, handing over the letter.

"I don't know if I can," Harp said.

Logan smiled at him. "I do."

For several seconds, silence threatened to take over again. Then Harp looked down at the words in front of him, the words he had written as a child, and began to read aloud.

"Dear Tom…"

ABOUT THE AUTHOR

Brett Battles lives and writes full time in Los Angeles. He is the author of ten novels, including *Little Girl Gone*, the first Logan Harper thriller, and *The Deceived*, winner of the Barry Award for Best Thriller 2009. More info available at www.brettbattles.com.

Made in the USA
San Bernardino, CA
10 June 2013